SCRIES LIKE AN OWL

OWL STAR WITCH MYSTERIES BOOK 11

LEANNE LEEDS

Scries Like an Owl
ISBN: 978-1-950505-78-4
Published by Badchen Publishing
14125 W State Highway 29
Suite B-203 119
Liberty Hill, TX 78642 USA

For permissions contact: info@badchenpublishing.com

CONTENTS

Chapter 1	1
Chapter 2	19
Chapter 3	37
Chapter 4	51
Chapter 5	69
Chapter 6	87
Chapter 7	107
Chapter 8	125
Chapter 9	145
Chapter 10	163
Chapter 11	181
Chapter 12	199
Chapter 13	217
Chapter 14	235
Chapter 15	253
Chapter 16	271
Chapter 17	289
Chapter 18	305
Chapter 19	325
Chapter 20	343
Chapter 21	359
KEEP UP WITH LEANNE LEEDS	371
Find a typo? Let us know!	373
Artificial Intelligence Statement	375

SCRIES LIKE AN OWL

CHAPTER ONE

 y sisters, Ami, Althea, and Ayla, and I would always gather in the kitchen in the mornings when my mother was still alive, the warm yellow Florida sun shining in through the windows. We'd be sitting around the kitchen table, wearing our nightgowns and with puffy eyes from sleep, with my mother always at the helm, eagerly awaiting breakfast from our aunt's hard work at the stove.

The scene unfolded as usual this morning, but my mother's chair, which had been empty for several months, remained vacant.

My siblings and I accepted the void as a fact of life.

Well.

Ami, Althea, and I felt a void.

My younger sister Ayla, on the other hand, still experienced a form of those mornings thanks to her ability to see and hear ghosts. She would occasionally glare at the chair and respond to a question that none of us could hear.

"No, I don't think we've ordered the incense yet," Ayla said one morning.

"Huh?" Ami wondered aloud, her eyes half-closed. Her blond hair was mussed from sleeping, and she rubbed her eyes as she struggled to stay awake.

"Jeez, have some coffee, already, Ami." Ayla reached out her arm and pushed the steaming mug toward Ami. "Mom's just reminding me to remind you all that we haven't placed an order for the incense in the shop yet," Ayla replied.

Cerberus, Ayla's dog—the actual three-headed underworld guard Cerberus, though he currently resembled a large black and white bulldog with short fur—barked.

"Oh, shut up," Archie, my owl, snapped at the dog.

Suddenly, Cerberus opened his mouth and let out a low, plaintive whine that echoed in the room. He stood up and walked across the room to Ayla, letting out an occasional whimper as he went to her for comfort.

"Hey, cut that out." Ayla had a stern expression on her face as she pointed her finger at Archie. "Don't be mean to my dog," Ayla warned him. "I don't discipline you."

"You literally just corrected him," I told her with an eyebrow raise.

"Well, someone needed to."

"You know, I love how Mom reaches out across time and space from the underworld, only to remind us we're not running Athena's Garden as well as she did." Althea was holding a piece of bacon between her thumb and forefinger while Lily, her crow, perched on her shoulder. "Is she telling us how much she loves us? Apologizing for any mistakes she made?" The golden-eyed crow blinked and shuffled contentedly against Althea's neck. "Nope, not at all. Criticism. That's what we get."

"It was just a reminder," I told her. "Where did you get that bacon?"

"It was not a reminder, it was criticism. And I grabbed a piece from the kitchen."

The owl's eyes narrowed and furrowed into a deep frown, his beak slightly agape in annoyance. Archie's feathers ruffled and his ears drooped, as if in protest of the situation. "You know, you could have done that," he grumbled.

"Death does not always change people," Lily, the crow given to my sister by the goddess Hecate, spoke from Althea's shoulder.

Before the dark bird could say anything else, Aunt Gwennie rushed in from the kitchen, carrying a tray overflowing with breakfast favorites. The aroma of bacon and eggs filled the air as she placed the tray on the table.

"Good morning, everyone!" Aunt Gwennie said cheerfully.

"Ugh. Stop being so cheerful," Ami mumbled.

"Nonsense. I hope you are all hungry." She dished out omelets with mushrooms and cheese, bacon strips, and crispy hash browns onto each plate. "I figured since it's Sunday, we should treat ourselves to something special for breakfast–I also made some blueberry pancakes and cinnamon rolls." She looked up. "The broom fell in front of the door, so I wanted to be prepared."

"Ugh." Ami balanced her fork on the edge of her plate, surveyed the steaming omelet filled with vegetables and cheese. "I hate company," she said, picking up her fork again. "I wonder who's coming."

"You know, Ami, you're such a grump lately,"

Althea told her. "Do you like anything these days?"

Ami didn't argue.

I hoped it wasn't Ayla's father, Hades. (Yes, the ruler of the underworld.) I remembered the last time I'd been around him for an extended period —it had been a nightmare, resulting in both my mother and boyfriend being sent to his realm. Which, to be honest, wasn't all that bad.

The underworld realm, I mean. I was there. It wasn't bad.

Mom and Jason dying and winding up there permanently?

That was terrible.

Archie sat on a wooden chair next to me, eagerly eating the piece of bacon I had placed in his beak. His small, bright eyes were fixed on me as he chomped methodically with his beak open, his feathers slightly quivering with each bite. "Don't be stingy with that bacon. Aunt Gwennie made plenty."

"Of course I did, now that we have two more mouths to feed around the table." She smiled at Lily and reached down, fingers spread wide apart, to stroke Cerberus' back. "Speaking of more mouths to feed, how's Emma doing?"

I couldn't help but smile when Aunt Gwennie

asked the question. Emma Sullivan, my best friend, was so pregnant she looked like she was about to burst. Eddie Renzo, her boyfriend, had moved his werewolf pack from Palm Beach to Forkbridge to be with her, and now everyone was looking forward to the arrival of the newest, tiniest member of the Forkbridge Pack.

"Emma is doing well," I said. "She's expecting their little one any day now."

Aunt Gwennie nodded, her face softening into a pretty smile. "I can only imagine how excited they must be! I remember when you, Astra, arrived—it truly was an amazing experience to watch a life come into this world. Such a miracle! We should all remind ourselves of that every once in a while, don't you think?" Aunt Gwennie looked around the table expectantly.

There was a chorus of grumbling murmurs around the table.

"Well, girls, try not to sound so enthusiastic." Aunt Gwennie looked disappointed.

"Yeah, whatever." Althea pushed away from the table. "Ayla and I are going to be in the potion room all day," she said. "We're working on something that should help take the burden off her with the whole 'Mom's dead' thing."

"Oh?" Ami asked, perking up for the first time. "What are you two working on?"

Althea shrugged. "It's nothing, really. Just something we're trying out. Nothing special." She stood up and grabbed her plate, then walked away before turning back to the table and adding, "Aunt Gertie's helping."

Aunt Gertie was our other aunt.

She was a ghost.

Ayla and her dog dashed out after Althea, leaving behind a plate of uneaten food on the table without a second glance.

"Ayla, your plate! Take it to the kitchen, please," I called after her, but the dog's happy barking got further away.

Ami let out a sigh. "Althea's always so mysterious about what she does in that potion room of hers, isn't she? What do you think it is this time? She never tells us anything!" Ami looked at Ayla's plate. "And what's with that? Ungrateful little—"

"Oh, it's nothing, Ami. I'm sure she just forgot," Aunt Gwennie said, grabbing it. "I've got it. It's no problem at all."

Ami sighed again and rose to her feet. "I'm going back to bed," she said, her voice trembling from exhaustion. Her head bowed in sadness as she trudged away from the table and down the hall.

I glanced at Aunt Gwennie.

"Everyone moves through grief in their own time," my aunt told me quietly.

* * *

IT WASN'T JUST my mother's death that Ami was grappling with. This past Yule was ridiculously chaotic.

Even crazier than last year, and that's saying something.

After years of wondering who each of our fathers was, my sisters and I discovered that we were the daughters of gods. My father? Apollo. Ami's father? Hermes. Althea's dad was Poseidon, and Ayla's father was Hades. They'd promised our mother—Athena's High Priestess—they would stay away from us.

Eventually, they decided not to, and that's where the drama started.

There were journeys to the underworld, a meeting with Hecate that netted my sister Althea a magical crow and a new goddess, baby daddy reveals galore... All of that might have been bearable.

With Persephone's revenge on my mother, though, things took a turn for the worse.

Mom died.

Jason died.

We all returned from the underworld dazed and distraught over what had happened, but Ami had found the entire experience particularly surreal and overwhelming. It had left her with a deep sense of anxiety and unease.

Actually, who was I kidding?

My sister was clearly depress—

"Hey, watch it!"

I came back to reality in the middle of an aisle at the Punktex grocery store, with a cart full of groceries. Their eyes followed me as I moved to the side, apologized and tried to get back on track. "Sorry."

"She's a witch," I heard someone say behind me. "And yet she has no idea which way she's supposed to be going?"

"Oh, stop it, Dora. Maybe she was having a vision or something."

I thanked the woman who had stood up for me and hurried away from the disapproving stares. I had a lot to finish up, and it would not happen mulling over the past in the middle of the cookie aisle.

I grabbed a package of Double-stuffed Oreos, Ami's favorite.

I passed by the Chips-A-Hoy, Ayla's favorite.

I did not grab a box.

That girl, I sighed.

She didn't deserve cookies.

My youngest sister, Ayla, had become extremely rebellious since my mother's departure. Was there a curfew? Not for her. Homework? Naw.

It was no surprise she left her plate on the table for someone else to clean up. She wore her indifferent demeanor as a badge of honor now, her posture and expression daring anyone to challenge her.

Some of it was normal. She was a teenager and naturally had her share of attitude.

Some of it was…well, not due to her age.

I'd hoped Mom would be around to keep an eye on her, because Ayla could communicate with and see the dead—but I had the feeling half of her rebellious behavior was an act for Mom's benefit.

Even if it was, it was difficult to see Ayla turn into somebody who no longer exhibited any concern for those around her.

"Astra Arden!"

The voice was harsh and demanding, breaking

through the store noise and causing everyone to stop and turn in its direction.

"Uh-oh," I heard someone whisper behind me. "It's the police."

I turned around.

It wasn't the police.

It was Lillian Thornton, the mayor of Cassandra and the mother of Jason Bishop, my now deceased ex-boyfriend. Chief Daniel Harmon, my former boss, stood beside her looking like he wanted to be anywhere but the Punktex in aisle five in front of the Sunday shopping crowd.

"Lil, let's not do this here," Harmon said, his face worried.

"Oh, no. She's been trying to avoid me. This is where we're doing it," Lillian shrieked. She charged at me, her face scrunched up in fury. "You!" She leveled an accusatory finger at me. "You murdered my son! It's all your fault!"

She had already said these things to me.

Many times.

I'd already apologized.

Many times.

Mayor Thornton remained mired in her grief and blame no matter what I said.

I stepped back, but she followed, her voice

growing louder as she spoke. I frantically looked around for an escape route, but the only way out was blocked by the crowd that had gathered around us.

Great.

In the military, this is known as a BOHICA situation. (Bend over, here it...well, you get what it means.) All I could do was stand there, speechless, as Lillian Thornton unleashed her rage on me on a Sunday afternoon.

In Punktex.

In aisle five.

By the cookies.

I'd already heard all of her rage. I'd had to face her shock, anger, and intense grief the day we returned from the underworld. Jason, who assured me he wasn't too disappointed to be dead, handled his own death far better than his mother.

Lillian Thornton was aware of two things.

One? Her one and only son was a ghost.

Two? Her only son died because of his involvement with me.

Those two facts led to a state of rage whenever she saw me or any of my sisters.

"You killed my son!"

"Lilian, please," Chief Harmon said, stepping toward her.

I said the only thing I could think of saying. "I'm sorry."

"Sorry?" Lillian barked out a laugh, and the crowd that had gathered around us tightened together. "Sorry? That's all you have to say for yourself?"

I should have kept my mouth shut.

Nothing I said helped.

"Lillian," Harmon warned.

"No way, Daniel. She must be punished for her actions. She murdered my son!" She turned back to me. "You horrible b—"

"Lillian!" The chief attempted to stop her cursing, but she was far angrier and louder than he was.

"Mommy, the lady used a bad word." A young girl pointed to the mayor, her eyes wide with wonder.

"Hush," the mother whispered, her eyes locked on the scene.

"Oh, you're just horrible," Lillian said, her voice dripping with disgust. "I don't even recognize you anymore, Astra. I've lost my son. I've lost my son because of you! Even when he was alive, you were terrible to him, but I didn't think you'd kill him!"

I felt a chill in the air as her voice echoed in my eardrums, and I could've sworn I felt Jason's presence lingering around us. It was almost as if he were trying to comfort me, to calm his mother down and let her know everything would be okay.

Her eyes focused on the area next to me.

I knew it.

Jason was there.

"Don't you make excuses for her!" Lillian's face softened ever so slightly and then hardened again, her eyes narrowing as she turned to face me once more. "If you didn't know this trollop, you'd still be here, Jason! Yes, that's her fault!"

A few onlookers let out a collective gasp as she spoke.

"Is she talking to her dead son?" someone whispered.

"I swear, this town is weirder than a one-legged duck swimming in circles."

Lillian's face changed from angry to disappointed. Whatever Jason was saying seemed to get through to her. But then the red flush of rage returned to her face. "No way! I'll never forgive her!"

"Mayor Thornton, please," I said, my voice confident but quiet. "I didn't kill Jason. He died because of forces beyond our control, and no, it wasn't fair. But you can't keep blaming me for that."

"Maybe the crazy mother is right. He was always running, so how come he died of a heart attack at such a young age?" someone pointed out in a hushed whisper.

"Maybe she really was the one who killed him," another chimed in.

Lillian's face twisted in rage as her gaze locked ferociously on mine. Every emotion she was feeling was written across her face: pain, hurt, sorrow, and anguish.

I truly felt sorry for her.

But I was also feeling sorry for myself.

"Fair?" She spat out the word like a curse. "Life isn't fair—you should know that by now." Her gaze softened slightly and I could see the love she had for her son behind the anger in her eyes. "He loved you, Astra," she said softly, "but he shouldn't have given his life for yours."

"Lil," Chief Harmon tried to stop her again.

"No," the mayor turned to face him. "She doesn't deserve to live."

"Lil," Harmon tried again.

"She isn't even human, Daniel." The mayor's eyes turned back toward me. "She'll never have a human life. Why should I let her live? Why should I let her do this to some other man? Some other mother?"

I noticed a strange tingling sensation in my fingers and wondered if Jason was trying to tell me something. I could feel the door behind me almost pulsing as if it was calling me. I had no idea where the thought was coming from, but it became more powerful as Mayor Thornton reached toward Harmon—

Oh.

Oh, boy.

My eyes fixed on the gun that the mayor had pulled from the inside of Harmon's jacket. She wrapped her long, slender fingers around the handle and pointed the barrel directly at me. "I hate you, Astra Arden."

Fair enough.

Dead in the cookie aisle.

I'd fought in magical wars, tracked criminals all over the world, and won fights with some of the most powerful paranormals on the planet, but I would die from a bullet shot by a psychic mayor in the cookie aisle of a Florida Punktex.

Great.

"No!" Harmon shouted, stepping between us, his back to me. "That's enough, Lillian! Give me that."

"Get out of the way, Daniel." Her voice was cold and steady, as if she had finally found the strength she needed.

I stepped closer. I kept my gaze fixed on her, not daring to look away. I could feel the crowd behind me, waiting, expecting me to do something witchy and sparkly and miraculous. "Lillian," I said softly, "put down the gun. You don't want to do this."

"Yes, I do."

"Put it down, Lillian," I said firmly. "This is not what Jason would have wanted. He wouldn't have wanted you to hurt anyone else because of him. You know that. Please... put the gun down."

My words—to my utter and complete shock—seemed to hit home.

At first, she didn't move, but then, slowly, she let the gun slip from her grip into Daniel's waiting hands. The crowd exhaled with relief as he tucked the gun away in his pocket for safe keeping.

"Lil, let's go home now," he said softly. "It's over." He put a comforting hand on her shoulder and gently guided her away from the scene. Everyone else silently watched them leave.

As I watched them walk away, a wave of emotion washed over me: relief no one had been hurt or killed; sadness at what had occurred; and regret this was probably not the last time all of us would go through this.

* * *

MAYOR LILLIAN THORNTON vanished later that afternoon.

Vanished. Without a trace.

And because of that public confrontation in the Punktex?

Obviously, I was the prime suspect.

CHAPTER TWO

I was still trying to process everything that had happened when I stepped out of the grocery store (without my groceries) and into the scorching Florida sun—and nearly walked into a werewolf. He was tall, with tanned skin and silver-streaked black hair.

And an annoyingly mischievous smirk that never seemed to leave his lips.

"Ugh. It's you. What are you doing here?" I asked, my voice cold.

Lothian Pennington flashed me a crooked grin. "Always great to see you, Astra. Especially when I'm greeted with such irrepressible enthusiasm," he said.

"Ha ha. You're hilarious."

"I was over at the drugstore and I heard you had yourself quite a situation at Punktex. I wanted to make sure you were okay."

My fingers twitched from the desire to punch him right in his broad, masculine face so I could wipe all that radiating self-confidence off.

That would prove I was basically fine, right?

"Well, as you can see, I'm fine. So you can go now."

He shook his head slowly, still wearing that infuriatingly sexy smile of his. "Not until I know what happened," he said firmly.

"Why do you need to know what happened?"

Before I finished the sentence, he grabbed my arm and pulled me close enough so our noses nearly touched. His skin smelled like night-blooming jasmine mixed with sea salt, and his breath tickled my ear as he whispered: "Let's not do this dance. You know Eddie and Emma will race out of the house and show up on your doorstep if I don't. Work with me, Astra."

Lothian let go of my hand and stepped back, giving me space to breathe again.

I sighed heavily and ran my hands through my hair in frustration. "Okay," I said reluctantly. "I'll tell you what happened. But let's go somewhere else—I'm not sure I want to be here anymore."

He nodded and motioned for us to walk away from the store. We stopped at a nearby sidewalk café, and he bought us coffees while I recounted what had happened in Punktex a few minutes before.

When I finished the story, Lothian shook his head in disbelief. "That was brave of you to step in like that—most people wouldn't have had the guts to do it. You should be proud of yourself."

"Oh, shut up, would you?" I told him, irritated. "I could have taken her and the chief down in a matter of seconds, but I...ugh, I just didn't want to cause her any more pain or grief. I get why she's acting the way she is. Jason's death is the tragedy of her life."

Lothian nodded in understanding. "I'm sure it is, but that doesn't mean she can run around in grocery stores and pull guns on you, Astra. You would have been perfectly within your rights to take her down. I'm sure the chief would have backed you."

Chief Daniel Harmon fired me the day after I returned from the underworld and before Jason Bishop's body was six feet under. Lillian Thornton demanded that I be drummed out of every legitimate job in town.

I guess she won't be happy until she runs me out of town.

And the woman doesn't even live here. She's the mayor of the next town over, a spiritualist community of people that talk to the dead.

"Maybe," I said finally. "But probably not."

"You can't let her get away with this, Astra. She had no right to treat you like that."

"What do you suggest I do?" I asked, suppressing a sigh as I took a sip of my coffee. "She's a grieving mother, and she's dating the chief. The woman just took a gun off him and pointed it at my head in the middle of the cookie aisle, and she didn't leave in handcuffs. What am I supposed to do?"

Lothian shrugged. "Show her you won't tolerate it anymore."

"Things are always just that easy for you, aren't they?"

He smirked. "Pretty much."

"That's not how life works," I told him hotly. "You can't just go around making demands without consequence. People are complicated and unpredictable, and they don't always do what you want them to."

Lothian raised an eyebrow skeptically. "That may be true, Astra, but I never said that they do—

I was simply suggesting that you take a stand and defend yourself against someone who is clearly taking advantage of your refusal to fight back. You have every right to protect yourself from this woman if she continues to act in such a hostile manner toward you. I think your tolerance and understanding has been extended far enough." He sipped his coffee. "Has Jason lifted a finger to help?"

"Don't," I warned him.

But Lothian wasn't deterred. "Well, has he? Jason should do more to head off these confrontations. He knows how his mother is. We know they can talk to one another, and yet it seems like he has done nothing to try to stop her from coming after you like this."

I clenched my teeth, trying to suppress my rising anger. "I don't want to talk about Jason with you, Lothian. Can we please just drop it?"

Lothian nodded reluctantly and took another sip of his coffee before changing the subject. "Emma punched Eddie last night when he tried to…encourage her to go to bed early."

I couldn't help but laugh. Emma was tough but very pregnant, and Eddie was a werewolf alpha with muscles on his muscles. "What did he do?"

Lothian chuckled as he recounted the story. "He tried to pick her up and carry her off to bed, so she punched him in the nose. He dropped any idea of force in about a second, and she just waddled away laughing. She's got guts, I'll give her that."

"She does indeed."

Lothian said that Eddie had been shocked and embarrassed by her boldness. He was also a little impressed, though he would never admit it. The rest of the pack backed off after that incident, leaving Emma to go wherever she pleased.

We talked about other topics until our coffee ran out and we decided it was time to go home. As I watched Lothian walk away, I couldn't help but feel a little grateful to him. His invitation to coffee gave me some breathing room, and I walked toward my Jeep feeling much calmer than I'd felt before.

* * *

ALTHEA HELD up a spray bottle with a glowing blue liquid that looked almost otherworldly. It was swirling and whirling within like a miniature whirlpool.

"This is it," Ayla said. "We created this glass

cleaner that makes the mirrors into a portal to the great beyond. Think of it like FaceTime for ghosts. You can see them, hear them, and even talk to them regardless of whether you have the death speaker power. It's like a bottled death speaker."

Ami stared, unimpressed. "So, how is this supposed to help us?"

Althea stared down at Ami. "It will allow you guys to communicate with ghosts through the mirror, dimwit."

"I'm not a dimwit."

"Are you sure? Have you looked at yourself in the mirror lately?"

"What? Because I look like hell, I'm stupid?"

"No, that's not what I meant," Althea said. "Look, just forget I said anything."

"Let's get back to this, please. Jeez." Ayla handed me the spray bottle and some newspaper. "Simply spray some of the liquid onto any mirror surface, wipe it down just like you were cleaning the mirror to spread it around, and then stand back—you should see images or hear voices soon enough. It works best on full-length mirrors but will still work on any mirror, really."

I took the bottle from Ayla. Ami seemed

intrigued too, so I offered her a chance to try it out first.

Ami nodded, her eyes brightening with anticipation. She slowly stood up and took the bottle in her hand. She walked over to the large mirror that Ayla and Althea had brought in and sprayed it with the solution.

The mirror had an ornate gold frame that glistened even in the dim light. The glass itself was dark and appeared to be an abyss, with an unfathomable depth that seemed to go on forever. Faint shadows of figures seemed to flicker in it from time to time.

There was a gentle whooshing sound as the liquid spread across the glass, illuminating the mirror with a deep, eerie blue glow. Ghostlike images appeared in the glass, with faces from the past and present occupying the mirror's surface. The figures in the glass seemed to move around as if they were alive.

After a few moments of stillness, ghostly whispers and faint voices that seemed to come from far away.

Ami handed the bottle and newspaper back to me. "I mean, it's pretty," I said, unsure of its practicality. I glanced down at the wet newspaper in my hand. There was an article on Siltwater

Investments, a nonprofit that had recently started up in Cassandra.

"Astra! Astra, can you hear me? Astra!"

I looked up.

I knew that voice.

That was Jason's voice.

My heart skipped a beat as I stepped closer to the mirror.

Ami gasped as a figure took shape.

Finally...there, in the center of the glass, was Jason's face.

"I can hear you, Jason. I can see you, too." His face was illuminated by the blue light, but he looked just like I remembered him. "You're very blue." I glanced at Althea. "How long is this going to last?"

"We think about four to six hours. Give or take. Over time, the image will fade a bit, and the voice will grow a bit more faint, but it's the best we could do."

Jason stepped closer to the glass, his eyes wide with awe and wonder. He slowly raised his hand and placed it against the mirror, as if he were trying to touch me.

"Astra, I'm so sorry about what happened. My mother...she shouldn't have done that. She was wrong, and I am so sorry she pulled a gun on you and got you fired. It was completely out of line. Please forgive me."

"His mother pulled a gun on you?" Ayla asked, shocked.

"When did this happen?" Ami added.

"This morning at Punktex. I'm fine. Everything's fine. I didn't want you guys to worry."

Jason nodded in agreement. "Astra was incredibly brave. I tried to convince Mom to give up her anger, but she just...she just isn't listening to me anymore." He glanced at Ayla. "She thinks your father is controlling me somehow, that because I'm in his realm, I'm not able to think for myself."

"That's ridiculous," Ayla said.

Jason's reflection in the mirror appeared to shimmer and ripple like a watercolor painting, his blue eyes and pale skin blending in an ocean of softness. "She won't listen to me, no matter what I say. She believes Hades is using me as some kind of tool to do his bidding and that I don't have any freedom anymore."

"We can help you, Jason," Althea told him without hesitation. "We're here for you, no matter what happens."

Ami stepped forward and placed her hand on

the glass as if she were trying to reach out to him, but she knew it was useless. "Yes. We could try."

"We can do more than try," Ayla told her.

I met his eyes. "You don't deserve this treatment from your own mother—and I don't blame you at all for the treatment I'm getting from her, either, so don't you dare feel guilty. We'll figure something out, I promise you that much."

Jason gave a faint smile and nodded once more before turning away from the mirror, the blue light fading away slowly until he was gone again.

* * *

MY MOTHER APPEARED in the mirror, her eyes misty with tears. She looked so much older than I remembered, and she seemed to have aged years in a matter of months.

"I should've known better," she whispered. "I should've done something before this happened. Something to stop what was coming—but I didn't know how. Now look at what it has done to our family."

Ayla had a talent for rolling her eyes with a remarkable amount of contempt, but this time she seemed to outdo herself. "Sure, Mom." She looked directly at our mother in the mirror, her gaze challengingly unyielding.

Althea stepped forward and glared. "That's all you can say? Your crappy behavior reverberates through all of this! Including Jason's mother bringing a gun to Punktex, threatening Astra—"

"Come on, Thea, that's not Mom's fault," Ami said.

Ami's face was filled with compassion and understanding, her hand resting on the cool glass surface of the mirror. She seemed to beg Althea to accept our mother's apology as Mom's blue face rippled and shifted in the mirror's reflection like a cloth caught in an invisible breeze.

"Not Mom's fault? Not Mom's fault? Are you kidding me?" Althea said, her voice rising in indignation. "Mom's manipulation of the gods and all her secrets—I mean, come on! She was so wrapped up in her own—"

"That's enough," I said.

Ami raised her voice, defending our mother. "But it wasn't entirely Mom's fault. We all make mistakes, and we have to forgive one another if we—"

"I said that's enough," I repeated.

Althea folded her arms across her chest with a

huff, not willing to let go of her anger just yet. "Maybe you can forgive and forget, but I can't— not until Mom—"

"It won't do any good to bicker over something none of us can change," I said firmly, looking at each sister. "Everyone has to learn from their mistakes and move on, but you can't force that on anybody. We have to accept this and move on. She'll deal with what she's done in her own time."

We all looked at each other, and then at our mother in the mirror. She seemed to shrink with each passing second, as if she were trying to make herself smaller, more insignificant.

"Fine," Althea said.

Mom nodded slowly, her eyes misty with tears once again, but her voice was steady when she replied. "I understand all too well your anger at me, girls. I know it will take a while to move past it. I want that, too…for all of us. I love you all very much."

Ayla rolled her eyes again, but wisely said nothing.

"Let's try to work together and figure out how we can go on from here." With that said, Mom turned away from the mirror and disappeared in a shimmer of light before any of us could respond further.

Althea's eyes narrowed as she spoke, her voice tinged with annoyance. "Astra literally had a gun pointed at her today, and Mom shows up here without even asking how Astra is doing?" A hint of judgment crept into her words.

Ami slammed her fists on the table, her face bright with anger as she looked around the room. Her voice broke as she cried out, "None of you will give her a chance! Not even the smallest of breaks!"

Ayla rolled her eyes again. "Oh, come on, Ami—"

Ami's eyes sparked with a fierce determination as she jumped up and grabbed the spray bottle. "I'm done with this conversation," she said, running out of the room and up the stairs. A few seconds later, she yelled down, "I'm not talking to Mom with you guys anymore!"

Her bedroom door slammed.

Althea turned to face us after staring at the stairs. As she spoke, her lips curved in a sly smirk. "You know, we made each one of us our own bottle." She bowed down to pick up another spray bottle and handed it to me. "There are also refills in the potion room. She had no reason to run as though I was about to ambush her."

"I don't know that she was running because of the bottle," I said, my heart hammering with worry. I hung the spray bottle off the pocket of my jeans. "She'll come around, eventually. She's probably just talking to Mom right now. Hopefully, that connection she has now will help her." I hope.

"Yeah, fine, sure, maybe—I mean, I know all that, but she still has no right to make a judgment on me," Althea said archly.

"The way you're judging her?" I looked over at Ayla, hoping that she would back me up. She didn't. "Look, guys—Ami is having a harder time than the rest of us because of what happened to Mom. Just give her some more time to work through it."

* * *

I CLIMBED THE STAIRS.

Despite their squabbling and secrecy, Althea and Ayla did an excellent job with the Mirror Potion. I couldn't wait to get upstairs and try to contact Jason privately, away from prying eyes and nosy ears.

I walked by Ami's closed door and stopped when I heard her sobbing quietly.

Damn it.

I slowly opened the door and stepped inside. With its pale blue walls and soft, cream carpeting, the room was warm and inviting. The curtains were drawn, shielding the room from the harsh sunlight outside as Ami sobbed under the covers of her bed.

I sat next to her on the bed, wrapping my arms around her shoulders and pulling her close. "Hey, what's going on? I've tried to let you work through it on your own, give you space—but I'm worrying, Ami. I'm not going to lie."

Ami's lips trembled and her eyes were brimming with tears. "I don't know who I am anymore. I'm part Mom, part D—...Hermes, and neither of them are really there for me. I don't understand why Mom did all the things she did, but at the same time, I feel like a part of me is still trying to be like her. But then my father, who's literally the messenger god..." She looked glum. "Well, he barely contacts me or even acknowledges that I exist."

"Oh, honey," I whispered. I hugged her tightly, trying to comfort her. "You're still you, no matter what your parents did or didn't do. That doesn't change you."

"You have Archie. Ayla has Cerberus. Althea has Lily." She sniffed and wiped away her tears. "I feel like everyone has got something to help them through this other than me. I just feel so lost and confused and alone... like I have no identity at all."

"So, first, Hermes' symbol is the caduceus, a winged staff intertwined with two snakes copulating," I pointed out. "I don't know if you'd want two amorous snakes to guide you on your self-discovery journey."

I chuckled, hoping to make her laugh.

Ami nodded and buried her face into my shoulder, tears streaming down onto my shirt as she cried out all of her pent-up emotions from the past few months. I hugged her tightly once again, and didn't release her until the tears stopped flowing.

"It's okay if you don't know who you are right now, or even who you want to be, considering everything that's happened," I whispered. "Sometimes we have to go through an identity crisis before we can figure out where our true selves lie."

I brushed a strand of hair away from her face, thinking of all the times she had confided in me over the past year or so about how difficult it was for her to reconcile Mom's expectations of her with what she wanted for herself; this felt like another layer peeled off to reveal an even more complicated situation beneath it all. "You don't need to figure out your identity right now—you can take it slow," I said as my fingers ran through her hair in a soothing pattern. "You're not alone in this—we're here for you always."

"We are," Ayla said quietly from the door.

Althea nodded. "Yeah, sorry, Ami. I didn't mean to come at you like that. Well, I did, but... yeah, I can be a real jerk. Sorry."

Ami sniffled and wiped her nose with the back of her hand. "Thanks."

We all hugged Ami, and I felt my heart swell with love for my sisters. It took a bit, but in the end they were there for her, like they were always there for me.

Like we would always be there for each other.

CHAPTER THREE

he next morning, Chief Harmon showed up at our house.

Looking for Lillian Thornton.

"Sorry to interrupt breakfast," the chief said, his hat in hand.

Aunt Gwennie's gaze fell warmly on the chief. She offered her hand and smiled. "Chief, won't you join us? I've made plenty extra."

I sat up straight and fixed my gaze on him. I didn't want him to join us. He'd fired me because his insane girlfriend blamed me for her son's death. I didn't want him here, and I didn't want to share my bacon with him.

Harmon surveyed the table and took in the unlikely sight of an owl, a crow, and a dog perched around it. Archie sat on an armchair, his head angled toward Chief Harmon, his piercing yellow eyes fixed on the cop. The crow perched on Ayla's head, her beady black eyes fixed on the chief. Cerberus was crouched on the floor, his dark brown eyes glancing up from the floor as if he was listening in on the conversation. "That's quite the menagerie you're assembling."

"What brings you here?" I asked, my voice tight and cold. My heart raced as I waited for his response; idle chit-chat about the adorable birds and dogs or the forecast for Central Florida was too unpleasant to contemplate.

It was Central Florida.

It would be muggy.

Chief Harmon scratched the back of his neck and avoided eye contact. "When I woke up this morning, Lillian was gone," he said. He nervously bit his bottom lip, his forehead furrowed with worry. "No note, no message on my phone, nothing. Her purse was still at the bungalow, and so was her car. I thought, considering what happened yesterday, she might have come here by taxi or something."

Aunt Gwennie frowned and gave Chief Harmon a sympathetic look. "That is strange," she said. "Perhaps she went to stay with friends somewhere else?"

I furrowed my brow, incredulous at the thought that after everything that had occurred the previous day, she was walking freely in the sunshine. "See, and I thought—considering what happened yesterday—she'd be in jail," I countered.

Chief Harmon turned and fixed me with a solemn stare. "Is that what you want? To put your deceased boyfriend's mother in jail for one moment of weakness? One slight slip—"

"—in public, in front of thirty people, with small children just feet from a crazy woman waving a loaded gun?" I finished. My eyes narrowed as I shook my head. "Chief, your girlfriend needs some help. Maybe you should get her some instead of coddling her murderous instincts like they're understandable."

Ayla speared a sausage with her fork and shook her head. "That's really corrupt, Chief. Jason's mom pulled a gun in a Punktex." She tilted her head. "Maybe you should check the swamp. That kind of thing is certain to make the pixies furious, I'd think." She crunched into the sausage, her eyes narrowing with determination. "Wouldn't you?"

"Pixies?" Chief Harmon asked, startled.

"You know what a pixie is, right?" Althea asked.

"Do I, um, know..." Harmon trailed off and looked baffled. "Mythical creatures that look like fairies?"

"Mythical creatures," Althea snorted.

Ayla nodded. "Alice Windrow, the owner of the Punktex chain? Yeah, she's dating a pixie. Pistachio Waterflash. He's a chieftain, too, so she's not dating just any pixie." Ayla leaned toward Althea. "And I know the guy. There's no way he'd be cool with guns waving around in the local Punktex. Not a chance."

"You know, I don't think we need to tell Harmon everything about the paranormals in Forkbridge, Ayla," I told her.

"Oh?"

I narrowed my eyes and set my jaw sternly, staring at the chief with a cold and unforgiving gaze. "Obviously, if he felt the department needed that information, he would have kept the witch they had on as a consultant."

"Let it go, Arden." Chief Harmon's face was a granite wall, his eyes as cold and unforgiving as the depths of the Arctic. "You were a liability."

I rolled my eyes. "Yeah. Right. Keep telling yourself that."

"Look," he said gruffly, his face reddening with frustration and embarrassment. "There are plenty of things that go on in Forkbridge that I don't understand. Vampires, werewolves—all sorts of weird things. And it isn't just the paranormals—there are plenty of people who live here who have secrets they don't want to share with the rest of us."

"Are you looking for some kind of sympathy?" I leaned back in my chair. "What you're describing is a town. Just a town, Chief. That's your job. To deal with these things. Do you want me to feel sorry for you because these things exist and you don't understand them?" I asked, an edge to my voice.

Chief Harmon clenched his fists and glared at me. "I don't need your sympathy, Arden. I need to know that this town is safe. That the people in it are safe. And right now, it's not. Maybe if you had just done what I asked of you in the job instead of running off to the underw—"

I didn't let him finish his sentence. "Keep people safe? Seriously? You can't even keep track of your own girlfriend when she's lying in bed next to you!" I slammed my palms down on the table and pushed away with such force that the chair screeched against the tile floor as I stood up. "You thought like a cop, so you left Cassandra and drove back to Forkbridge to ask me if I'd seen Lil Thornton. What you should have done was grab the nearest psychic so they could ask the dozens of ghosts that flit around that town what they saw." I stared at him. "Did you do that?"

The chief looked taken aback by my sudden outburst. He opened his mouth, but seemed unable to find the right words to answer. He blinked. "No. I asked people walking around outside her house if they saw her. If any of them were—"

"So that would be a no," I interjected, raising an eyebrow at him in disbelief.

He scowled at me and sighed heavily before speaking again. "Arden, please understand that my priority is the safety of this town—and its people—above all else. Anything else is secondary, including any personal grudges or misunderstandings between us."

"Oh, I get it, Chief Harmon," I said firmly but evenly. "But understand this: I won't be used as a stopgap measure when you can't figure out something yourself about the paranormal world that exists here in Forkbridge. You had that. You gave it up. And just a point—Lillian Thornton doesn't live in this town, so this isn't your case."

He appraised me with a penetrating look before acknowledging my words with a barely perceptible dip of his chin. "Fair enough, Arden," he said in a low voice before broadening his arm in the door's direction. "Thank you for the information. I'll head back to Cassandra and follow your advice."

"Good luck."

"I assume if she turns up here, you'll call me?" The chief eyed me suspiciously, an air of mistrust settling between us.

"Sure."

"Try not to turn her into a frog if she does."

Aunt Gwennie's brows drew together in an angry frown. "Well, that was just offensive," she murmured softly.

* * *

I STOOD ALONE in my bedroom, my back to the door, holding Althea's spray bottle filled with the brilliant blue enchanted liquid. It seemed to swirl and sparkle in the light, gently swaying and shimmering in a mesmerizing way, even when the bottle was still.

"What if your mother shows up?" Archie asked.

"That's what the Vinegar and water spray is for." I would not ignore Mom forever, but I wasn't in the mood to deal with her woeful regrets from the great beyond.

I brought the nozzle up to the mirror and sprayed it liberally, watching as it spread across the surface, twinkling and leaving behind a faint trace of smoke.

As the blue liquid cascaded over its surface, small sparks of magic flickered in the air. Wisps of blue smoke fluttered between my fingers as I danced the liquid around the mirror. "Jason," I called.

Nothing.

"Try knocking?" Archie asked from his perch.

I raised my hand and knocked on the mirror three times.

I mean…it couldn't hurt.

The blue liquid swirled faster and faster, creating a whirlpool of color that illuminated the entire mirror. As the light became brighter, an image appeared in the center of the mirror.

Jason, his eyes twinkling with mischief and his hair tousled by the wind.

He looked around curiously before turning

back with a smile on his face. "I thought you'd have this done last night. Not that I want to start off our first private meeting with a reproach." Jason smiled wider. "You look good, Astra." He tilted his head. "Though I knew that. I check in on your family every day for at least half an hour."

"I wanted to get this done yesterday as well, but my sister...she's really struggling. We all needed to spend some time with her," I told him. "Well, for her, really."

He nodded and sighed heavily. "I know, your mother's pretty insufferable down here at the moment."

I crossed the room and pulled up a chair in front of the mirror. As I sat down, I noticed Jason had done the same wherever he was in the underworld. "Speaking of mothers," I said, "Harmon just burst into our breakfast looking for yours. Do you know where she is?"

He shook his head and looked away. "I haven't seen her since yesterday, when she pulled a gun on you. I wanted to give her a day or two to calm down and realize on her own what a mistake she made, but I haven't been able to find her. It's like she's gone off the grid."

I sighed and leaned back in my chair. "Okay, I

know what I mean in this world when I say that, but you're a ghost. What do you mean when you say it?"

Jason smiled. "When you look at yourself in the mirror, what do you see?"

I looked at my reflection and studied it for a moment. "Well, I see my face, obviously. And yours."

Jason nodded and continued. "But there is something else that connects us, something that binds us together no matter where we are or what we are doing; a silver cord of love and understanding. That's how you could find me here. That's how I know when you want to talk to me. It's a literal cord or energy field that extends from your physical body to the spiritual realm to me—and also your mother, other people you love."

I squinted. "I don't see any kind of cord."

"You're still alive, so you won't. But I do."

I glanced at Archie briefly, who nodded. "So you have a cord that connects to your mother?" I asked Jason.

He nodded. "Well, I did until a few hours ago. I can't feel her presence in the afterlife anymore."

I sat up. "Wait, what do you mean?"

"She's cut us off from one another, like the

silver cord that usually binds us has been severed. I don't know how she did it or why, but I have no way of knowing where she is or what she's doing unless she comes back. I knew she was angry at me, but I didn't think she'd go this far."

"How can you be sure she did this on her own?" Archie asked in a low voice, his feathers softly rustling.

Jason's eyes shifted as if trying to spy something in the shadows, and his fingers twitched as if he wanted to reach out and grab whatever it was he was looking for. "I can feel it tugging every few minutes, but when I try to follow it, it just leads me in circles." His lips set into a determined line as he raised his chin. "She can try to hide from me all she wants–but I'll find her, eventually."

I'd never heard of this silver cord, but I had no reason to doubt what Jason was telling me— especially when Archie confirmed what he was saying. My senses, though, were tingling on high alert at Jason's dismissal of Lillian Thornton's silver cord snapping, and his assumption that she'd done it to herself. I knew enough about magic to realize that the cord might be interrupted by a good ward.

Or a protection spell.

Or...binding spell.

The thought made me shudder, and I felt a chill run down my spine.

"What are you going to do?" Jason asked me. "You have that look."

"I don't think I'm as convinced as you are that she did it to herself. I mean, it's possible. It's definitely possible. Maybe she was embarrassed about her behavior yesterday and she just needs alone time. Maybe she just wanted to be as isolated as possible so she could think things through."

But my mind raced with possibilities.

Grave possibilities.

Dangerous possibilities.

Or maybe the pixies had her. Somewhere in the swamps of Forkbridge she could be wrapped with vines from the murky depths coiled around her limbs, all because she brandished a gun in their territorial grocery store. Or maybe someone with magical abilities snatched her in some weird defense of me.

Or it could have nothing to do with us at all.

Had she been involved in the strange psychic politics of Cassandra, her weakened state of mourning for Jason leaving her vulnerable to some sinister plot?

"Astra?" Jason asked, his bluish tinged face undulating in the mirror. His eyes were wide, brows furrowed in concern as he stared into the glass. "You looked like you were a million miles away for a second."

I shook my head and smiled. "No, I'm here. I was just thinking. I think the best thing I can do right now is talk to the pixies and make sure she's not meditating somewhere in the swamp. I can start looking for her there, and if that doesn't pan out, then I'll look elsewhere."

"Okay."

"Harmon, if he has any ounce of intelligence, he ought to be scurrying back toward Cassandra to debrief the ghosts." I cocked my head. "Or better yet, why don't you do it? You'd be better at prying information out of them."

"I can, but just so you know—I have to be in the underworld for this mirror thing to work. Either here, or literally right next to you. You won't be able to call me in Cassandra."

"Can you come find me with that silver cord thing?" I asked.

Jason met my gaze, stroking his chin in contemplation. "I can. You'll need to keep a mirror sprayed with that stuff, though."

"I can do that."

Jason nodded, then backed away, fading into the darkness. "I'll be in touch soon. Good luck—and thanks. I'm not worried, but..."

"No, I get it."

He gave me a reassuring smile before he stepped back away from the mirror and faded into the underworld.

"Well," Archie said with a sigh, "that could have gone better."

"It went fine."

Archie looked at me. "You don't really think she did that to herself, do you?"

As we watched the faint glimmer of light from the mirror fade away into nothingness, I admitted silently that I did not think Jason's mother had suddenly discovered silver cord magic and then snipped her own to get some "me time."

"Yeah, you don't," Archie said. "I can tell."

"Let's get some more information. Then I'll tell you what I think."

We clearly had some investigation to do and the sooner we got started, the better chance we had of finding Lillian Thornton in one piece.

CHAPTER FOUR

"Did you know there's an International Bacon Day?" Archie shouted from the back seat of the Jeep, his head bobbing up and down as we drove along the muddy dirt road toward the ancient swamp where the pixies lived.

"No." I glanced over my shoulder into the backseat. Archie looked like his beak was drawn in a bewildered pout, and considering it was a beak, I had no idea how he pulled that off. The Jeep hit a bump, and the jolt sent us airborne.

"You really are no fun sometimes."

"I'm taking you off-roading, and we're going to a swamp filled with pixies." The road wasn't much better than a dirt track full of dips and potholes that kept us bouncing in our seats. "I'm fun a lot of times."

The thick trees closed in around us, blocking out the sun and creating a mysterious atmosphere. I heard a muffled yelp and glanced back to find Archie's eyes widened.

"Was that you?"

He vigorously shook his head no. "You didn't think she was going to stay home, did you?"

Not again.

I put my foot on the brake pedal and jerked the steering wheel hard to the right. The wheels locked and the Jeep skidded wildly, sending a billowing cloud of dust and gravel into the air. I leaped out of the car and raced around the rear. With almost frantic energy, I yanked on the pale blue tarp draped over something in the back and stared. "Really?" I asked, exasperated.

Ayla stretched casually and then climbed out of the back of the van. "Hey."

"You've got to be kidding me."

Ayla laughed, brushing a few stray strands of hair away from her face. "Well, now, Astra, come on. We've done this before and it all worked out fine."

I shook my head. "Do you know how dangerous this could be? What if the pixies have

Jason's mother? It's not like they're going to just welcome us in."

Ayla nodded solemnly, acknowledging the danger but not backing down from it. "I know, and that's why I came. You've got a compact in your back pocket that may or may not let you talk to Jason. And only if he's around."

Spies everywhere. "Who told you that?" I asked her.

"Aunt Gertie, obviously. I've got her with me, and I don't need magical sprays and mirrors to talk to her." Ayla crossed her arms. "That makes me pretty useful."

Aunt Gertie was our long-dead aunt who had returned to assist Ayla with her death-speaking abilities. I frowned, suddenly realizing she'd probably been summoned from the otherworld when she came back. Most likely another of Hades' "gifts."

I released a long sigh, wondering what else would look different in retrospect now that we knew about our divine fathers and our mother's…ethical challenges.

"Look, Ayla—even if your logic is solid and even if you're right, you should have come and talked to me about it."

"I know," she sighed, her mouth curling into

a smirk. "But I figured if I waited for you to say yes, we'd still be back at the house arguing about it in two days' time. So I just said yes for you."

I wanted to give her a piece of my mind, to lecture her on being honest and direct. But, as I looked into her eyes, I saw that cocksure confidence of youth that reminded me way too much of myself. I gestured toward the passenger seat and released an audible, heavy sigh.

"Oh, stop with the exaggerated sighs, will you?" Ayla said as she jumped back in the Jeep. "I know you don't care that much."

We trudged further into the swamp's murky depths. The engine roared, the wheels churned, and mud and dirt kicked up in our wake. Unseen creatures croaked and shrieked in the shadows, but we pushed forward, driven to reach our destination despite a strange fog settling around us like a blanket.

"Look, Ayla, I don't want to replace Mom in everyone's lives—"

"Thank Hades for that. Mom was a manipulative sociopath."

I rolled my eyes. "She wasn't a manipulative sociopath," I said, glancing up at the trees looming ominously as we passed. I frowned. "I

SCRIES LIKE AN OWL | 55

don't remember this swamp being so gloomy the last time I was here."

"I've never been here. Because you guys never let me go anywhere."

I shifted in my seat, knowing that Ayla had a point. "Quick reminder? That wasn't me, Ayla, and you know it."

"You never should have respected Mom. She didn't deserve it."

I wasn't sure what to say about that.

She might be right.

Mom refused to let my sister go anywhere, no matter how many times she begged. Maybe she was terrified that something might happen on the outside—that her witchy abilities might be discovered. Or maybe it really was that my sister would follow in my footsteps and flee…

Huh.

Now I wondered if my sisters were sheltered so Apollo, Hermes, Poseidon and Hades couldn't get their claws into their own daughters without my mother being aware of it.

I refocused on the present. "Okay, Ayla. It's easy to tell me what I should have done when I came home, but she's our mother. I did what I felt I could without telling her how to parent you three—because I'm not a parent. She was. I didn't have the right. I interfered as much as I thought I could. I was trying to repair my relationship with her."

For all the good that it did.

"Yeah, well, you took us on vacation," she admitted. "Hey—why do you think our fathers didn't show up then? Mom didn't come up with us. There was no one around."

"I don't know," I said honestly. "Maybe they were...afraid that the fish would tell Mom? Maybe they knew we were dealing with a situation that threatened paranormals? I really don't know, Ayla."

That was a good question.

One I'd spent a lot of time wondering about myself since Mom passed away.

It seemed like our fathers kept their distance supposedly because Mom demanded it, but even I had to admit they made reconnection with us overly complicated. I mean, kidnapped to the underworld? What was the point?

A phone call would have worked just as well.

And had they done it like normal people, Jason and Mom wouldn't be dead.

Then again, our fathers?

They weren't normal people.

"I really don't know. I wish I did," I repeated as

we pulled into a small clearing near the center of the swamp. A cypress tree stood tall and proud in front of us, its glossy leaves shimmering in the light. "But I think we're here."

Ayla opened her door and stepped out into the dusk, her eyes wide as she took it all in. I followed and felt a wave of nostalgia wash over me. It had been over a year since I'd last seen this place, but it felt just as magical now as it did then.

"Astra!"

* * *

ALICE WINDROW SEEMED to still be just as I remembered.

And yet she had undoubtedly taken on some of the pixie culture fashion with her dyed blue hair glimmering in the sunlight. Her smile lit up her face when she saw me, and her vivid clothing danced in the breeze as she sprinted across the meadow. "What are you doing here? Did Emma have her baby?"

I met Alice after the goddess Athena directed me—via glowing card—to keep Alice from being murdered. As the sole owner of the Punktex grocery chain after her uncle—who started the stores—passed away, she was exceedingly wealthy—and that wealth had made her a target.

"Nope, Emma's still pregnant," I told her with a smile. "It's been a while since we last saw each other and I wanted to check on you."

"Really?" Alice's smile faded as if she sensed something was wrong. "Are you okay?" she asked cautiously. "I heard about what Lillian Thornton did yesterday—pulling a gun on you like that. That's just awful. I know she loved Jason, but...I just don't understand where she's coming from."

I nodded. "Yeah, I'm fine. We resolved the situation without anyone getting hurt. How have you been?"

"Pistachio and I have been doing really great! I can't thank you and your sisters enough for what you did. I've been learning so much!" Alice then gave us some advice on paranormal creatures in town: what they liked to eat, where they usually hung out, and how not to anger them. "He's a fantastic teacher," she told me, blushing.

"I'll bet he is," Ayla said with a smirk.

I glared at her.

She quickly added, "That's what I hear, anyway."

With one more sisterly glare at Ayla, I turned and asked Alice where Pistachio was.

She responded that he had left early that morning for a couple of days. "He said something about needing to go on a business trip or something. I wasn't super clear about where he was going. Goodness, I was half-asleep."

"So, it was unexpected, then? How early are we talking?" I asked, a little more sharply than I intended.

Alice frowned. "Well, I guess it was really early. I heard the alarm go off at four a.m."

Pistachio Waterflash could have gotten in his car at four o'clock in the morning, driven to Cassandra, and kidnapped the mayor. Pixies could cause human confusion, and Lillian Thornton's kidnapping could have gone down without a struggle if a pixie was involved. Pistachio could have simply asked her to walk out with him, and she would have done it—and probably not have remembered she'd done it.

It was also possible that he would do something like this but wouldn't tell Alice to shield her from the consequences of his actions.

"Do you know what kind of car he was driving?"

"Do I—" Alice seemed to sense the suspicion in my voice and stepped closer. "What do you mean? What's going on? Is Pistachio in trouble?"

I took a deep breath and shook my head, trying to reassure her. "No, no, of course not! I just wanted to know what kind of car he drives. It's not that important. Just curious. The road in here almost bogged down my Jeep in a few places and I'm looking for a new 4x4, that's all. No worries."

Alice's expression softened, and she smiled again, relieved. "Oh, he has one of those new Broncos. He loves it so much! I got it for him for his birthday. It's so cute—it's white, and he's put metallic hot pink flames on the side to match his hair color."

I nodded.

"You know that Lillian Thornton has disappeared, don't you?" Ayla busted in, her eyes meeting Alice's with a stern look. "Right out of her bed this morning while a police officer slept next to her. Seems like something a pixie could pull off pretty easily, don't you think?"

Oh, jeez.

"No, I didn't, Ayla, but Pistachio wouldn't do something like that," she said firmly. "He might be wild at times, but he's always been a good person. He would never hurt anyone." Alice turned to look at me. "Is this why you came here and why you asked me about his truck?" She paused, waiting for me to answer, but I said nothing. "Astra Arden, I thought we were friends!"

"We are. I'm not saying that Pistachio is the person who took Lillian Thornton. I don't even know that the woman was taken by anyone at this point, Alice. I'm just asking some questions."

I had nothing tying Pistachio to the kidnapping of Lillian Thornton. I wasn't sure if Pistachio was guilty or not, but I sure as hell didn't want to take a chance on letting him get away with something that serious.

"You were interrogating me!" Alice said. "At least your sister was honest about it!"

I opened my mouth, then closed it.

What could I say?

The woman wasn't stupid.

"I'm sorry, Alice," I said after a moment. "I know you're in love with Pistachio and I should have been straight up with you. I just didn't want to alarm you if all of this was nothing."

Alice's eyes narrowed. "If you say so," she said, walking away from us. "You really hurt my feelings, Astra. I think it's time for you both to get out of our swamp. Now."

Great.

* * *

I CLIMBED BACK into the driver's seat of the Jeep, but before I could turn the ignition, Ayla and I were already bickering about the best way to interrogate suspects. Her arms were crossed over her chest, and her lips were pressed together in a hard line.

"You were dancing around it! I got straight to the point."

"Is that what that was?" I asked her. "You were too harsh, Ayla. You should have been more subtle. We don't want to scare her off or give her any reason to think that Pistachio is guilty. We want to get information, not make accusations without proof."

"I bet Emma would side with me." Ayla rolled her eyes and recrossed her arms. "I was being subtle! That's how you interrogate people—you put the fear of god into them so they give up their secrets. That's what she deserved for trying to hide something from us."

I glanced at Ayla, who's face was stormy. "She wasn't trying to hide something from us."

"Uh huh. Says you."

"Look, coming at someone may work sometimes, but not here. Alice is a gentle person, and she loves Pistachio—we don't want to make things worse by making her feel like an enemy or suspecting him of something he didn't do." I looked in the rearview mirror at Archie. "Did you see anything while we were getting our butts handed to us?"

The Jeep hit a ditch and bounced as Emma's voice filled the interior.

"Hello?"

I slammed on the breaks and stared at Ayla. "You called Emma to referee this? Seriously, Ayla?"

Emma's voice cut through the tension in the car now so thick the entire tribe of pixies could probably walk across it. "What's going on? Why are you two arguing like this?"

"Because Astra's wrong," Ayla said.

"Well, that happens twenty times a day, and it's not something you would call me for while I was a million months pregnant and ready to pop. What's going on? I heard a bump. Did you guys hit something?" Her tone was full of curiosity, as if she sensed that something strange was happening and wanted in on it, even if it was only at a distance. "Is everything all right?"

"Don't," I warned Ayla. "Eddie made me swear I wouldn't call Emma about any cases until at least six weeks after the baby is born."

"Yeah, so, the point is he didn't make me

swear. Sometimes, it helps to be overlooked by adults."

"Ayla, don't!"

"Don't listen to Astra, Ayla. Spill the tea, girlfriend!" Detective Emma Sullivan, jonesing for a crime to solve, encouraged my youngest sister.

"Oh, don't worry, Emma. I'll tell you. I don't take orders from boys," Ayla said with a sassy sarcasm. "So, Lillian Thornton disappeared this morning and Astra thinks the pixies might have something to do with it because the mayor pulled a gun on Astra yesterday in a Punktex."

I wondered which wards worked against werewolves.

Because Eddie was going to kill me.

Emma gasped, "What?! A gun? No one told me about this! Are you all right? Does Chief Harmon know?" Her voice was filled with equal parts concern and curiosity. I could almost picture her pacing (well, waddling) around in worry while she waited for an answer over the phone.

I sighed.

Yep.

Eddie Renzo was going to kill me.

I took a deep breath before explaining everything that had happened so far.

"I can't believe the chief let her get away with that," Emma said, shocked that he didn't arrest her for grabbing his piece. "He could lose his job for that!"

"I know," I told her. "But who's going to fire him? And like I said, twenty people—maybe more —saw it happen. Lothian was there, too. I'm surprised you didn't hear about it."

We told her about how we had gone to the pixie swamp to investigate, but didn't discover much that was useful because Ayla had been too aggressive toward Alice—

"I was not!" Ayla interrupted.

Emma sided with me. "You were, too, kid, so pipe down. Let me hear the rest of the story."

Ayla sulked as I explained what we thought might have happened to Lillian—that Pistachio Waterflash confused her, marched her out of bed, and took her because she'd pulled a gun on me in one of Alice's Punktex's.

"But it's only a theory, and that's as far as we've gotten," I said.

Emma let out a long sigh. "Okay, this is a lot to take in. Ayla, you need to be more careful next time you're dealing with pixies. I know it's hard for you to control your temper, but it has to be done. You don't want to get on their bad side because they can be powerful and unpredictable."

"Fine," Ayla answered, her tone sullen. "I mean, I never would have known that without your human advice. My being a witch and all. So thanks."

"Oh, young lady, your sass could keep a house warm on a winter night," Emma teased. "I wish I could wrap it around my big, swollen yet freezing feet. You know, you'd think all the body temperature water down there causing the swelling would act like an insulator or something." She paused for a moment, then said, "Okay, now, what needs investigation next? Let me think…you probably need to go to Cassandra and see if there's any surveillance showing Pistachio Waterflash's Bronco around the mayor's house at four."

"That's where I was headed," I told her.

"Smart, smart. You should also talk to Alice again—if you can manage it without Ayla getting too aggressive—and see if she has any more information about the pixies' plans or motives. Maybe Pistachio really is on a business trip—but if he is, where is he? Nail his alibi down. Honestly, he didn't strike me as a criminal mastermind, but he protects Alice from things without thinking sometimes. And then—oh, hey, honey!"

I listened to the muffled sounds of a kiss, followed by Eddie's voice, the pitch slightly softer and lower than normal. "Why are you still up, Em?" he asked. "I thought you were going to take a nap."

"Just talking to Astra," she responded. Her voice was way too mechanical and measured, like someone had hit the pause button on her emotions. "By the way, honey, did Lothian tell you about anything weird that happened in town yesterday?"

Silence.

"At a grocery store, maybe?"

Only static lingered through the phone line.

"To Astra?"

"Maybe," Eddie muttered, almost too low to hear.

"I love you, Eddie, but if a gun ever gets pulled on my best friend and you or your werewolves decide I don't need to know, I'm going to have my brother the vampire bite every one of you. Twice." Her voice grew louder as she focused on us once more. "I know it's a lot of work, but if you guys put your heads together, I'm sure you'll figure out what happened to Lillian."

"I think so," I told her. "There is something weird going on, though. Jason said his connection to his mother was severed. I don't know what it means, but it does point to some kind of paranormal thing going on here."

"Jason? Your dead boyfriend, Jason? That Jason?"

"Long story," I told her.

"Okay. Tell me later. Good luck!"

"Yeah. Thanks," I said, not able to hide the worry in my voice.

"Stop it. You've got this. Call me if you need me. And if the love of my life and father of my unborn child tries to control my communication like he's the boss of me, remember I'm the boss of me and you have my permission to blast him with whatever sparkly dust or fuzzy magic lightning will make him realize he's not the boss of me."

I let out a little chuckle, grateful for Emma's support. "Yes, ma'am."

CHAPTER FIVE

"**G**o over there," Ayla said, as we passed through the small town of Cassandra. She pointed toward a gas station tucked between a sleepy diner and a pawn shop advertising saddles, guitars and psychic readings in its front window.

"I don't need gas."

"No, but that's my friend's gas station. Remember Bill Platt?"

Yep. An unpleasant man that was not fond of witches, if I recall. I think he called us Satan's hags. "You're friends with Bill Platt?"

"No. His son. I bet he knows something about what's going on in Cassandra. Plus, the chocolate milkshakes are to die for."

"You're friends with Bill Platt's son?"

"Did I not just say that? I have friends, you know." She paused as we drove past an old barbershop and an abandoned church with broken stained glass windows. "Well, a friend, at least."

I pulled in to the gas station and parked, surprised at how nice it looked considering its size. It was an old-fashioned building with bright yellow paint and a red neon sign that read 'BILLS GAS & SNACKS' on the outside.

As we stepped inside, I was hit by the smell of motor oil and fries—a combination that was both mouth-watering and masculine. The walls were lined with shelves stocked full of all kinds of snacks, like chips, candy bars, and soda pops.

"Hey there!" Ayla said, waving.

A tall teenager stepped forward from behind the counter, his face lighting up when he saw my sister. "Ayla? What are you doing here?"

I blinked.

Was that little Melvin Platt?

Little Melvin Platt wasn't so little anymore.

In fact, Melvin Platt had grown from a scrawny adolescent to a tall, strong young man. The awkwardness of a couple of years ago gave way to a six-foot tower of confidence and

SCRIES LIKE AN OWL | 71

strength. His short, unkempt hair and rough stubble gave him an inappropriately sexy vibe. "That's Melvin Platt?"

"He goes by Mel now," she said. A faint flicker of emotion crossed her features.

Ayla was working overtime to keep her expression and body language neutral, but Mel didn't bother hiding his feelings. His eyes lit up the moment he saw Ayla, his face breaking into a bright smile as he stepped out from behind the counter to greet her.

How on earth had this happened?

"Hi, Mel."

"Hello there, Ms. Arden."

"I remember you from when we were here a few years ago," I said, extending my hand. "That business with the arson was nasty stuff."

Mel nodded politely and shook my hand. "It was just awful, but if it hadn't happened, I would never have met Ayla, I don't think." He kept sneaking glances at her as we talked, as if trying to commit every detail of her face to memory. "But I did, and it's all thanks to you bringing her here for Halloween, Ms. Arden."

"Is that so?" I eyed Ayla, and she blushed.

I wondered how they'd developed a friendship —and how Ayla knew about the superiority of milkshakes—when she was never allowed out of the house on her own.

I wondered, but I didn't ask.

I wasn't Mom.

"Yep, it sure is." Mel pulled out two chocolate milkshakes from behind the counter and handed them to us with a bigger smile. "On the house. Think of it as a thank you."

I shook my head. "I appreciate the gesture, Mel, but we really need to—"

"Come on, you know you want one." Ayla said, nudging me with her elbow. "They're delicious. I promise. One milkshake will not derail what we're doing. It might even help explain why we're here."

She had a point, and I reluctantly accepted it, taking a sip as Mel looked on.

Ayla wasn't wrong. It was even better than I expected–thick and creamy, with a hint of chocolate that sent my taste buds into overdrive. "Okay, that's a fantastic milkshake," I admitted.

Ayla smiled as she watched me take another sip. "See? I told you they were good." She gave me a smug glance, followed by a knowing look at Mel. "I told you, and now you see it for yourself. They never listen to me."

"I'm drinking the milkshake, Ayla. Let's not be overly dramatic."

Mel grinned. "So, I'm thrilled to see you and everything, but what are you doing here with Astra?" He glanced toward the garage. "No offense meant, Ms. Arden, but you know that the town isn't a huge fan of you since Jason died."

The town wasn't a fan of me before Jason died, either.

"I know," Ayla told him. "We're here because of Lillian Thornton's disappearance. We just want to find some answers. Have you seen or heard anything strange lately? Anything at all?"

"Disappearance?" Mel looked away, his face growing serious. "Well...yeah, actually. I opened up the shop for Pops this morning, so I had to get up really early. I heard screams coming from the woods between here and my house."

"Screams?" Ayla asked, startled.

"What kind of screams?" I asked him.

"Not like...fun screams, you know? Like screaming for help, almost. It sounded like someone was being attacked or something." He paused and shook his head before continuing. "Anyway, I was going to help, but Daniel came out of the woods and told me he was just practicing for a play, and not to worry about it. No one else came running out, so I figured the ghosts weren't concerned. But…still, it freaked me out a little."

The town had a spectral early warning system —the ghosts that inhabited Cassandra monitored things and reported any craziness to the proper town authorities. It was an incredibly effective system. There was almost no crime in Cassandra…

Well, except for the arsons.

And a few murders.

But mostly very effective.

"Daniel? Who's Daniel?" Before Mel could answer my question, my phone vibrated on my hip. "Hold on one second, Mel." I tapped the screen and held it to my face. "Hello?"

"A package came here for you. From your father," Althea said.

"Go ahead and open—"

"Right. Like I was calling you for that. I opened it already. It looks like a toy jail, almost— for some reason, your dear father is sending you a miniature prison."

"Did you say a toy jail?" I asked, struggling to comprehend the oddness of this situation.

"Yep, that's what I said. Try to keep up," she said in a tone that made it clear she was trying to hold back her annoyance. "And there's a pixie inside. It looks like Pistachio Waterflash."

My mouth hung open.

"And there's a note, too. From your father. He says he saw your need for the pixie and wanted to ensure that you had what you needed."

Gee, thanks, Dad. How the heck—

Oh, right.

Apollo was a god of prophecy, so that was possible.

"Pistachio's not hurt, is he?"

"Not as far as I can tell. He's not happy, but he looks...safe, I guess? I mean, they shrink down themselves, anyway. And honestly, he's probably safer in there than he would be out here. If Apollo shrunk him down forcefully and he can't expand back to full size when we let him out, Cerberus might use him like a chew toy, chieftain or no."

I had so many questions.

Questions about what was going on in Cassandra.

Questions about what was happening back home.

So many questions.

I wondered why there wasn't a search party set up to look for the mayor in these woods. Was this town really so odd that blood-curdling screams were just shrugged off, even when the mayor had gone missing? And who was this Daniel guy that claimed he was rehearsing a play during the night on a dark path in the woods?

Did Apollo know something about Lillian Thornton's disappearance? Or did he just think that having a pixie would help us in some way?

So many questions.

Too many questions.

"Look, just keep him in the box for his own safety and because we don't know what's going on. Ayla's friend Mel heard something in the woods last night that I want to check out. Then I'll be home."

"Sounds good."

* * *

"C'MON," Mel said, pointing toward the door. "I can show you where those screams were coming from." He grabbed a flashlight from under the counter and spoke briefly to a coworker as we stepped out the door and into the parking lot.

As we trudged along the edge of the station toward a dense cluster of trees in the distance, Mel explained that Daniel Caldecott was the interim mayor who had recently moved here from San Diego.

"The interim mayor? Already?" I asked.

He held up his phone. "The town emailed."

"So, you knew about Lillian Thornton being missing?" I said.

A chorus of crickets chirped, and then a great horned owl hooted somewhere in the distance. I looked up through the canopy and saw Archie gliding above it. Hopefully, he would ignore his wandering eye and snack-hungry belly and concentrate on the task at hand.

"Sort of. I mean, I knew she couldn't perform her duties. The ghosts keep everyone pretty well informed of things in this town, Ms. Arden," the young man told me with polite seriousness. "After the email, Pops told me this morning before I left that one of the neighbor's roommate ghosts told her that Mayor Thornton was really rattled about what happened yesterday. You know, when she pulled a gun on you and all?"

I frowned. "Oh, I remember."

"Well, she took some time off because of that. You know, get her head on straight."

"I see."

But I didn't, not really.

Everything transpired at such a rapid pace, so

quickly that I couldn't believe the story. Well, that and that Lillian Thornton's breakdown in the fifth aisle of the local Punktex would make a convenient excuse for her disappearance if, in fact, someone wished her gone.

"So tell me more about this Daniel fellow." It wasn't a name I'd ever heard before, and Cassandra wasn't exactly a town where strangers could come in and gain a foothold fast.

"Daniel Caldecott?"

"Yes. If you don't mind?"

Mel explained that much of what he knew about the man comprised the various rumors he'd heard. One was that Daniel was a rich developer from San Diego, and he had a spiritual awakening and moved here. "But I don't know if that's true. He's always so secretive," Mel said with a shake of his head. "Really surprised he's interim mayor, honestly."

Okay, I thought Cassandra wasn't a town where strangers could come in and gain a foothold fast.

Just then, Ayla stumbled over a protruding knotted root, her arms flailing as her weight was thrown forward. Before I could think about helping, the young, stubbled Mel Platt was beside her faster than I could blink. He pulled her upright, his face etched with concern. "Are you all right?"

"I am, thanks," she said with a nod.

"Glad to hear it, Ayla. Back to Daniel for a second. What did you mean by secretive?" I asked, eyeing Ayla's hand in Mel's. I noted she was stable and the kid had no reason to keep holding it.

I also noted I was starting to sound like my mother.

"He's been seen with a few different people in town, but they're people no one seemed to know. Pops grumbles about him all the time, that he must be pushing more out-of-towners to come here," Mel explained. "As you can imagine, Dad hates that."

Bill Platt, Mel's father, was head of the Merchant's Guild in Cassandra. He was all for attracting more tourism, which would mean more money—he just didn't want to attract growth. "The people should show up, spend their money, talk to their dead relatives, tip their psychics, and then go back to where they belong," Bill told me once.

Mel explained the ghosts had seen Daniel going into several abandoned buildings on the outskirts of Cassandra, meeting people, and then returning to his apartment in the center of town. "Sometimes he has a briefcase, they said," Mel added.

Briefcases usually contain documents or cash —and carrying either when leaving a deserted building after a secret meeting with a mysterious stranger seems suspicious.

Ayla tensed suddenly, her eyes darting from side to side before settling on a spot in the distance. She shook her head, as if to clear away whatever it was she had heard. "Jason's here," she said. "He wants to speak with you. Get out the mirror."

My fingers scrabbled through my coat pocket for the familiar, round shape of my makeup compact. I opened it up and quickly sprayed it with Althea and Ayla's blue spray. Holding it in front of me, I carefully scanned the clearing for Jason's presence.

"What's she doing?" Mel whispered.

"Shh," Ayla told him.

After a few moments, a faint silhouette of a figure emerged from the background of trees and shadows.

"Well, that's not what I was hoping for," I muttered. "I can barely make out his face. Are you sure it's even him?"

"It's a small mirror, Astra." Ayla defensively crossed her arms, "What more do you expect? You picked a powder compact. Maybe if you brought a hand mirror, you'd be able to see him a little more clearly. And yes, it's Jason. Who else would want to spend their eternal rest chasing after you?"

I dropped the mirror to my side in a single, swift motion. "That was a little uncalled for, don't you think?"

Ayla's eyes locked with mine, and she didn't flinch one bit. "No. Don't give me that look," she said. "He follows you around like he's your own personal shadow, more than my poor dog ever follows me. You can't even let him go in—"

Abruptly, Ayla paused, her attention focused on the empty air where Jason's spirit had been last. She nodded and rolled her eyes as if she was hearing something nobody else could.

"Jason is griping at you now, isn't he?" I asked a little smugly.

Ayla whipped her head around and shot me a look that was equal parts exasperation and annoyance. "Oh, he is lecturing me about how I should stop ragging on you and how I should show more respect for your decisions," she said with a roll of her eyes.

I looked at Mel, and he shrugged. "I'm used to it. I grew up here. The ghosts have a lot of opinions."

Ayla turned back to the empty air. "Listen here buddy," she said in a voice that was both stern yet snarky all at once. "I'm not being mean when I call Astra out about her choices. She's—wait, what?" Ayla paused. "Where?"

"What's he saying?" I asked her.

Ayla turned and faced me again, her expression unreadable as she crossed her arms and said, "He says I should stop ragging on you. That no matter what I say, it won't make a difference in how he feels about you or how much time he spends with you. He says whatever choices you make, they're your own—and that I should respect that the way I want you to respect my choice."

My boyfriend was great with kids. "Okay, that's—"

"And that he's standing on the necklace he gave Lillian Thornton for Mother's Day last year."

I stared at her. "You could have led with that."

"Yeah, I guess I could have."

* * *

I DROPPED to my knees and searched the ground.

Then, nestled deep between two blades of grass, I spotted it—a small glint of silver that shimmered like quicksilver in the sun. No larger than a coin, its reflective surface flashed and twinkled like a star.

I picked it up carefully and held it in front of me.

I remembered this necklace.

In fact, I'd gone to the jewelry store with Jason to help him choose it. It was an ornate silver locket with a rose and the words 'I love you, Mom' engraved on one side. On the other side, 'Forever and always, Jason' is inscribed.

"He's right," I said as I looked up. "This is his mother's necklace."

"Are you sure she even wears it now?" Ayla asked.

I felt my eyelids squeeze shut, picturing her from the day before. Her gaze burned into me, her jaw clenched, and I could sense Jason's anxiety rising like an energy swirling around me —then I saw it.

I glanced down to Lillian Thornton's neck and saw the glimmer of the necklace I held in my hands, nestled between the open buttons of her blouse.

"Oh, man, I don't want to read this," I said quietly, opening my eyes and looking down. The clasp was still locked—the chain itself had snapped. I hoped Mayor Thornton had done it herself, as a way of leaving a distinct breadcrumb trail for us to follow instead of...

I shuddered.

"Read?" Mel asked.

Ayla nodded. "Astra's witch power—well, one of them—is psychometry."

He frowned. "You mean psychoscopy?"

"It's the same thing," I said, cutting off the occult vocabulary debate. "I touch things, and I see things that happened around them." And the more deeply an object was in touch with and connected to a person, the stronger the emotions would be around that contact.

I fixed my gaze on the necklace. My hands felt heavy, almost hot.

She most likely wore it every day.

I didn't want to think about Jason's mother being mistreated to the point that her necklace broke in the scuffle, and I certainly didn't want to see or experience that in a mental video. I absolutely, totally did not want to be the person who told Jason his mother's life was in danger.

Despite how warm it was, I felt a chill run down my spine.

I dreaded doing this.

Everything was still and quiet, as if nature itself was waiting for us to discover what happened to Lillian in that clearing. Something the forest's flora and fauna already knew.

Ayla kneeled beside me and reached out. "Astra—"

"I know. Don't touch me." I said it a little harsher than I intended, but Ayla seemed unaffected and moved back slightly. "Jason, if you're close to me, you need to step back," I told him, hoping he was still nearby (while also hoping he'd left.) "I don't want any energy pollution. Okay?"

"He's moved back," Ayla told me.

I closed my eyes, gripped the necklace tightly, and concentrated on the pulsing energy. Silver has memories, and it is old. Because silver ore can take millions of years to form, reading it can be...challenging.

The voices of the dead and their memories of the past inundated my mind like a flood, each clamoring to be heard above the others. I sifted through their words like a child at the beach looking for a specific grain of sand on a specific beach at a specific time.

"I've got it," I whispered.

"Hello?" Lillian called. "Hello? I'm here. Are you here?"

The vision came in flashes, like a fast-forward movie montage. Lillian Thornton stood in the clearing, her face distorted by indignation as she yelled at someone she couldn't see. Someone—a man—stepped forward, his face somehow dark and menacing, even as his identity was obscured by shadows. His movements were swift and sure as he grabbed her to drag her away, the necklace skittering across the dirt.

"No!" I cried out and opened my eyes.

Ayla and Mel stood over me, looking concerned. "What did you see?" Ayla asked quietly.

"Lillian was walking on the path when someone grabbed her from the shadows. She couldn't see who it was—it was too dark—and she dropped the necklace in the struggle. Then... she was gone." I looked around the clearing. "Someone took her."

CHAPTER SIX

The path that led to this place was well trodden—it couldn't have been a chance encounter. Whoever had taken Lillian must have known her route and lain in wait. I shivered, imagining the unseen person grabbing her. I could only hope they had not hurt her.

Or worse.

"The path starts in your parking lot," I said, pointing back the way we came, and then gesturing in the opposite direction. "But what's that way? Do you know?"

Mel nodded. "If you follow the path down, it will soon fork. Veer right to make your way toward the swamp, or left to head into the middle of downtown Cassandra. You'll pass the public hall coming out, right near the Visitor Center."

The swamp—which meant pixies.

The center of town—which meant the interim mayor and council.

Great.

My gaze lingered along the length of the trail, taking in its winding curves and meandering through the trees. I tracked it until it eventually disappeared from view. What was Lillian doing here in the dead of night? It seemed like she had a rendezvous with someone if the words I heard her say were any indication, but what could have possibly brought Jason's mother to this place alone in the early morning hours?

"What do you think?" Ayla asked.

"I don't know what to think, honestly," I said, my gaze tracking the horizon. "Jason's been hanging around his mother. Did he see anything, overhear anything?"

Ayla stood with her head inclined to one side and her brows furrowed, as if listening. It was always a little odd watching her talk to someone she could perceive in the empty air before her, but that I could not. "He says she was pretty angry at him for taking your side yesterday, so she told him to leave her alone."

"Taking my side?" I asked, confused. Then I blinked. "As in Jason not wanting me shot dead? To her, that was him taking my side over hers?"

Ayla nodded. "Step off, Astra. We all know she's off her rocker at the moment. Don't be so judgmental."

"I'm not being judgmental, Ayla. I'm trying to figure out what happened."

"Shouldn't we call someone?" Melvin asked. "About the necklace?"

I took out my phone and flipped through the numbers until I was staring at the entry for Chief Daniel Harmon. I felt a mixture of dread and anticipation, not wanting to call him yet feeling as though I had no other choice.

"Who do you call?" I asked him. "You don't have a police department. I know you have fire tenders for fires. Do you have...um, crime tenders for crimes?" I waved my phone. "I can call Chief Harmon, or the county. But the county is going to tell us that someone needs to be missing twenty-four hours."

"What about the screams?" Ayla asked.

"The interim mayor accounted for those," I pointed out. "All we have right now is a lost necklace in the woods, and a concerned boyfriend that also happens to be a cop. The county sheriff isn't going to give the time of day to psychic visions or ghost evidence."

I looked around again.

The path was surrounded by thick trees that offered plenty of cover for anyone wanting to remain hidden—there were plenty of places to hide in or escape from, depending on one's needs. It seemed likely that whoever took Lillian had chosen this spot for its concealment, but why?

"We can keep looking, but I just don't have enough information right now." I looked at Ayla. "It's Jason's mother. What does he want us to do?"

Ayla stared blankly ahead, her brow furrowing and her eyes growing distant. After a few moments of silence, she slowly shook her head. "He says to call Harmon. He trusts him to make the right decision. And he's sorry—he knows Harmon fired you because of his mother's influence, and he can see that you're still hurt by it."

"I'm not hurt," I said, and dialed the number. "It's fine."

My former boss answered on the third ring. "Harmon here."

"It's Astra." I explained the situation: the screams Melvin overheard, the necklace in the woods, and my concern that the county would

SCRIES LIKE AN OWL | 91

take none of this seriously until tomorrow. "Just to be clear, I'm not helping you," I told him flatly. "But Jason's mother is in trouble, and I'm not going to stand by and do nothing just because I think you're a complete—"

"No need to get into specifics, Arden," he responded gruffly. "Take the path to the center of town. I'm with Daniel Caldecott in the city hall office."

"You are?" I blinked. "Are you questioning him?"

There was a long pause. "Why would I be questioning him?" he asked.

I'd mentally rushed through the information I'd given and realized I hadn't told Harmon that Daniel Caldecott was on the same trail and in the same woods where the screams were heard.

Instead of letting him know, I simply replied, "Well, he took your girlfriend's place awfully quickly, didn't he? It would seem to me he might have something to gain from her disappearing."

"He's just helping out, Arden, that's all," Harmon said quickly.

Helping out? By seizing control of a village usually ruled by a female and a person gifted with supernatural powers in the middle of the night? I've heard less suspicious forms of help offered by a shady car-salesman to a naive college student holding Daddy's Amex Black Card in his sweaty palms.

"All right, Harmon. We'll be over there in about twenty minutes," I said, and then I disconnected the call and began walking.

As we ventured further down the path, it became clear that someone had taken care to keep it in as good a condition as possible. The grass was cut short and every once in a while, a tree root snaked across our path, appearing out of nowhere. "Who takes care of this path?"

"The path tenders," Mel answered.

Of course.

Four minutes later, we arrived at a fork in the path.

The trail to our left was manicured and lined with orderly, symmetrical trees that all seemed to point directly toward the center of town. To our right, however, the path snaked through a dense overgrowth of wild vegetation, the darkness of the pixie swamp encroaching upon it from all sides.

"Cassandra doesn't maintain that path?" I asked, pointing off to the right.

"I don't know. Not many people go that way," Mel answered.

I spotted a large, flat rock a short distance down the path toward the swamp. It was partially covered with white quartz chips and a circle of small stones in blue, green, yellow and red. It was clearly a place where offerings were left for the pixies.

I fumbled through my pockets, finding a few pieces of chocolate tucked away in the corner. Placing them on the rock as an offering, I hoped it would be enough to get me out of trouble for capturing the pixie chieftain back home.

Well, I mean...I didn't capture him.

Apollo did.

Technically, I had nothing to do with it.

To the pixies, though, I suspected that would be considered a distinction without a difference.

* * *

"WELL, HULLO THERE!" the man exclaimed, his dark eyes twinkling with joy. He wore a broad, inviting grin that stretched from ear to ear. "A real life witch! Never thought I'd have the pleasure of meeting one in all my days. No sir!" His forceful grip almost crushed my hand as he shook it enthusiastically. "The name's Daniel

Littlefeather Caldecott. Call me Littlefeather. A pleasure to make your acquaintance."

Well.

That was certainly a hodge podge of cultures stuffed into one name.

His cotton shirt was decorated with a pattern of alternating white and green spirals, and his long braid was adorned with feathers of different colors and beads that glittered in the sunlight. The intricate beaded jewelry around his neck looked Native American.

"What tribe?" I asked, pointing toward the beadwork.

"I am of the clan of the wandering nomads," he answered easily. "I am in touch with my ancestral roots and honor them in spirit."

Great non-answer. "So, Apache?"

He smiled pleasantly.

"Navajo?" I prodded.

Daniel's face tightened, the amiable smile fading from his lips. "I do not wish to speak of my past. I am here now to help you and the town of Cassandra," he said. He waved his arm toward the glass window overlooking the center of town. "Dan here tells me you are concerned about the mayor. I can assure you that she's fine. She's simply off on a vision quest."

Ayla snorted. "The rite of passage for young males?"

Littlefeather cast a proud, determined look at Ayla. "Modern vision quests are much more egalitarian now, young one." His words were delivered in a sweeping, poetic cadence, sounding almost too perfect to be true as he went on and on about unity and understanding, his voice slowly building to a crescendo as he proclaimed, "We must be like the wolf, and howl at the moon together!"

Oh, barf.

My phone buzzed, and I looked down to find a text from Ayla. *I googled 'clan of the wandering nomads' and there were literally no results. None. Zip. Zilch. Zero. Mayor Moron over here is some white pretendian dude culturally appropriating. It's offensive.*

I looked up to find Ayla's furrowed brow, her lips pursed in disapproval, and her eyes filled with the unmistakable judgment of someone who knew she was right about the offense.

And to be fair, she probably was right.

I was more concerned, though, that he was suspicious.

There was something more to his presence—an air of dishonesty that seemed to hang around him like a fog. His voice was smooth and his words were reasonable, yet there was a slight edge to them that made me uncomfortable. He felt...oily.

Harmon watched my face, noticing the subtle changes in my expression. "What's wrong?" he asked.

I ignored his question and turned my focus back to the temporary mayor. "How did you wind up being interim mayor, Mr. Caldecott?" I asked him. "It seems a little strange that it happened so quickly, and in the middle of the night. You weren't even in the government, were you? Did the guru appoint you?"

"Please, call me Littlefeather."

Even though Caldecott was wearing an intricately woven shirt and his long braids were adorned with yellow and red feathers and traditional (to my eye) Indian beads, I just couldn't bring myself to. "Are you not going to answer my questions?"

"Of course I will! It was a strange night, to say the least," Caldecott began. "I was at home when I received a call from Mayor Thornton herself. She said that something in her spirit told her to reach out to me. That I was the one to help guide the town of Cassandra during this difficult time, and to guide her so she could resolve her issues with her son's death and your role in it."

I knew Lillian Thornton.

She did none of that.

I could buy her shooting me in the head in the Punktex cookie aisle more easily than I could buy his story.

"And yet you're here, and she's not."

His eyes shifted around the room, never holding contact for more than a few seconds. I could feel an underlying tension fill the air, like there was something he was hiding from me. "Well, Astra, there is more to this story."

"Awesome. We're all waiting."

Caldecott leaned back in his chair and steepled his fingers. "I met her at my doorstep and she seemed frantic and disoriented as she told me her story of the day's events. I didn't know what to make of it, but it felt like something...something greater than myself was guiding me in my decision. I agreed to take over for her while she goes on her journey for guidance."

Every word out of his mouth was slow, almost sickly sweet, like he was trying to trap me in a web of his own lies. "You're saying you know exactly where she is?" I asked. "Right now, you know where we can find her?"

"Well, of course I do."

He had the same mixture of feigned holiness and overconfidence I had seen in many snake oil salesmen. "And she is…where then?"

"I was just telling Chief Harmon that before you three arrived. The vision quest is four days. The mayor will be back at the end of the four days."

"That's not what I asked you," I said.

"No, Astra, it's easy," Ayla said. "He can just take us to her."

Caldecott shook his head. "I'm sorry, I can't do that. It's a sacred ritual, and the location is a secret. All I can tell you is that she will return in four days."

"Of course you can," I assured him. "We'll just peek in. She won't even know we're there."

Caldecott shook his head once more. "It would be inappropriate to disrupt her journey and interfere with the spiritual growth she is experiencing. You will just have to wait until she returns. The mayor must complete it on her own and find her own answers."

"Jason's not happy," Ayla said. "Like, beyond not happy. He thinks this guy is full of it."

"I'm so sorry to hear that." Caldecott's face gave nothing away, and if he had a reaction to Ayla's statement, he didn't let it show. He smiled his serene smile, seemingly oblivious to the ill will building around him. "The best thing for Cassandra is for the mayor to complete her vision quest uninterrupted. Let Jason know."

Wait a minute.

He asked Ayla to tell Jason.

He didn't just tell Jason himself.

"You can't talk to ghosts," I said.

Caldecott stepped toward me, and I shifted, subtly moving back and away from the guy. "I'm not a death speaker, no," he said, shaking his head. "I speak to the ancestors differently than the people here in Cassandra."

That got my attention.

He called the power to talk to ghosts "death-speaking."

That's not what the folks in Cassandra called that ability.

That is, on the other hand, what witches called it.

The witches he claimed he'd never met.

Until us.

* * *

I SPRINTED AWAY, my shoes sinking into the damp grass as I dodged stones and roots. Mel and Ayla followed close behind me, their quick breaths coming in gasps.

"Where are you going?" Ayla yelled.

"Archie!" I shouted back over my shoulder.

"Astra, wait!" Chief Harmon bellowed.

I returned my gaze to find the chief's face crimson and glistening with sweat beads running down his brow. He pushed past Mel and Ayla, the coins in his pocket clinking with each step as his tie flapped in the breeze.

As a thin sheen of sweat glistened on Ayla's forehead, her jaw was set in determination. "I will not let that old dude beat me," she yelled, then pushed herself to run even faster.

I chuckled, knowing Jason was probably getting a kick out of this.

"Shut up, Jason! I know!" she snarled and picked up the pace, her feet pounding against the pavement. "I should have practiced more. I get it!"

Yep.

He was getting a kick out of it.

I burst through the tree line and scanned the tangled branches for Archie. I heard rustling and a few quiet curses as the three slower runners picked their way through the trees, their faces red and sweaty. "Archie, where are you?" I called.

The brown and white owl stretched his wings and glided silently from the tree tops, then made a graceful landing on a leafy branch that hung low in the tree near me. "I'm here. I see nothing in the forest," he said, his head cocks sideways. "No sweat lodges, no saunas, no steam rooms. There are no Turkish baths or Russian banyas or anything out there."

"What's a Russian banya?" Chief Harmon asked.

I crossed my arms, lifted my chin, and looked him in the eye. "I could tell you," I said, a hint of defiance in my voice, "but I'd have to bill the police department for the time it took me to answer, and I can't do that. Since you fired me."

"You're not going to let this go, are you, Arden?"

A sly smile curved my lips. "I could answer you, but—"

"Okay, Arden, you made your point," he said, cutting me off. "That's enough. Why didn't you tell Caldecott about the necklace you found in the woods? Oh, wait," Harmon said, and then reached into his pocket to pull out a worn wallet. He withdrew a twenty-dollar bill, the paper crinkling as he handed it to me. "This should do it. Why didn't you tell Caldecott about the necklace you found in the woods?"

I grabbed the twenty and slipped it into my back pocket. I would not wave the chief's offer away so he could consider the matter closed. "Why didn't you tell Caldecott about the necklace I found?" I asked him. "You could have. You had plenty of time to tell him while we were traipsing through the woods to the office."

"You're right, I did."

"You did what?"

"Had enough time to tell him," Harmon responded.

"I know," I told him. "I just said that. But you didn't tell him."

"No."

"Why not?"

Harmon studied our faces one by one, his gaze lingering on each of us as if debating how much to tell us and how much to keep hidden. "Because I don't trust him, that's why. Lil didn't trust him, either. Which is why I don't believe his story."

"Which part?" Ayla asked. "That he's Native American, that he saw the mayor last night, or that she's on a vision quest?"

"If his lips are moving, he's probably lying," Harmon responded. He glanced out toward the street and lowered his voice. "Look, Lil asked me to look into him. He showed up a few months ago and started to social climb like everyone's head was a ladder rung. I've never seen anything like it. Her, either. It made her nervous."

"What did you find out?" I asked.

Harmon studied me intently, his expression thoughtful.

I pulled out the twenty he had given me earlier and held it out.

"You two really need to get over this," Archie pointed out. "Twenty dollars buys a lot of beef jerky. It's not something to be trifled with."

"Noted." Harmon took the twenty-dollar bill from me and tucked it back into his pocket. "He's a developer. He swoops in to small new age communities, runs everyone out or buys everyone out, and replaces the town with enormous luxury high rises and expensive new age day spa resorts. He's done it to four communities so far."

"And you think he's targeting Cassandra?" I asked.

I don't even know why I asked the question.

Obviously, he did.

Harmon nodded slowly. "I do. I think he sees the potential here and wants to capitalize on it. He'd been asking questions about the mayor, her plans for the city—anything that might give him an edge. Lil caught wind of his activities—buying up land and such—and became suspicious."

"When was that?" I asked.

"Right before Jason passed," Harmon said. "She'd asked me to look into him, but by then it was too late; Caldecott had already bought a bunch of cheap property, and sold it to big developers from New York and Chicago. And Jason...well, Lil took her eyes off the town's issues for a while." He looked at me. "What I can tell you is this: Lil never would have made him interim mayor. That signed decree is fake, or he forged her signature."

"But it was her signature, Jason said," Ayla argued. "He said he'd recognize that crummy scrawl anywhere."

"Maybe he forced her to sign it?" I said.

"That's possible." Harmon shook his head in frustration. "It could be that this whole vision quest thing is a ruse, a ploy to get her out of town so that he can swoop in with his cronies and take over."

"If she didn't trust him, she wouldn't go on his

vision quest or whatever. I think we have to accept that the story he told is just complete bull. It's more likely he kidnapped her to keep her out of the way for a few days," I pointed out.

"What can he really do in four days?" Mel asked, startled.

Harmon shrugged. "A lot, if he has the right people in his pocket. He's a sly one, that's for sure —if he has his eye on this town, he won't stop until he gets what he wants. But, to tell you the truth? I don't care about any of that." He looked at all of us. "I just want to find Lil."

CHAPTER SEVEN

*A*yla had a puzzled look on her face. "So, I'm a little confused," she said from the passenger seat. "You called Chief Harmon so we could work with him, right?"

A white-tailed deer darted across the road back to Forkbridge, and I braked. "I did. Reluctantly."

"Then why didn't you tell him about the screams in the forest that Mel heard? And Daniel coming out of the woods right after?"

I glanced in the rearview mirror and saw Harmon was following.

"Because I don't trust him. He fired me from my job, and he did it because of his personal connection to Lillian Thornton and not out of any concern about the town," I explained. "When we first got to that office, I honestly didn't know if he was buddies with Caldecott or if he suspected him. He told me on the phone he wasn't questioning him, so…yeah, I just needed to observe for a bit before revealing too much."

Ayla nodded slowly, understanding crossing her features. "That makes sense." She looked out the window. "But once he told us he didn't trust Caldecott, why didn't you tell him then?"

Because I still don't trust him, I thought.

There was only one person I told everything to during a case, and that person was sitting with her feet up on a couch incubating a half-werewolf baby.

Instead of explaining that, I told her, "Just because you align with someone, Ayla, it doesn't mean you show them your entire hand."

"So, what do we do now? Are we just going to ignore this lead?"

I shook my head. "No, we're still going to look into it, but just not with Chief Harmon's help. I'll admit it seems obvious Daniel has her—"

"Or he killed her," Ayla said.

"She's not dead."

Ayla's eyes widened in surprise. "How do you know?"

I smiled briefly and glanced at her before turning my attention back to the road. "If she were dead, she would have gone straight to Jason. There's not a doubt in my mind that woman would scour the spirit world until she was reunited with him again. He hasn't heard from her, so I'm almost a hundred percent sure she's alive."

"What if someone trapped her spirit or something?" Ayla asked, reminding me that Jason's cord to his mother had faded and was being blocked by someone or something.

"She's the most powerful medium in Cassandra. She's an expert in the spirit realm and afterlife. I'd like to see someone try to lock her spirit in something. Honestly, Ayla, I just don't see it happening. I didn't see anyone kill her in the woods. I saw someone take her."

"They could have killed her after they took her," she argued.

"Sure, that's possible. But if they wanted her dead, it would have been easier just to do it right there in the middle of the night, in the dark, in the woods. Whatever's going on, I think it's happening on this plane, and she's alive."

"But you have no evidence of that."

I gave her a small smile. "That's why you have

to learn to trust your instincts, Ayla. You've spent years studying the supernatural and living in the world of magic and myths, so you know how it works—logic isn't always enough. It starts with logic. You take what you know, and you make a judgment call."

"What's your judgment call?"

"My gut is telling me that wherever Lillian Thornton is, she's alive...and she needs our help. Instincts are a powerful tool, and often the best thing you can do is just go with them."

Ayla nodded, falling quiet for a bit before she asked in a casual voice, "So, just curious. What do you think of Melvin Platt?"

I realized she had been secretly seeing the teen and was trying to discover what I thought of him. I smiled, amused by her abrupt change of topic. "He seems like a good kid," I said carefully. "Polite. Why? Are you asking me for a specific reason?"

Ayla blushed and looked away. "No," she mumbled.

I chuckled and nudged her with my elbow. "You like him, don't you?"

I could almost feel her blush deepen, but she didn't deny it. Instead, she shrugged and stated, "Just maybe I do. We're good friends, at the very least, but I'm…I'm not sure if it could ever grow into something more."

I looked over at her. "Ayla, that boy clearly has feelings for you."

"Seriously? He's been so cool to me since we met. He's always around when I need someone to vent about my day or just want someone to chill with. We get along pretty well, but…I mean, I think it could be deeper if I finally just let myself open up to him."

I reached over and gently squeezed her shoulder. "He seems like a really nice guy and he's lucky to have you in his life, Ayla. You don't have to rush things, though; take your time and get to know him better before making any serious decisions. After all, you're both young."

Ayla nodded, her eyes wide with worry. "I know," she breathed. "I'm trying to get close to him but, like, it's so freaky. I care so much that it's gonna be catastrophic if I get my heart broken. Whatever. It's like an Arden family curse or something. Look what happened to Jason."

"Jason died because of something Mom did years ago," I told her. "It had nothing to do with some Arden curse. That's not something that's going to happen to you or Melvin. You two will be fine as long as you take your time and get to know one another better."

We rode the rest of the way home silent, and both of us, I suspected, were thinking about all the ways being an Arden witch and member of this family sometimes felt like more trouble than it was worth.

But only sometimes.

With so much power came so much responsibility—responsibility that often weighed heavily on our shoulders. It wasn't easy to manage—and yes, it torpedoed our dating lives—but it was something we had grown accustomed to over the years and something that united us as a family.

And for that, I was grateful.

* * *

"THE BOX JUST CAME. Like Archie and the toy soldier. The doorbell rang, I opened it, and there it was sitting on the stoop," Althea explained.

The miniature jail had been painstakingly crafted in minute detail. Its walls were dark, aged wood with iron bars framed in gold trim. The jail door was heavy and wooden, but it swung open easily. "Where's Ami?" I asked.

"She's running the store today," Althea said with a jerk of her head toward the new age shop. "We have to make money, especially now that you're not working. Unless you plan to ask Daddy for some cash to pay the bills since yours is the only one that has money. All I can ask mine for is some fish from the other side of the world. Or maybe lobster." Althea looked around. "By the way, does anyone want lobster for dinner?"

"Hey!" a small, tinny voice squeaked out from the jail as Chief Harmon walked in. "Look, dearies, while I find your witchy banter on your daddy issues quite endearing, I would find it even more so if you kindly let me out of this contraption?" A tiny head with a shock of bright hair appeared in the barred window, his little hands hanging over the sill. "I thought we were friends, Astra. Is this how you treat your friends?"

"We are friends, Pistachio, but something's going on." I stepped closer to the jail and leaned down, squinting at his tiny face. "What do you think you're doing in there? Why would a god jail you and imply you might have something to do with Lillian Thornton's disappearance? Have something you want to tell me?"

Althea frowned. "That's not what—"

My foot connected with Althea's shin bone.

"Ow!" Althea said as she stumbled backward, wincing in pain. "Jeez, Astra, that's going to leave a bruise!"

Pistachio Waterflash shook his head in disbelief. "I don't know why I'm here. I was just minding my own business, flitting around like a good pixie should, when suddenly this box appeared out of nowhere. I leaned in to check and—"

"Out of nowhere where?" I asked.

"In my swamp, of course. Next thing I know, I'm thrown into jail and being accused of something. What kind of nonsense is that?" He crossed his arms and stuck his nose in the air. "This is beyond absurd. Someone needs to explain to me exactly what is going on here."

I ignored his ranting. "Alice said you got up at four this morning and left. Where'd you go?"

That got his attention.

The pixie's expression grew wary. "When did you talk to Alice?"

"This morning. First thing."

An uncharacteristically quiet Chief Harmon stared at the tiny talking pixie like Pistachio was a possessed troll doll, straight out of a horror movie. His mouth hung open in awe, and he looked a little green.

"Harmon, are you all right?" I asked.

"What kind of creature is this?" he asked, his voice barely above a whisper.

"He's a pixie, Chief Harmon," Althea said with an amused smirk. "Pistachio Waterflash is one of the few remaining members of an ancient race that used to inhabit these lands. Now they live—"

"Where we please," Waterflash said quickly, cutting her off.

Harmon blinked several times and rubbed his eyes, as if trying to make sure he wasn't dreaming. "A pixie," he drawled. "I've never seen one before."

"Awesome. Super happy for your expanding paranormal horizons, dude," Althea said with as much sass as she could interject. "Could we get back to the question?" She turned and looked at the pixie. "You and I spent all morning together, and you didn't say a thing about leaving your girl in the middle of the night to go run an errand."

"It's not like I have some burning desire to tell you where I was going when I don't even know why I'm here." Pistachio sighed and crossed his arms, his face a mask of annoyance. "The situation as it stands doesn't inspire much trust, Althea. I'm being locked up in a box like some kind of criminal. How do you expect me to believe that I can trust any of you when this is how you're treating me?"

He had a point.

"You're still a chieftain?" I asked.

Pistachio nodded. "I am." He glanced back at the jail. "Which is why this is slightly humiliating. Astra, you must admit this isn't right. If someone has something against me, then they should come out and say so openly instead of locking me away in this tiny prison."

I had no leverage over Pistachio, and locking him up had done nothing but make the pixie mistrustful. "Okay. You're right," I said. "I'm sure there were reasons for doing this, but I don't know what they were." I opened the door and motioned for him to step out. "Come on."

Pistachio's eyes lit up as he gazed at me. "You are a genuine friend, Astra," he said.

Sure.

I'm a genuine friend whose god-dad snatched the pixie chieftain out of thin air, shoved him in a mini-jail, and sent it through the supernatural post to appear on my doorstep.

With friends like me...

I moved closer to the mini-jail and held my hand flat in front of the door so Pistachio could climb on to my palm. I carefully lowered him to

SCRIES LIKE AN OWL | 117

the ground, and as soon as his feet touched the floor, he grew back to his full human size.

"Now that we are equals once again, you may ask me your questions," the chieftain said, his head tilting. "I will choose, as is my right, whether to answer." He narrowed his bright eyes. "You, as a friend, will respect that."

* * *

I EXPLAINED Lillian Thornton's disappearance, including the silver cord's dimmed connection. "Since Mayor Thornton pulled a gun on me in a Punktex, I was concerned the pixies might have gotten miffed at her."

"You know, for attacking Astra? Since you're friends," Althea said.

"Or for putting people in danger in one of Alice's stores," I told him.

It was sweet that Althea thought the pixies would run to defend me, but they were far more likely to be motivated by a risk to Alice's stores than by some defensive loyalty toward me.

Pixies didn't hold grudges, but they also didn't remember favors.

Pistachio looked at me. "Are you implying that you think I might have been angry enough to kill

Lillian because she waved a gun around? Surely you think more of me than that."

I shook my head. "No, I don't think you would ever do something like that. Well, not over what happened in Punktex, anyway," I admitted. "But I don't think Lillian Thornton is dead."

He raised his neon eyebrow.

"Did you see her in the woods last night, or did you take her to the pixie swamp to give her a talking to about pulling a gun in one of Alice's stores? Alice said you were gone at four in the morning."

Pistachio narrowed his eyes. "Why is four a.m. significant?"

"There were screams heard in the woods on the path to the pixie swamp around that time," I said, glancing at Harmon's face, which registered surprise.

Pistachio sighed and ran a hand through his hair. "I didn't see her, no. But I heard those screams, now that you mention them."

"Oh?"

"It was around four in the morning, maybe a little after. It seemed to be just before dawn broke over the horizon. I thought it might have been kids getting too drunk and wandering into the woods, but now..." He trailed off and looked away from me for a moment as he considered what he had said. "I know what it was. It sounded like woo-woo-woo, repeatedly."

I frowned. "That's weird."

Ayla touched my elbow, and I turned. She cupped her hand over her mouth and made the very Hollywood, very fake, hand-over-mouth war cry. "Like that?" she asked Pistachio when she was done.

"Okay, that was offensive," Althea said, appalled.

"You think that was offensive? You should meet the new mayor of Cassandra," Ayla said with an eye roll. "Dude's last name is Caldecott, and he's playing like he's Native American, but he won't even answer what his tribe is. He's so fake. Like, man, he's so fake. It's just gross."

"You cannot judge someone solely by their name," Pistachio said. "Well, not generally. Here, though, you are correct." A stormy expression roiled his face. "Daniel Littlefeather Caldecott is a fraud."

"How do you know that?" I asked.

"He is not Native American, as he claims. He is actually a descendant of European settlers who have always tried to capitalize on the mistreatment of minorities. He has no true understanding or appreciation of the culture and beliefs he claims, and Caldecott's attempt to pass himself off as something he's not is insulting."

Well, Pistachio, tell us how you really feel.

Ayla frowned. "If that's the case, how did he rise so high in Cassandra's society so quickly? I mean, he's the mayor now."

"Because those idiots wouldn't know a real indigenous person if they came up and whacked them in the head with a tomahawk steak." He paused for a moment, took a deep breath as if to calm himself, then added in a softer voice, "I know it can be hard for someone who doesn't share your heritage to understand it, but it's important that we respect each other's cultures and beliefs at least enough to recognize when they're being exploited."

"White people, am I right?" Ayla asked with a shake of her head.

I glared at her and then turned back to Pistachio. "How did you come to know all this about him?"

Pistachio stared at me.

I looked back.

He looked at Chief Harmon, then cleared his throat and looked back at me once more. "I will tell you and your sisters, but I will not speak in front of that man."

Harmon's jaw clenched, and his eyes widened with offense. "Excuse me?"

Pistachio nodded slowly. "It is not just that you are human. It is that you are law enforcement for humans and involved with the political leaders of Cassandra. Your towns border our swamp. I will not speak in front of you. I'm sorry, but I have a tribe to protect." Pistachio looked at me with an expression of regret on his face, shrugged apologetically, and waited.

Harmon seemed to swell with indignation, his eyebrows furrowed and eyes hard as he stared at Pistachio. "Lillian is my partner, you rainbow-colored fool!" he said through gritted teeth.

The chieftain shrugged. "That changes nothing."

I quickly stepped forward, placing myself between the two men, and looked an angry chief in the eye. "Harmon, please calm down," I said. "Pistachio is just trying to protect his people. I'm sure you can imagine how important that is to him. He didn't mean any disrespect to you."

Harmon took a deep breath and let it out slowly. "Pistachio," he said, his voice still tense. "I understand your caution, but if you don't start talking, I'm afraid I'll have to arrest you and put you in a real jail."

"Now, hold on a minute—" I started, but he kept going.

"You're right that it's important to protect your people, but I'm here to do the same. I need to ensure that justice is served and those responsible are held accountable for their actions. And I need to find the woman I love before she's harmed."

Pistachio looked at Harmon with a mix of sympathy and defiance. He set his jaw and crossed his arms over his chest. "As I said, that changes nothing."

The air in the room seemed to thicken as both men squared off, their postures tight. I could feel the tension increasing with each passing second. "Now, look, gentlemen—"

"You have no power here, human," the pixie said, his voice calm but serious. "I am not some criminal that you can lock up in your human jails, nor can you arrest me for speaking the truth. You may think that you're protecting justice, but I'm trying to protect my people; people who have been exploited for far too long." He stepped closer to Harmon and jabbed a finger into his chest, emphasizing every word.

"You may have the power of your law behind you, but mine comes from something far deeper —from the ancient wisdom of my people. I will not be intimidated by a badge or a uniform or threats of punishment that you have no ability to enforce."

"I thought pixies were supposed to be happy, silly little things?" Harmon sneered.

"We were," Pistachio said with another shrug. "Once."

"That's it," Harmon growled. "You're under—"

"I warned you."

"Guys," I said, holding my hands out to keep them apart. "Let's just take a breath."

Pistachio's eyes narrowed, and he angrily swept one arm forward in a wide arc to push me aside.

Harmon jumped back as glittering, multicolored pixie dust flew at him.

"Oh, you will not shrink the police chief," I whispered, stunned.

The dust swirled around Harmon, seeping into his skin and hair and clothing, making him shimmer in the faint light of the fire's embers. When the sparkles, smoke, and magic fire cleared, Pistachio delicately scooped up the six-inch chief of police off the floor and placed him in the jail the pixie had previously occupied. There was a tiny clinking sound as the door shut.

"Get me out of here!" Harmon squeaked. "Now! Astra! Get me out of here!"

I looked at Pistachio, who had a satisfied smirk on his face.

"I warned him," he said simply. "Now, let us get to this business at hand. Place a ward around that jail so he can hear nothing, and I will tell you what it is you want to know."

CHAPTER EIGHT

"Six months ago, I found two surveyors in the swamp," Pistachio began. He leaned forward in his chair, his sharp, angular features shadowed by the bright sunlight that filtered through the window. "I heard them speak of expansion. How to drain the swamp, how to build up foundations," he said, his voice low yet intense. "I think even now that the government of Cassandra has a plan, and that plan is to expand the development of their psychic village into the pixie swamp."

I'd lived in Florida long enough to know real estate development in a swamp is an arduous and expensive process requiring detailed planning and execution, environmental impact studies, water level studies, soil studies. It's incredibly complex, and not something I would immediately believe the town of Cassandra was capable of.

The folks there were a little...well, hippie-like would be the kind way to put it.

"Do the psychics in the town even know about the pixies? Half of them don't even believe we witches are real," I pointed out.

"We allowed them to settle here years ago. Some among their number could see us. I don't know that they knew what we were." Pistachio's eyes shone in the bright light of the sun-filled room. "But I can't understand how they would not be aware that we live in the swamp just to the south of their village. We are their neighbors."

Ayla stared at Pistachio in disbelief. "You mean to tell me that the government of Cassandra is going to encroach on the pixie swamp?" she asked, her voice betraying an indignant offense.

Cerberus, who had come in to sit at Ayla's feet, whined.

"I know, right, Cerbie?" Ayla was poised and determined, ready to take to the streets in an impassioned display of dissent outside of

Cassandra's grand hall. "Did you talk to the surveyors or try to talk to the mayor about it?"

"I stayed hidden from them so I could hear them speak freely," Pistachio said.

"You did? Then how do you know it was the leadership of the village that sent them?" Althea asked. She glanced at me. "I mean, isn't this Caldecott dude a developer? Maybe he was just doing his due diligence before he put his plan into place. Whatever that plan is."

"I know it is Cassandra because the surveyors were accompanied by Mayor Thornton and that man there," Pistachio said, pointing to the chief. "The four of them spoke openly, believing no one could hear them."

Althea stared at Pistachio in shock. "Are you sure?"

The pixie nodded.

"Jason, do you know anything about this?" Ayla asked the area to the right of her. She glanced at me. "He said it was the first he heard of it."

Was Mayor Thornton plotting something so secret she hid it even from Jason?

I looked over at Harmon in the tiny cell. It was warded so he couldn't hear what we said and was oblivious to what was being discussed around him. Even so, the chief's stoic expression suddenly seemed darker and more menacing.

I thought I knew him.

I thought I knew them both.

Was it possible I didn't?

* * *

THE STILLNESS WAS DISTURBED by a barely audible flapping. Archie and Lily, Althea's crow, suddenly appeared in the window.

"Keep up, featherbrain!" Archie growled. His eyes darted to the crow, watching it with annoyed contempt.

Archie swooped onto my shoulder, settling in with a proud elegance. Lily soared through the air and nestled atop Althea's head, her glossy feathers shimmering like midnight stars. "If you just went where you were supposed to go instead of flying in circles like you were performing some kind of aerial ballet—"

"It's called a search grid, you moron!"

"Hey!" I said sharply. "Did either of you see anything?"

"We scouted the skies, spun in dizzying circles, and hopped along branches searching for

Lillian Thornton. But we saw nothing that would point us to the current location of the woman," Lily told us with a bow of her iridescent head.

Archie rolled his eyes and shuddered so hard his feathers vibrated. "She's right. But she could have said it with thirty fewer words. Just 'no' would have gotten the point across." Spotting the tiny jail, he squinted. "What's that?" Archie thrust his head forward. "And who's that?"

I drew a deep breath. "That's Harmon."

Archie and Lily exchanged a glance. "Your old boss?" Archie asked.

I nodded.

The crow beamed in agreement.

Archie, however, looked perplexed, his eyes wide and head tilted. "Was the job really that important to you that you'd shrink him down and throw him in a little jail just to get back at him?"

"That's not why he's there."

His confusion was clear. "Tell."

"Pistachio wouldn't talk to us unless we put him in a quiet space."

"You thought you gave me an answer, but I gotta tell you, I'm exploring a veritable labyrinth of questions." The owl looked around the room, his gaze lingering on the chief and the tiny bars that confined him. "What's the pixie even doing here?"

"Astra's dad, Apollo, sent him shrunk down—"

Archie exploded at Althea. "Whoa! Wait a minute, hold up, hold your unicorns—none of you said anything about any of the gods being involved in this!" He turned to Lily. "Did you hear them say anything about the gods being involved in this?"

The crow shook her head no.

Archie leaned out and stared down at Cerberus. "How about you, slobber monster? Did they tell you that there were—"

"Archie, we get it," I said, amused that he complained the crow was too wordy. "What's your point?"

"What's the point? What's the point?" Archie stared at me while waving his wings. He turned and looked at Lily. "She wants to know the point. Can you believe this?"

"Archie, I'm running out of patience," I said.

"What?" Archie's beak opened in feigned shock, his feathers ruffled in agitation. "Fine. Anyway, my point is that it's weird the gods would be involved in something like this."

"And you were making fun of my crow for

being too wordy?" Althea said to Archie, a smirk playing on her lips.

"You, too, Althea?" Archie muttered.

I sighed and rubbed my temples. "We don't have time to ponder the motivations of the gods right now. Maybe Apollo's just trying to ingratiate himself to me. Maybe he really had some random vision and saw I would need to talk to Pistachio, and this was his clumsy way of helping. Who cares why he did what he did? We need to focus on finding Lillian Thornton."

"Who cares?" Archie asked, shocked. Lily and Archie exchanged another glance. "Did you hear that? Who cares, she said."

Lily's arrival providing Archie with a comedic snark partner was pushing me toward my witty bird banter limit, and I felt my annoyance growing.

"What?" I asked, exasperated. "What now?"

"Maybe you should talk to Apollo," Lily suggested. "Or Poseidon, or Hecate, or Hades."

"Or Hermes," Archie added.

Althea, Ayla, and I all looked at each other in surprise. "Why should we talk to any of the gods?" Ayla asked the feathered divine wonder twins. "What could they possibly tell us that would help us find Lillian?"

"Because they're gods, child," Lily said. "They will know something about Lillian Thornton's disappearance that we don't, and if they don't know it when we begin the conversation, they will certainly have the full picture by the end of the question. After all, they are divine."

Pistachio stared at me, his eyes wide with awe. "You know all those gods?"

"Yes. Anyway, let's—"

"You know them...personally?"

"Yep." I nodded. "Now, we need to—"

"Please." Pistachio leaned forward, his face filled with fascination. "Tell me."

"Tell you what? We more than know them, buddy," Ayla told him.

"That's true," Althea agreed. "But we know nothing about the gods' involvement in this. Talking to one of them might shed some light on the situation." She looked at me. "Especially Apollo, since he sent the Pistachio here."

"It couldn't hurt," Ayla said. "Even if we think we know what this is about, we obviously don't even know where to look for Lillian if the birds can't find a trail. But the gods would, right? I mean, they're immortal and have access to knowledge that we can't even fathom. We should ask them for help."

I noticed my Aunt Gwennie watching me silently from the kitchen.

"I hear what you're all saying. I really do," I said. "But we're all grown women, and this isn't our first rodeo." I looked around the group, my gaze finally settling on Archie and Lily. "Are you really suggesting we call our daddies for help? I mean, that's just insulting."

The two birds exchanged a glance before Archie spoke. "Look, your mother did it all the time—she reached out to Athena. We're suggesting that you reach out to the gods because they've already stuck their noses into whatever this thing is, and as much as you think you have this all figured out already, you don't—because you haven't found Thornton," he said. "They may know where she is. Heck, they may have her."

That idea startled me. "You think Apollo did this? Isn't just helping, but may have done this?"

"It's a possibility," Lily said. "We can't ignore the possibility that one or more of the gods might be involved. You're Apollo's daughter, Astra. The mayor pulled a gun on you. You don't think your father, divine as he is, would be upset by that?" Lilly cawed and shook her feathers. "I've seen people drawn, quartered, and fed to dragons for less divine offense."

Cerberus barked.

"She's right." Archie leaned forward and looked me in the eye. "It's possible. Nothing's out of the realm of possibility for gods."

My eyes moved and scanned the room. "They might be right. But it's a risk. If it turns out the gods had nothing to do with her disappearance, then we might be worse off than we are now. We'll have wasted time and possibly have gotten Apollo's attention." I turned and looked at the free-standing mirror Althea had pushed to the side of the room. "Get Jason a window so he can speak. It's his mother. He should get a vote."

Althea nodded. "Good idea." She walked over to the mirror and sprayed it down from top to bottom, causing Jason to appear in the glowing, rippling blue glass. "Jason, what do you think? Should we take time to talk to the gods or keep going the way we're going?"

Pistachio gasped. "What is this magic? You're dead, are you not?"

"I am." Jason nodded, and then frowned. "The silver cord fading between my mother and me makes me suspicious that maybe the birds are right. Who else could block something like that other than the gods?" He looked around the room and sighed. "You should do it. But I also think you should do one other thing."

"What's that?" I asked.

"Call Serena Bliss and get her here," he said, mentioning his ex-girlfriend (and the right hand of both the mayor and the guru in Cassandra.) "If anyone knows what's going on with this land development deal, it's her." He crossed his arms. "She's also supposed to be the interim mayor or interim guru if one of them needs to take time off. You need to find out how Caldecott could maneuver around that."

I nodded. "Okay." I looked around the room. "Is everyone in agreement?"

The others nodded.

"Let's do it," Althea said. "You try talking to your dad, and I'll call Serena Bliss and ask her to come here."

"All right then, let's do it. We'll start with Apollo and Serena and then take it from there." I stood up and grabbed my bag. "Let's go, Archie. I want to talk to Ami really quick before I call Dad."

* * *

AMI STOOD BEHIND THE COUNTER, her slim frame bent slightly as if her weight was too much for her shoulders to hold. She wore a white tunic, her long blond hair pulled back in a messy bun. Her usually cheerful face was still a far cry from its usual state, but she seemed to look a little better.

"Hey!" I called out, Archie riding along on my shoulder. "Busy today?"

Ami looked up, her gaze meeting mine. "Not too busy," she said. "Just a few customers in and out."

"I know the answer is likely no, but have you heard anything else about Lillian from anyone?" I asked, coming closer to the counter. I doubted she would have, and the question was a long shot, but I wanted her to feel involved in the case.

Ami shook her head. "No, nothing. None of the customers seemed to know anything about it. But honestly, no one really thinks about Cassandra all that much, you know? The locals just ignore it exists."

I nodded. "We're going to find her," I said confidently.

Ami nodded. "I hope so."

"So, you're the sister with the tarot cards and crystal balls. We decided I should probably check in with Apollo since he sent Pistachio here in the mini-jail. I'm just a little concerned about sticking my foot in something I'm not prepared for, though. Can you give me a reading?"

Ami blinked, taken aback by the sudden request. "You want me to give you a tarot reading?" She studied me carefully, as if my request was some trick. "Or scry for you? Really? I don't think you've ever asked me that before."

I definitely had never asked her that before.

I nodded. "Sure. I mean, I'm not sure what I'm going to find, but I think it would be helpful to have some guidance if the gods are involved. Would you mind?"

Ami smiled, her eyes showing a little more life in them. "Of course I wouldn't mind. That's really smart, too. Let me get everything ready. I haven't read in…well, in a while." She disappeared into the back room and came back out a few minutes later with a deck of tarot cards. "Okay. Let's see what we can find out."

I leaned against the counter as Ami shuffled the cards.

After a few moments, she laid them out in the shape of a plus sign, one card at the center surrounded by one card each above, below, and on each side. "The Wheel of Fortune is in the center. Hmm. Interesting," she said, pointing to each card in turn. "Surrounded by the Tower, the Sun, the Page of Pentacles, and the Star."

"It's pretty," I said, having no clue what I was looking at.

"The Wheel of Fortune in the center is usually associated with luck, fate, and destiny," she said. "It can also be interpreted to mean that something is beyond your control." She looked up. "These are all Major Arcana cards, Astra. So it's all—well, almost all—big energy."

I nodded. "Big energy. Got it."

Ami looked up at me. "I think the cards are telling you that you need to be careful. The Tower represents upheaval and danger—a warning that something may collapse or be destroyed if we don't take action soon. The Sun... I feel like it's shining a light on an alternative path, a new path—the new path might be Apollo. He's always associated with the sun, so that would track."

I nodded. "Who's that?" I tapped a card.

"The Page of Pentacles? The Page of Pentacles has to do with money and resources; it could mean that someone is manipulating the development deal for personal gain. The Star is a sign of hope and healing—but you have the star power, so that might not just mean what it normally means." She tapped the Star card. "You may have to zap someone. Anyway, the whole reading tells me that in order to find Lillian, you'll need to use your wits and trust in the universe."

I nodded slowly as I took in Ami's analysis of the cards. "So, I'm not sure if you're aware, but trusting the universe has never been my strong suit," I told her. "The universe can be one heck of a tricky mistress."

Ami smiled. "That's true. But you have the power to make a difference here. You can do this." She gathered up the cards. "Can I ask a question, though?"

"Shoot."

"I was listening to what you guys were saying—"

I blinked. "Wait, hold up. How were you doing that?"

"Mom had intercoms all over the house," Ami said. She pulled out a speaker with small buttons on the top marked with all different rooms in the main house. "When there was no one in the shop, I just turned it on so I could listen."

I stared at her. "Are you telling me Mom had us under surveillance? In our own house?"

Ami shrugged. "I wouldn't put it that way, but sort of. Aunt Gwennie used it, too."

No wonder those two old women always had a "sixth sense."

"Well, that's definitely one way to keep us in line." I turned my attention back to her question. "Sorry. What were you going to ask?"

"Well, I was listening to what you guys were saying about the land development deal and it made me think—what if there's something beneath all of this? A bigger problem that's causing all of this?" She held up her cards. "The whole time I was doing the reading, I felt like the cards were saying you should look deeper. That something else was influencing it, something that's bigger than what we know."

"I don't know," I said slowly. "Maybe. It's possible that we're missing something."

"It's more than possible," Archie said.

"Caldecott appeared to be behind everything simply because he was near the forest where Mel heard the screams, and he had—well, probably has a motive. We have seen no evidence of something happening right now that would benefit him being mayor for the next four days." I frowned. "But we haven't looked that deeply yet, either."

"Right." Ami nodded. "I still feel like there's something…bigger."

Ami was being maddeningly non-specific with her vague references to something bigger, but she wasn't wrong. The big things weren't adding up completely, and the little things around the situation seemed…odd.

Like Chief Harmon.

He knows the county sheriff. I know he does. I've seen them together before.

Now, granted—they're not exactly friends, but they're certainly friendly.

Harmon could have easily traded on his badge to a fellow cop to get the county to open Lillian's case early—unless he came to us specifically because he wanted no real law enforcement looking into the case.

And if he doesn't…why doesn't he?

What was he hiding?

And what about Pistachio?

He still hadn't explained why he left Alice unexpectedly at four in the morning, or where this supposed business trip was to—if there had been one at all.

Or how he knew so much about Daniel Caldecott.

I had an instinctive wariness of pixies. After

all, their mischievous nature and penchant for trickery could not be ignored. Heck, if you looked up scheming in the dictionary, you'd probably find a picture of a pixie next to it. My gut warned me never to even consider the possibility of relying on them fully for anything.

And yet, as much as I wanted to believe that he might be up to something sinister so I could hurry and solve this, I couldn't help but feel a sympathy for Pistachio. It sounded like his swamp was under siege.

And yet…even that made no sense.

Alice was rich.

Why couldn't she just buy the swamp if it was up for sale?

I sighed heavily. "We need more answers."

"Agreed," Ami said. "So, what are you doing first?"

"I'm going to talk to Apollo," I told her. "Maybe he saw something in that prophecy he forgot to mention." Or, I thought, maybe he was behind the whole thing, would admit it, and I could head over to Emma's so we could argue over baby names. "Can you have Althea track down the paperwork for these land deals? Maybe Pistachio can help with that. We'll compare notes when I get back."

Ami nodded, her eyes brightening. "If you see Hermes, can you tell him I said hello?"

I nodded. "If I do, I will."

Ami smiled. "Good luck."

I thanked her and headed out the door, my mind spinning with possibilities.

Something was going on here.

I just had to figure out what it was.

CHAPTER NINE

I left the house to drive to my father's (even though it was a precaution I felt a little silly taking.) I could've just called him up and invited him over. After all, the man—er, the god—was my father.

Even for all my mother's political and power-hungry shenanigans at all of our expense before her passing, she never deliberately put me in harm's way that I could recall. I doubted he would.

But...my father was Apollo.

He was a god.

I couldn't ignore that.

And I wasn't sure he'd keep me out of harm's way.

After all, Persephone almost killed us.

"You know full well that the moment you bring this to him, he's going to jump headfirst into it, right?" Archie asked from the backseat. "He's a god. The gods are nosy. He won't be able to resist sticking his nose into this problem as soon as you mention it to him."

"I guess you know him better than I do, because I didn't know that."

"I don't know him. I know history and myths and the perils of getting the gods involved in your business," he responded.

"Boy, your tune's changed."

"Athena alone is one thing. These gods together? Quite another."

"Look, Apollo's already involved in this. He jailed and mailed a pixie chieftain," I told Archie as the highway opened up and I pushed the Jeep to go faster. "But yes, I know what you're saying."

"To be honest, Astra, I'm not sure why he'd bother getting involved. You never bother to thank Athena for the gifts she's given to you—"

I stepped on the gas and passed a slow Cadillac. "Archie, I don't need a lecture right now."

"—but she's distant, so I can sort of understand." The owl flapped his feathers. "Your father, on the other hand, is doing his best to respect your need for independence while still being there for you when he feels like he can help. But give him an inch? He'll take a light year. Believe me."

Would he?

I didn't know.

I didn't know the gods as…well, gods.

For years, I didn't even believe they existed.

And while I now believe in them, I sure as heck don't trust them.

Our previous encounters with divinity in Florida were not exactly successful mortal-divine partnership endeavors. It seemed to me the gods had their own way of dealing with mortals, their own agendas for getting involved, and their own ways of solving problems. Sometimes what was easier for them was not, in fact, easier for us.

So I had no idea how he would handle this situation.

Would he launch into an all-out assault on the villain—if he even knew who that was? And if he knew, would he tell me? Or would he try to handle the situation to not draw too much attention to himself or too much heat on me?

I just hoped whatever he did, he wouldn't make matters worse.

"Ugh, what am I doing?" I asked myself in a whisper. I felt a little nervous—which was uncharacteristic for me. I didn't get nervous.

"What? What was that?" Archie asked.

"Nothing. Never mind."

I was doing what I had to do, I told myself. There was nothing to be nervous about. Apollo had already pulled himself into this, and it was up to me to go to the god and learn what he knew. That's all.

Super simple.

It was even easier now than it was before. Apollo lived in this world as a psychiatrist...or maybe a psychologist. He went by the name of Dr. Delian Loxias and had moved from Palm Beach to a shaded woodland area along the water just ten minutes from Arden House. He did it—I assumed—to be closer to me.

Why did a god need to be geographically closer to me?

No idea.

He could travel across the world in the blink of an eye.

But move, he did.

"I hate that he's gotten involved in all this," I said as the sign for Two Isle Lakes—the tiny township just south of the pixie swamp—whizzed by. "You know, the last time I dealt with him, everybody nearly got banished to the underworld forever. Jason and Mom died. I feel like we should stay away from these gods, distance ourselves, and keep them as far away from us as possible. Dads or not."

"Banished? You weren't banished. If you were banished, you wouldn't be here. You wouldn't be alive. Your father loves you, Astra," Archie said. "Sure, it's an odd love, all wrapped up in some weird ancient and divine package, but he wants what's best for you. Your mother made her own bed, and Jason's death was…unfortunate."

"Tragic," I corrected him.

"I know it hurt you."

"Hurt him more," I muttered.

Archie was oddly supportive. It was…weird.

Lily's presence in our lives seemed to impact how he interacted with me. Gone were his snide jabs and insulting observations and, in their place, a newfound encouragement. It was as if Althea's sharp-tongued crow had become the sole recipient of Archie's barbed comments, freeing him up to be nicer to the rest of us.

I wasn't sure what to make of it.

But I was grateful.

"Well, we're almost there, so let's hope you're right," I said. "Let's hope he can help us."

With that, I pushed down the gas pedal and sped toward Two Isle Lakes, eager to get to my father's home and see what he knew about the mysterious disappearance plaguing Forkbridge, Cassandra, and the pixie tribe with problems.

* * *

IT WAS the first time I'd been at Apollo's new house.

I liked it.

It was a simple two-story structure with a wraparound porch and another white picket fence with gorgeous rosebushes lining the front. Walking toward the door, I thought I spotted a small garden in the backyard. It was cute. Homey.

And it was a million miles—and millions of dollars—away from his lavish oceanfront estate in Palm Beach.

I was about to knock when the door opened. With a smile on his face, Apollo stood in the doorway. His hair was longer than I remembered, and he was dressed casually in a black t-shirt and jeans with a casually tussled Sunday-morning air about him. The godlike figure he once was wasn't readily apparent, but I could sense it.

"Astra," he said warmly, a genuine smile gracing his handsome face. "It's been too long. I'm so glad to see you. Come in, come in. I'm so glad you finally came to the house. I thought I'd never see you here."

I stepped inside.

"Yo," Archie said to the god from his perch on my shoulder.

"Hello, Archimedes. You decided to accompany Astra, I see," Apollo said.

"Always," Archie said.

Apollo chuckled as he stepped back and let me fully enter. He shut the door behind me, and I was struck by the sense of mystery that seemed to pervade the entire house. It was as if there were secrets beneath the surface that only the gods knew.

"Can I get you anything?" Apollo asked.

"No, thank you," I replied. "I just have a couple of quick questions, and then I really have to get back. I'm working on a case."

The expression on his handsome face shifted briefly to one of slight disappointment, and then immediately morphed to a more composed and agreeable look. "Yes, of course. Let's go into the sitting room," he said.

The house was filled with warm tones and comfortable furniture, from the plush armchair in the living room to the ornate dining table in the kitchen. As we walked, I could see trinkets on dozens of shelves and artwork on the walls from all over the world. "I like it," I told him, gesturing toward the art.

"I'm glad."

When we finally arrived at the sitting room, it was surprisingly simple, with two plain chairs and a small ottoman in the middle that seemed to serve as a focal point for conversation. The room reminded me of a therapist's office.

"Are you still doing therapy for people?" I asked.

"As they need it. Have a seat," Apollo said, motioning to the chairs.

I stood still and looked warily at the chair that had been offered, trying to read if the invitation meant that I needed it. Apollo's face was kind and inviting, yet something in his gaze made me uneasy. I weighed my options, uncertain of what was expected of me.

With a twinge of reluctance, I took a seat.

Archie perched on the ottoman in front of me and began preening.

Finally, Apollo sat down across from me and looked at me, his gray-green eyes twinkling. "Now. What can I help you with, daughter?"

"Do you know where Lillian Thornton is?" I asked him point blank.

His face didn't change, but his eyes narrowed. "The mayor of Cassandra, correct? And your boyfriend's mother," he said slowly. "Why do you ask?"

I noticed he did not answer me.

"I saw someone grab her in the forest. On a path near the pixie swamp. Well, I didn't see it happen, but it was in a vision. I wasn't there."

If I had been, she wouldn't be missing.

I guarantee that.

Apollo's expression grew serious. "That is a very dangerous place to be right now, Astra. Who did you see placing hands on her?"

"Wait—back up. Why did you say that? That it's dangerous?" I asked.

He shook his head. "It's not important right now. What did this person look like?"

"Don't just dismiss my question," I said, narrowing my eyes. "Do you know anything about Lillian or not? Why did you say that path was a dangerous place to be?"

"You're a very stubborn young woman." My father's face was stern, but his eyes held a hint of amusement. "There are...forces at work in Cassandra. Forces that don't always play nice. Do you understand?"

Obviously, no.

Because he wasn't really saying anything specific.

"And it appears," he continued, "that Lillian has been caught up in their games. You must be very careful, Astra."

I sat upright. "Are you talking about Daniel Caldecott?"

"I know of him." Apollo nodded. "He's not the only one, the only force. There are other people and creatures who are even more dangerous, and if you want to find Lillian, you must tread carefully." He paused, then added, "I will do what I can to help you, but you must stay safe."

"I'm fine. She's not. I need to know what she's gotten herself into."

Apollo smiled, but it didn't quite reach his eyes. "Of course. Then answer my question. What did the person who took Lillian look like?"

I described the man I had seen, but Apollo

shook his head. "I don't recognize him, though it would be very difficult to recognize anyone from your description. You did not see much at all."

Ouch.

"But I will keep my ears open for any news about Lillian." Apollo stood and gestured for me to follow. "Come. I have something to show you."

I shook my head, my mind racing with questions. "You realize you haven't told me a single thing I can use, right? I don't want to see anything. I need answers. Why did you kidnap the pixie chieftain and send him to me?"

Apollo paused, looked at me, and sat back down. "The pixie chieftain? What pixie chieftain?"

"You sent him to me. Shrunk down in a little tiny jail." I slapped my pockets and pulled out the note Althea had found on the box. "This was with it."

Apollo scanned the paper, his eyebrows knitted together in confusion. "No, Astra. I did not send you this. I have never heard of this pixie chieftain." He peered at me, his face heavy with concern. "Come."

"Where?"

"Trust me."

"That isn't much of an answer," I replied, my voice sharp with suspicion.

"If you follow me, your question will be answered."

* * *

THERE WAS a large fountain in the center of Apollo's backyard.

It had a statue of a woman holding a pitcher in her hands with her hair pulled back into intricate braids. Her dress was ancient-looking, and it flowed down from her shoulders in long folds as she held the pitcher outward.

I stared at the woman's face, then I uttered a vicious oath. "That's—"

"Yes. This is the fountain of Persephone," Apollo said.

My eyes narrowed as I stared, every muscle tense as though I was ready for a fight. "Why the heck would you bring me out here?" I asked him, rage radiating from me like the heat from a noonday sun.

I wished with every inch of my being that I had something in my hands so I could smash the statue's face in.

"Astra, breathe and get your emotions under

control, please." My father stepped forward, and the surrounding air seemed to crackle with a magical charge.

"Answer my question," I said flatly.

Nothing would bring Jason back, but I would blame Persephone for his loss for the rest of my life. I felt my hands sizzle with the destructive magic Athena gave me. All it would take was one bolt, one well placed—

"I mean it. Stop," Apollo said.

"Why should I?" I asked, not even trying to hide the disbelief in my voice. "She doesn't deserve my respect. She destroys innocents."

Apollo stepped forward and put a hand on my shoulder. "Astra," he breathed. "I understand your anger, but this is not the place for it. Persephone is not entirely to blame for what happened."

"Are you kidding me?" I bit my lip, trying to rein in my fury. "The whole vengeful plan was hers."

Apollo shook his head. "No. Things happened the way they were supposed to happen, and everyone went where they were supposed to go. If it was not meant to end as it did, it would have ended in an entirely different way."

"Oh, get real." I looked at him. "You're trying to tell me it was all fate?"

"Yes," Apollo said softly. "Against fate, even the gods have limitations." He squeezed my shoulder. "Let it go, Astra. Let go of your anger and focus on finding your friend's mother. Her fate is not yet decided."

* * *

"THIS FOUNTAIN," he began, "is pulling water from the southern tip of the pixie swamp." He pointed to the edge of the fountain. "See, the water is sloshing north as if it wants to go back in that direction."

Once I focused more on the fountain as a whole (and less on where I should hit it to make the whole thing crumble into dust), I could feel the power of the fountain in the air. The water churned like a living thing. "Yeah, fine, I see it. What does that mean?"

"We gods have been blessed with holy wells," Apollo said, his hand immersed in the cool liquid. "Those sacred springs have linked both the divine and mortal worlds together. The waters of Persephone's fountain are beyond the physical domain, crossing into the gods' realm."

"Can you explain it in plain English?" I asked. "I don't understand."

"What does it do? If I dive in, will I show up in the underworld?" I looked at the clear water and frowned. I wished I'd brought Althea with me. She'd probably have bottled up a month's worth of this stuff for study already. "Does it let us make cell phone calls to Olympus if we drink it? What?"

"I'm sure you know that my sister-in-law dislikes being in the underworld for half of the year," Apollo said, his fingers trailing the surface of the water.

"Everyone's aware of that. It's probably what made her such a bitter—"

My father cleared his throat to cut me off. "This fountain severs the connection between her and Hades, and makes it far more difficult for him to find her and bring her back with him to the darkness of the underworld."

"So…it's like a protection spell for her?"

"Yes, and a powerful one." Apollo stepped back. "This fountain has been around since time immemorial. It will remain until the end of time. But not necessarily in this physical place. It moves as Persephone moves, shifting and changing as she changes her focus on the earth. Her focus has been on your mother, and so now her sacred well is here."

"But Mom died months ago," I told him.

"No one knew her focus was on your mother, and so no one knew the sacred well was there. Once Persephone's plot was revealed, so was the location of the fountain." Apollo pointed beyond his backyard toward the trees. "This house is at the southern edge of what you call the pixie swamp. I purchased it so I could monitor the well and who was using it. And for what purpose they were using it."

"Okay," I said cautiously, my mistrustful hackles already rising. "But you've never heard of the pixie chieftain?"

He shook his head, his expression dark. "As a deity, I have much bigger problems to worry about than the pixies and their squabbles. But I can tell you this—many people have found the sacred well within the waters of the pixie swamp, and because of the pixie magic shielding it, I have been blind to what is happening there."

"You have no idea who's using the water?"

"No. I only know that there have been several people." He looked at the water. "If you've spoken to this pixie chieftain, and he didn't mention Persephone's well, Astra?"

I drew in a deep breath and let it out slowly. "He's hiding things from me."

Apollo nodded. "Yes. There is no way a pixie would not know about this."

I frowned, feeling frustrated and helpless. "So what do I do now?"

Apollo smiled, his expression filled with understanding. "You do what you do best, daughter. You find the truth."

CHAPTER TEN

*W*ith a thud, I placed several thermoses on the kitchen table and looked at Althea, repeating Apollo's information about the water severing connections. "Be careful with it. I wanted to know what it does, but he was so cryptic. I'm still not sure if I'm clear on what the heck it does," I told Althea.

"I'll be careful," she reassured me with a solemn nod.

"What else did you find out?" Ayla asked.

"That gods talk in riddles, and they like to be mysterious," I replied.

"It's true," Archie agreed, ruffled feathers betraying his frustration. "Half the time, I feel like their words just bounce around in my head like marbles in an empty jar."

"I don't think that's because of the marbles, jarhead," Lily murmured.

Archie glared with beady eyes at her. "What?"

"Nothing. I said nothing." Lily preened her wings as she averted her gaze. "You must be hearing things."

Althea slowly lifted the bird to the crown of her head, her expression thoughtful. "At least he gave you some of the water so I could study it. We'll figure it out. We always do," she said.

"She found out more than that," Archie interjected, his eyes wide. "Tell them about Pistachio. You know—that Apollo didn't send him here."

"You just did." I turned. "He's right. Apollo told me he didn't send him to us. He claimed not even to know who he is."

Ayla's face twisted into a mask of unease. "That makes even less sense. So, how did he get here? And who has the power to shrink down a pixie chieftain and a jail to put him in it?"

"I don't know." I looked around. "We probably should ask him. Obviously, he wasn't telling us the whole truth. Or maybe any truth. Where is he?"

Althea and Ayla exchanged an uneasy glance.

"What?" I asked. "What's that look?"

"He's gone," Ayla told me. "He said he had to go back home and see Alice."

Althea nodded slowly, with a hint of dissatisfaction on her face. "You let him out, so we figured we didn't need to keep him here."

"The chief leave, too?" I asked, assuming Pistachio had expanded Harmon back to his standard size before he left.

Althea shook her head. "He's still here, and he's still tiny. I have a potion that will reverse pixie dust, but it needs to simmer a bit longer before reaching full potency. Pistachio said leaving him like that might give him time to think about his attitude toward the pixies."

"The pixies he didn't seem to know about until today? Sure. Or he wants him out of the way," I said.

"Well, yeah. Or that."

"Are your cases always so convoluted?" Ayla asked me.

"Cases are, by nature, convoluted, Ayla," Althea answered like the in-house expert on missing persons. She turned to me. "So, what do we do now?"

"Now?" I pointed to the thermoses on the

166 | LEANNE LEEDS

table. "We study this water. We must understand what it does before determining who would want it and why. So far, we only know that everyone's been trying to get their hands on the pixie swamp. I think this water might be the reason."

"And by we, you mean me, right?" Althea grabbed the thermoses and tucked them under her arm. "Got it."

"At least we know Lillian is probably alive," I said. "This water is likely why Jason can't find his mother in the spirit world. Someone probably made her drink it."

"Or they have her underwater," Althea's crow added.

"She'd be dead if she were underwater," Ayla pointed out.

Althea shook her head. "Not necessarily. There are underwater caves. Remember when Mom took us to Devil's Den? Oh, by the way, Astra—Ami was looking into the paperwork while the store was empty. She's got my laptop, and she scried for some information. She wanted to talk to you before telling us about it."

"Why?"

Althea shrugged. "No idea."

I sighed and rubbed my temples. "Fine. I'll go talk to Ami."

* * *

ALTHEA'S glowing laptop illuminated Ami's determined face as she sat cross-legged, her fingers clicking furiously at the keyboard.

"Hey," I said.

Her eyes darted up at me. "Hey. You're back."

"I am. Althea said you have some information?"

Ami's words came out in a rapid stream of information. "Okay, so I looked into who owns the pixie swamp land. But it's not just about who owns it now; it's about who owned it before, and who wanted it, and…okay, wait. Let me back up. So, first, a real estate lesson—land speculators avoid wetlands. They are just super unlikely to be purchased. Like, crazy unlikely. They call swamp land 'constrained' land. It has no development value. No one wants it." She glanced up. "With me so far?"

I nodded.

"Okay, so that's true, except for this swamp. It had no development value. It's constrained land, and it's not in a great location that someone would go through the expense of changing it to something people can build on. Someone bought it, and they paid an awful lot for it." She pointed to the laptop, and I walked over to look. On the screen was a map of Central Florida with the small town of Cassandra, Forkbridge, and the pixie swamp highlighted. "It's now owned by a company called Siltwater Investments. They paid a fortune for it. Overpaid, really."

"Siltwater." I stared at the map. "That name sounds familiar."

"It should. It was on the front page of the Forkbridge paper a week ago." She typed for a few seconds before turning the screen again. It was a news article about a newly founded nonprofit company Siltwater Investments and its goal of wetland protection. "The Windrows started Siltwater Investments." Ami looked up. "Well, Alice Windrow.

"And if it involves Alice, we can assume it involves the pixies."

"Right. They bought it seven months ago when the owner, Ima Nelson, put it up for sale."

"This isn't suspicious, though. It's not surprising that the pixies would overpay for the swamp. I mean, it is their home." I frowned. "Ima Nelson. That name rings a bell, too."

Ami nodded. "Ima Nelson is a psychic from Cassandra. She put the land up for sale because she was getting too old to take care of it. The mayor wanted Cassandra to buy it, but Ima and Lillian Thornton got into some kind of kerfuffle. Ima refused to sell it privately to the town and instead sold it at auction, so she had no control over who that land was sold to. It was a huge, dramatic mess in Cassandra, too—people were furious at her for opening the border of Cassandra to outsiders."

"How do you know all that?"

She pointed toward the crystal ball. "That, and Althea hacked the private Cassandra mailing list."

Of course she did.

"Okay. I assume the auction happened?"

Ami nodded and typed a few more times. "There were five bidders. The towns of Cassandra and Forkbridge, Siltwater Investments, S.T.O.R.M. Enterprises, and another company called Aether Enterprises." She glanced up from the screen before continuing. "But Aether Enterprises dropped out of the bidding right before it was sold."

"Do you know anything about either of those companies?"

Ami shook her head. "Not really. I looked into S.T.O.R.M., but I couldn't find anything. They're a mystery. As for Aether Enterprises, I didn't move further since they dropped out. You think I should?"

"Maybe they dropped out because they figured out a better way to get the land," I told her. "Like by kidnapping the mayor of Cassandra."

Ami's fingers hammered on the keys rapidly. Her head tilted and then swiftly swung to face me. She swiveled the laptop around, pointing to a page filled with the image of a handsome man in a spotless suit, his smirk oozing with confidence.

"You must be kidding me."

"Nope. Lothian Pennington," she said. "He's the owner of Aether Enterprises."

"That can't be right," I muttered, shaking my head in disbelief.

"It's right. What on earth is he doing wrapped up in this? Well, at least there's no way he kidnapped Lillian Thornton." Ami looked at me. "Right?"

"Look, I know Eddie would never tolerate it," I replied grimly. "But I don't think Lothian tells Eddie everything he does. And this isn't the first time I've seen Lothian involved in magically infused liquid and a shady land deal."

Ami's eyes widened. "So you think…"

"I think I need to go talk to Lothian."

* * *

I RANG the doorbell of the werewolf lodge, a sprawling two-story building surrounded by sturdy trees and lush vegetation. A few moments later, the door opened, revealing Lothian Pennington, the owner of Aether Enterprises.

"Astra, what a surprise," he said, his voice dripping with sarcasm. "Here to visit Emma?"

"No. I have some questions for you," I said, my voice cold.

He scrutinized me with a penetrating gaze, then stepped back and opened the door to let me through. "Very well," Lothian said, motioning me to follow him down the hall and into a study. He sat behind a large desk, and I stood across from him. "Ask me your questions."

"What are you doing in wetland protection and a land deal involving the pixies?" I asked as Eddie and Emma walked into the room.

Well, Eddie walked in.

Emma waddled like a duck, her belly swollen with pregnancy.

Lothian gave Emma a soft smile before swiveling toward me, his facial expression unreadable. "I fancy myself a bit of a steward of the environment, Astra," he said with false sincerity. "You should know better than anyone how important it is to protect what little wilderness we have left. And for a wolf, obviously, this is a top priority."

"Is it now?"

"Astra, what's this about?" Eddie asked.

I gave Eddie a quick rundown of the situation as Norden, one of the other werewolves, brought extra chairs to the office to accommodate Eddie, Emma, and her gigantic girth. He shot a curious glance at Lothian when I detailed his werewolf's sudden appearance in my sticky paperwork wicket of a case.

"Is that true, Lothian?" Eddie asked.

"Which part?" Lothian steepled his hands on the desk in front of him and nodded. "That I was interested in buying the wetlands? Yes, it is. Once I knew we were moving, I'd wanted to purchase the land to cover my bets here, but some pixie approached me and asked me not to purchase their home." His facial expression was unreadable, but his posture was tense and alert. "Walnut? Almond?"

"Pistachio," I told him.

"Right, that was him. I felt protecting the land from development and ensuring the pixies have a safe home was important, so I bowed out of the auction." He shrugged. "I thought it was the right thing to do. Let the pixies own pixie land. It looked like they had deep enough pockets to do it."

Emma nodded, not surprised by the answer. "Why did you get involved in wetland protection in the first place? It seems like something unrelated to your business." Emma winced. "Oh, man, my feet hurt."

"Sit," Eddie pointed.

Emma sat down with a thunk.

Eddie knelt before Emma's chair and gently cradled her feet in his hands. Without a word, he kneaded the arch of her foot, slowly working out the knots of tension that had built up in her muscles. "Better?" he asked.

Lothian caught me watching. "We're good at that."

"What, being a considerate mate?" I asked.

"I was talking about foot massages," Lothian replied with a wink. "But that, too."

"Are you flirting with me?"

Lothian winked again. "Of course not, Arden."

Sometimes I thought Lothian wanted to kill me, and other times I thought he liked me. It was like figuring out what a cat was thinking or reading an alligator's facial expression.

Impossible.

A sudden movement inside Emma's belly caught everyone's attention. Lothian's gaze fell on her, and his expression softened with uncharacteristic warmth. "That is just bizarre," Lothian said. "I guess the baby's awake."

I had been watching him for months and still hadn't figured him out. He was an enigma. Standing across from him, I wondered if I could figure this guy out—if it were even possible, it would certainly not be easy.

"The baby's always awake," Emma said, patting her belly.

"Are you okay?" Eddie asked, poised to jump into action.

"I'm okay—" Emma suddenly gasped, catching her breath as the baby inside her moved again more ferociously than before. "It feels like this kid has his feet hooked onto my ribcage, and he tries to stand up now and then." She rolled her shoulders and then looked up at me. "Are you the only one looking for Lillian Thornton?"

"I've got some help," I told her. "Archie's doing flyovers looking for clues. Althea is looking into...some things about it," I said, quickly deciding not to say anything about Persephone's well. "I also have Ayla, Lily, and Cerberus. Ami's googling stuff. We're doing okay."

Lothian eyed me with interest. "Do you all have any leads?"

I pointed. "You're my latest."

Lothian faked a hurt expression. "Astra. I'm wounded. Even after all this, you think I'm still a suspect?"

"After all of what?" I shrugged. "You barely told me anything. You're not off the list yet."

Emma stood up, her hand on her back. "Astra doesn't trust you."

"Like that's news." Lothian smiled. "Fair enough." He leaned back in his chair and looked toward the window. "I'm not sure I can do anything to change that."

Eddie cleared his throat. "Well, maybe there is. I think it would be good if Lothian accompanies you on your investigation," he said, looking between Lothian and me.

"No, you don't," Lothian told the wolf pack leader.

"Oh, no, I do."

"I think that's a great idea," Emma said firmly. "You can tell Astra all about your swamp land deal—because we both noticed that you didn't say why you were involved in buying it in the first place—and I'll feel better that she's got someone with her that's only slightly less dangerous than my gun."

Lothian muttered something under his breath but nodded reluctantly.

Eddie stood up from the table. "Well then, it's decided. Now, if there's nothing else?" He looked around the room expectantly, but no one spoke up. "I'd like to get Emma back to bed."

"That's how I got into this predicament in the first place, wolf." Emma's body leaned softly against Eddie's, and her eyes sparkled with amusement as she teased him.

It was good to see her so happy.

As we made our way out into the hall, Emma reached out to me for support. "Walk with me," she said. "I walk slower than anyone else." Eddie seemed to get the message and carefully handed her to me. "I'm sure Eddie and Lothian want to talk."

Eddie nodded, and the two walked ahead of us.

Emma lowered her voice so that only I could hear her words. "Be careful with Lothian," she warned me in a low whisper. "I trust him, but only to a point. He may not always be what he seems, and his agenda's not always clear."

I nodded as we both stepped outside—where I found Lothian climbing onto his motorcycle. "Um. No."

"No?" There was a soft creak as Lothian adjusted himself in the seat, followed by a subtle rev as he twisted the throttle back to life. "What do you mean, no? Get on."

"We're not taking that thing. I'm driving," I said as I stared down Lothian.

He grasped the handlebars with determination, and I could see the tension in his shoulders. "No way. My motorcycle is much faster and more reliable than your Jeep."

Lothian had a point there, but I would not give in easily. "My Jeep has better off-road capabilities, and this case involves a swamp."

"Unless it's got an airboat mode, that's a dumb argument."

"There's no way two people will fit on that tiny thing you call a bike."

We continued this debate for several minutes.

I won't bore you with the details.

Finally, after much bickering and heated words, we agreed to take both—me in my Jeep and Lothian on his motorcycle—and meet up at our destination.

Eddie pulled me aside. "He can be a handful,

but he's loyal. And he cares about you, Astra. It doesn't seem that way sometimes, but he does."

"You're right," I said with a nod. "It doesn't seem that way sometimes. But I appreciate you saying something. I'm sure he'll be a great help whenever I'm not distracted by the urge to punch him in the face," I told Eddie as we watched Lothian drive away on his bike.

A sense of dread washed over me as we approached Cassandra, the small town where Lillian Thornton had last been seen. The streets were oddly empty, and the buildings seemed dark and desolate even though it was early evening.

Lothian swung his leg off the side of his motorcycle in one smooth movement, his hand still firmly clasping the bike as he surveyed the street. "This is strange," Lothian murmured. His voice was hushed, and a strange uneasiness laced his words.

"I know." I looked right and left as I locked my Jeep. I'd never seen a tourist town so uncharacteristically still—still until a deafening cry shattered that stillness, at least.

"She was the one! She killed Lillian!" a woman yelled.

An enraged mob materialized from the shadows, the woman at the center.

She was pointing at me.

Lothian stepped in front of me, shielding me. "What's going on?" he demanded.

The mob shouted back, accusing me once again of murdering Lillian Thornton. "First, you killed the son, and now you killed his mother!"

"I did not—"

"Stop talking. Quick," Lothian said, grabbing me protectively. "We have to get out of here. We'll work through it once we're away from them."

"But I—"

"Astra, just do what you're told for once!"

We dashed toward the outskirts of town, weaving through the streets and easily avoiding the angry mob—they were out of shape, and we were quick and crafty. Lothian's gaze was on me now and then as we passed by an empty street or hid behind an abandoned house. He seemed uneasy and stayed close.

"There." I spotted a small clearing with a dirt road winding through it, part of the forest path that led in multiple directions through Cassandra and the pixie swamp. "There," I whispered. "Go there. The townsfolk don't go toward the pixie swamp path."

We made a mad dash toward the tree line and hid behind bushes as the mob moved past us, unaware we were there. We waited until they had moved out of sight before slowly emerging from our hiding spot.

"We should be safe for the moment," Lothian said. He turned toward me, his face full of concern. "Astra... why do they think you killed Lillian Thornton? What exactly happened back there?"

I shook my head, still trying to process what had just happened. "I have no idea."

But I knew one thing.

I had to find out what was happening in this crazy town before the mob found us again. We had to get to the bottom of this mystery and fast.

CHAPTER ELEVEN

The marsh turned into an otherworldly landscape of inky blacks and emerald greens as the sun went down. The dense cover of shrubbery and thickets dissolved into darkness. It was alive with frogs croaking, the gentle rustle of wind through the trees, and the occasional splash of something slinking through the murky water.

The only sound of civilization was our footfalls on the graveled path—a path that grew more uneven and unkempt as we progressed away from Cassandra and toward the pixie swamp.

Oh, and Lothian's voice.

I could hear Lothian's voice.

Heck, the werewolf was so loud I suspected people gathering on the deck of a seaside restaurant for dinner in Daytona could hear Lothian's voice.

"I know Florida has a reputation for a bit of weirdness," he said as we walked, "and I can attest to that. I've visited the white sand beaches of Destin, the mangroves of Pensacola Bay, and the hidden coves of St. Augustine. I've partied on the streets of Miami and tripped on the bridges over Tampa Bay. I've seen the glorious foliage of the Everglades and the forgotten relics of the past in forgotten inlets all along the coast. I've even been to the Kennedy Space Center and Cape Canaveral," he continued.

"Are you writing a travel ad?" I asked. "What could possibly be your point?"

Lothian's lips curled into a slight grin, his eyes bright with amusement. "You know, Astra, I've read my book lounging on the balcony of the Ritz-Carlton in Fort Lauderdale," he said, gesturing with his hands as if indicating the vastness of the experiences he was sharing with me. "Incredible hotel. Five stars. Fantastic views. And the food? Magnificent."

I gritted my teeth and tried to ignore the

sound of his constant rambling, but it was like a mosquito buzzing around my head that I couldn't swat away. "I don't care."

"Oh, sure you do. I've seen the dirty parts of Florida. I've seen the idyllic and the hellish—"

"Oh, dear gods, do you ever take a breather?" I snapped. I wished he would just shut up and leave me alone so I could focus. "Just stop talking for two seconds, will you?"

I could see Lothian's smirk widen as he watched me, his eyes twinkling with amusement. "Why, Astra, whatever do you mean?"

"At least get to the damn point, then," I snapped. I balled my hands into fists that twitched with the desire to clock the werewolf hard enough to break his jaw. An act of violence that would, hopefully, make his mouth stop moving.

Though I suspected even that wouldn't get him to shut up.

I heard a light, amused chuckle escape him, a clear indication of his delight at my growing frustration. "Of course, Astra," he said, still smiling. "My point is that, despite all that I've seen, there is no place stranger in this state than the odd trio of towns, Forkbridge, Cassandra, and this very faerie swamp. If you've ever watched the horror movie 'War of the Worlds,' I'd wager it's simply a retelling of a typical week here in Florida."

"Are you from Florida?" I asked.

"Nope."

"Then be quiet. You don't get to say that." We had reached the brink of the swamp, the heavy air heavy with the cloying scent of decay and rot, a strange combination of honeysuckle and moist earth, tinged with the barest hint of sulfur. "And it's a pixie swamp."

"What?"

"It's a pixie swamp," I corrected him. "Not faerie. Faeries and pixies are not the same. Pixies are small, mischievous beings associated with nature and the outdoors. Fairies are more ethereal and otherworldly, associated with magic and the unseen realm."

"Yeah, none of that means much to me." Lothian shrugged, uninterested in the finer points of my folklore lesson. "Whatever. I just wanted to point out that no matter how weird the rest of Florida is, this place takes the cake."

"I think you just like to hear yourself talk."

I had to admit that he had a point (silently and without saying anything to him.)

Even though I'd grown up in Forkbridge, moved to Paranormopolis, and joined the witch military, I'd never encountered anything as strange as some of the things that happened since I came home. And I'd seen some pretty weird stuff. "Maybe my mother hid all this weirdness from us growing up the way she hid everything else," I mumbled.

Lothian elbowed me. "What was that?"

"Nothing. Let's keep walking. I want to get to the swamp before it gets completely dark out."

Lothian and I trudged side by side, our gazes fixed on the murky depths of the pixie swamp ahead. I could feel the tension in the air, but it was almost comforting in its familiarity, and I found myself grateful for this moment of respite—

"So, before?"

Oh, dear gods.

I knew he couldn't shut up for long.

"I'd heard you clearly, actually." Lothian shot me a sideways glance, eyebrow raised. "And hearing what you said, I just realized you and I never talked about what happened in the underworld."

"What's there to talk about? And what does

this have to do with what you overheard and then lied about overhearing?"

Lothian shrugged. "I just thought it might be good for us to discuss it. To get it off your chest. I mean, we're not related. I was there the whole time. It might help to talk through what happened with someone unrelated to you. Or female."

"I'm fine," I said, picking up my pace. The sun kept setting, casting a hazy orange glow over the western trees and shrubs. "Perfectly fine."

"I didn't say you weren't."

"Good." I could feel his eyes on me, but I refused to look back.

"But obviously, what's going on right now has something to do with Jason, his mother, and his death. Maybe talking it out with me would help?"

"Help what? That's not why I'm here. That's not why you're here. I'm here to figure out what's happening in this swamp and find Lillian Thornton. That's it. I'm not here to talk about my feelings."

"Okay, okay." He held up his hands, palms outward, in a gesture of surrender. Lothian opened his mouth to say something else—because the man truly could not shut up—but a loud screech cut off whatever he was about to say.

We stopped. I glanced up, hoping it was Archie, but I didn't see him.

"What was that?" Lothian asked, his voice low.

* * *

THE SOUND of the animal grew closer and more ominous. It was like a wild cat's hiss combined with a hawk's sharp cry and just a hint of something wild and primal that made me uneasy.

Lothian's body tensed, and his body hunched over as if he was getting ready to shift. He kept his eyes forward, looking into the trees and then back to me as if ready to shield me from whatever was coming our way.

"I don't need you to protect me," I whispered.

"You remember saying my sparkling conversation wasn't why I was here? Well, you were right. Protecting you is why I'm here, and I don't need you to tell me how I'm supposed to do that." "Now, be quiet, and listen." his body shifted into an athletic stance, one foot stepped back and his arms instinctively curled up slightly in preparation to fight, ready to throw a punch or deflect a blow.

"I wasn't the one launching into a monologue

while whatever that thing is creeps closer and closer to us," I hissed.

"Oh, Athena, wise goddess of war, could you tell them to shut the hell up?" Archie shouted full-throated from the branches above.

We both spun around and stared up into the trees.

Archie flapped his wings and flew down from his perch, settling on my shoulder with a tight talon grip. "Finally, some common sense. Now, I suggest we all be quiet because I think that thing is coming closer." He pointed with his beak in the direction of the noise. "And it doesn't sound friendly."

Lothian and I glared at each other briefly before returning to the sound coming our way. We both held our breath, straining our ears in an attempt to make out whatever it was that was approaching.

The sound of a twig snapping in the darkness made my heart leap.

I felt my body tense, ready to fight or run.

Then I blinked.

The pixie was a tiny, shimmering figure in the dim light. His glittery silver eyes sparkled with puckishness and a grin spread across his face, revealing a shock of lavender hair. "Hello," he said with a playful tone.

"That's not what screeched," Archie whispered.

As he stretched upward and outward, the pixie grew, his frail and slender body expanding and becoming more sturdy. A smile played across his lips, implying a playful personality and as his features became clearer, he transformed into a human-sized pixie, exuding a cheerful aura.

"Hello," he says once more, his voice rich and deep. I could have sworn I detected a hint of chimes in his words, like delicate crystal tinkling. He fixed his gaze on me. "You're a witch," the pixie stated, then flicked a glance toward Lothian. "And you, a werewolf. But not in this moment. And you are in the pixie swamp. At night." He tilted his head. "You're either fearless or foolish."

"Don't want to guess what I am?" Archie snapped.

The pixie regarded Archie with a glimmer of admiration in his eyes. "You're quite the talking bird, aren't you?" he said. "And clever too, I see. Four bullfrogs devoured since your arrival in the swamp just an hour ago." He clapped his hands together. "So, what brings you to me today?"

I didn't recognize this pixie, and considering my dealings with them, I should.

There weren't many of them.

You think there should be a lot of them in this swamp. The swamp's the size of a small town—several hundred acres easily—and they generally went about life at no more than six inches tall. But even though the land could support hundreds of them, there were no more than twenty-five or thirty pixies in Pistachio's tribe.

"We're looking for someone," I said, deciding to be direct. "Her name is Lillian Thornton, and she's been missing for the past few days."

When Lillian's name was mentioned, the pixie's eyes glowed with recognition. "Lillian Thornton," he said, carefully enunciating each syllable. "I'm aware of her reputation. Is she not the leader of the psychic town in the northern region? The woman who is said to be in a secret relationship with your village's not-so-bright police chief?" He looked at me with keen interest.

The northern region?

I half expected the pixie to tell me winter was coming.

"Can you tell me where I can find Pistachio?" I asked.

The pixie's eyes flashed, and he smiled. "Ah, so

that's why you're here. To find the leader of the pixies. Well, I can certainly tell you where you can find him, but it won't be easy." He paused, then continued. "He's in the center of the swamp.

"Thanks. And your name is?"

He bowed slightly in our direction before disappearing into the shadows.

* * *

LOTHIAN AND I SHARED A LOOK.

"So," I began, "we need to find Pistachio in the center of the swamp."

"Looks like it." He nodded his head and made to take a step forward. "Let's go."

"Wait." I grabbed his arm, stopping him in his tracks.

His gaze shifted to me, eyes wide with surprise. "Wait? What for?" he asked. "Suddenly decided you want to talk about things?"

"You know, I was on your side a couple of weeks ago, but after spending a mere half an hour with you, I have to admit Astra was right," Archie told Lothian with a huff. His wings were slightly spread, and his talons clenched me tightly as he glared. "You might be the single most annoying human being on the planet."

"I told you," I said to Archie while rolling my shoulder. "And don't stab me, dude."

"I am not," Lothian said with a half-smile.

"You totally might be." Archie's brown feathers ruffled, and his eyes practically glowed with annoyance. "Totally. Might. Be."

"I'm not a human being, oh divine feathered one," the werewolf reminded the bird with a grand gesture. "I'm a werewolf. And werewolves are not annoying. We are strong, fierce, and loyal. We are majestic. We are powerful, strong, and wise."

I let out a snort of laughter. "You're something all right."

Lothian shrugged. "At least I can admit it."

"I wish you could admit you're totally annoying. Acknowledgment of a problem is the first step toward fixing it," I said, reaching up to pluck Archie off my shoulder and set him on the ground. "Now, let's focus. We need to find Pistachio, and if what the pixie said is true, then he's in the center of this swamp. So let's go."

"If what the pixie said is true," Archie muttered as he took off. "The pixie we didn't even get a name from? The one we've never seen before? The one who couldn't be bothered to introduce himself? That pixie?"

"Let's just go," I said, starting off once more.

Lothian followed behind me, his steps sure and steady. We navigated the thick foliage, occasionally using Archie's guidance. As we moved further and further in, the fog grew denser, and the trees began to look more and more sinister. I could almost feel something in the air, something watching us and waiting.

But that was probably just paranoia.

As I trudged through the swamp, my thoughts returned to Lothian's suggestion that we talk. We were from two different worlds and had nothing in common. What was there to say? It was likely to be more awkward than meaningful.

But despite my misgivings, I found myself drawn to finally talking with someone whose opinion I didn't care about. I was pretty sure it wouldn't help us find Pistachio or Lillian faster. It wasn't going to make things easier between us. There wasn't a cosmic power left in the universe that could do that.

But I had been feeling lonely lately.

I didn't particularly enjoy admitting it.

But I was.

I continued on my way, my thoughts wandering to those who had once played a vital role in my life but were now consumed by their own affairs. My Aunt Gwennie, who had grieved silently and alone for months following my mother's passing. Emma, who was entirely absorbed with Eddie and the arrival of their new baby. And Jason, who was adapting to his new existence in the afterlife.

It was no wonder I felt a little adrift.

We continued walking until we reached the center of the swamp, a large clearing surrounded by a circle of trees and shrouded in fog. In the middle sat a large boulder with a small but ornately carved door set low on it. It looked ancient and eerily familiar, like it had been through a hundred lifetimes before we arrived.

Lothian and I shared a look before turning our attention to Archie, who had circled us and was now perched in front of the small door.

"So," he said, preening his feathers, "shall we?"

Archie stepped forward and knocked on the small door with his beak.

After a few moments of silence, we heard a loud thump, and the door swung open to reveal a tiny figure with an angry expression on her face. "Who are you? And what do you want?" she snapped, her voice like the crack of a whip.

Lothian stepped forward, his manner calm and confident. "We're looking for someone," he said slowly. "Your chieftain. A pixie named Pistachio. Have you seen him?"

The pixie crossed her arms over her chest and narrowed her eyes at us. "What makes you think I know where he is?" she demanded.

"We were told that he was at the center of the swamp, and this boulder marks the center of the swamp," I said carefully. "We need to speak with him or Alice."

The pixie sighed and stepped back, gesturing for us to enter the small hallway beyond the tiny, doll-sized door. "Pistachio is in the back," she said, gesturing to a small hallway. "Alice is with him."

Lothian and I exchanged a worried glance. It seemed obvious to everyone but the pixie that the door was far too small for us to pass through.

The pixie laughed at our confusion. "No need to fear," she said. She waved her tiny hands from the doorway and released a spore-like cloud of glittering pixie dust that flew toward us.

I felt like a tiny speck of nothingness in a gargantuan world, the trees and blades of grass towering above me. Archie, who now seemed the size of a four story building, stood hovering above us, a scowl etched on his face.

"Wow. You're huge," I said. "Now I understand

why the rabbits run like hell when you get up in the morning. Seriously, Archie, you're terrifying."

Archie peered down at us with an amused expression. "No need to worry," he said with a snort. "You're way too sour for me."

Lothian gave me a nudge, and I stepped through the small entrance, feeling like Alice in Wonderland.

"Next time, ask," I said to the pixie. "Consent is a thing, you know."

"You knocked, witch," she responded with a shrug. Then she pointed. "That way."

The walls were lined with intricate patterns and symbols, creating a magical atmosphere. Sweetness lingered in the air, almost like honey or nectar, and the air was thick with the sound of pixie laughter and song. It made me feel oddly calm and relaxed despite my annoyance.

We found Pistachio and Alice deep in conversation at the end of the hallway. They both looked up as we approached, surprise and recognition flashing in their eyes.

"Astra! Lothian!" Pistachio exclaimed. "What are you both doing here?"

"Why didn't you tell me Alice bought the swamp six months ago?" I asked him.

Pistachio grew suddenly still and looked

down at the ground, avoiding my gaze. I could tell he was concerned by my question but remained silent momentarily before finally speaking. "It's complicated," he said.

"Pistachio Waterflash, you tell her what's going on!" Alice said hotly.

"But—"

"Now!"

So he did.

CHAPTER TWELVE

*P*istachio cleared his throat, his face visibly flushing from Alice's stern gaze. "About six months ago, I was approached by a group of pixies from a swamp in California. They told me that a company had gathered in their area, bought the land, and then systematically emptied the swamp of pixies to develop condos and high rises. They asked for my help—they wanted me to buy this swamp and keep it safe from whatever was out there. They also asked me to allow them to stay with us."

"You're sure it was six months ago?"

His shaggy red hair fell over his face as he nodded.

"Why didn't you tell me any of this when you

were at my house?" I asked him. "Or tell me that Alice's company had purchased the swampland?"

Pistachio shrugged. "I don't usually divulge pixie matters or affairs to witches, Arden. Especially those who associate with human law enforcement," he added, emphasizing the last words. "Need I remind you, the police have never been particularly benevolent toward our kind." He rolled his eyes heavenward. "Don't give me that look. You didn't need to know, so I didn't see fit to inform you."

"Now she needs to know," Alice said with a nod.

"I do?"

"You do," Alice answered.

"Why is that?" Lothian asked.

Alice ignored him. "Astra, I can see you're suspicious, but pixies aren't liars by nature," she said as she leaned closer to us. "Yes, they often misdirect people for the laughs or some agenda, but they're not dishonest. Pistachio didn't intentionally mislead you to hurt you. He is a chieftain. His people come first."

That was a mighty fine hair Alice was splitting. From where I stood, he misled me. Or, at the very least, lied by omission.

"Just so you know, I went to see my father

before coming here," I told the pixie and his shrunken human girlfriend. "He said he had nothing to do with your capture and didn't send you to my house. I think he's telling the truth," I continued, "but someone put you in a box and dropped you on my doorstep. If it wasn't my father, who was it?"

Pistachio's eyes were wide with surprise, and his jaw hung slightly open as he stared at me. "I have no idea. We figured it would have had to be a god. Who would even know about pixies, much less be powerful enough to capture one?" His hands were clenched tightly in frustration as he tried desperately to find an answer.

"Do you have any guesses at all?" Lothian asked. "Any issues with witches, maybe?"

I looked at Lothian. "Witches? Why witches?"

"Well, who else would send him to you? Dragons?"

"I honestly have no idea," Pistachio said with a shake of his head. "I can't think of any being powerful enough to capture me or why they would want to in the first place." He sat there, sweat beading on his forehead as his mind raced for an answer. "It could be anyone—a powerful witch, god, or deity that's not your father. That's a guess, though. I don't know."

Pistachio touched on an uncomfortable new monkey wrench in my life.

Athena wasn't the only god I had to worry about now. I also had to consider Apollo, Poseidon, Hermes, and Hades. Otherwise known as the Deity Dad brigade.

I couldn't make heads nor tails of why Pistachio was captured and mailed to me in this Florida real estate dilemma. Was I missing something obvious here? Was he snatched away to keep him out of harm's way? Or did someone want to point the finger at my dad, Apollo?

Because the answer seemed to be obvious. Like it was staring me in the face.

And yet the pieces didn't quite fit together.

Not completely.

And I still didn't know where Lillian Thornton was.

"Maybe we'll never know," Alice suggested gently, giving Pistachio's arm a reassuring squeeze. "Is it that important, Astra? What would it tell us?"

"Oh, we'll know," I told them. "Just not right now."

Lothian squinted, his chiseled jaw clenched tight as he scowled in my direction. "What do you mean?" he asked with a demanding gruffness.

"I need to go back home and put my hands on the little jail Pistachio locked the chief of police into. I might be able to see who came up with the idea."

"Right," he nodded. "I keep forgetting you have powers. Since you, you know, never bother to use them."

I raised my arm toward the werewolf, my power crackling like a spring storm. "I may not use it often, but I can do it. Would you like to see just what I'm capable of?"

Alice's laughter pealed through the room like a bright bell, and she directed a smirk-filled smile in our direction. "Maybe everyone can take a step back. We're all aware that everyone here—except me—is quite magically capable. Astra, you were telling us about reading the miniature jail?"

I dropped my hand. "It might be the only way for us to get some answers about this whole situation and figure out why someone decided to lock your boyfriend up like that." I frowned. "If that crazy mob in Cassandra lets me get back to my Jeep, anyway."

Pistachio gave me a vigorous nod. "I'm game to tag along," he said with a wink. "Let me know if there's anything I can do to help."

"My brave pixie man," Alice said. "Be careful, okay? We don't want to lose you again."

Lothian glanced between us, his eyes growing ever more narrow. "Wait, hang on. I know I heard wrong. Are you seriously telling me that Pistachio shrank the chief of police? Against his will?"

I nodded. "You heard right."

"I heard right." His tone indicated he didn't believe the pixie had accomplished such a feat. "And he's still shrunk in a tiny jail at your house?"

I nodded again.

"With your sisters?"

I gave a final nod. "Your point?"

The werewolf slowly rotated to face the pixie. "You want to explain why you did that?" he asked. His eyes then shifted toward me. "And maybe you want to explain why you don't seem concerned about this at all?"

"I wouldn't say I'm not concerned," I corrected him. "I'm just confident in my ability to handle the situation." I gave a small smile and gestured toward Alice and Pistachio. "They're here. He's there. No one's causing any trouble at this very moment. I call that a win." I shrugged. "That, and the dog might use him as a chew toy if I let him roam around the house until he snaps back to normal size. I wanted to make sure he was safe until the pixie dust wore off."

Lothian leaned back in his chair, giving himself a moment to contemplate the situation. Finally, his face softened with understanding. " I guess you have a point there," he relented. "But why'd you have to shrink the police chief? What kind of beef do you have with him?"

Pistachio moved toward the entrance hallway, gesturing for us to follow. "Come on, let's get going. I'll tell you what's what while we walk."

* * *

ONCE WE RETURNED to our regular sizes, we walked back through the swamp on the gravel path toward Cassandra. The night air felt cool and crisp on my skin, and I could see stars twinkling in the sky above us.

"It was October, six months back," Pistachio began as we strolled along, "that we first heard the mumblings. The locals on the street were talking about something big coming our way. A mysterious figure that would stir up all sorts of trouble. We pixies knew that whatever it was, it wouldn't be good."

"Is that before or after the other pixies showed up asking for help?" Lothian asked.

Pistachio nodded. "Right before. We'd heard reports throughout the summer that some strange activity was happening in and around various pixie enclaves, but we had no idea what it was or who was behind it."

"Did you look into it?" Lothian asked.

"How would we? How could we possibly accomplish such a thing? We stay close to our swampy home. That's how we like it—traveling the world at this point? That's not our cup of tea," Pistachio said with a shrug. "If word gets to us, we hear it. If it doesn't, we figure we didn't need to know."

"But then the other pixies showed up," I said.

Pistachio nodded. "That's right. They told us about someone powerful that had been wreaking havoc throughout pixie tribal lands, and they were desperate for help. Or, well, maybe not help, but at least somewhere to stay that was safe."

We kept walking through the swamp, each of us pondering our thoughts as Pistachio led us toward the town of Cassandra.

"I still don't understand why you shrunk the police chief," Lothian said after a few moments.

"I told you. Oh, no, wait—I told her and her

sisters," Pistachio said as he hopped over a fallen log, narrowly avoiding its gnarly roots.

"So, do tell me, please," Lothian said with an exaggerated bow.

Pistachio cast a sidelong smirk toward Lothian as they forged ahead, his eyes twinkling with amusement. "We heard them talking about draining the swamp. We can see their ghosts, you know. Talk to them sometimes."

"You can?" I asked, surprised.

"Of course we can. We talk to the ghosts. The ghosts talk to the psychics. We know that they know we are here." His arms are crossed tightly over his chest as he continues to walk, stomping his feet and shaking his head in frustration. "They've never bothered to talk to us, though. Never sought to make a neighborly alliance like the Ardens." Pistachio frowned. "They are arrogant."

"Are you sure that's what they said?" I asked him. "The thing about draining the swamp?"

"I'm small, not deaf," Pistachio told me with a tense glance.

"I didn't say you were, but you also didn't tell me exactly what they said."

"I told you," Pistachio responded. "Obviously, the mayor and her moron boyfriend worked with whatever group is taking over all the pixie lands. They were getting a head start on their plot to eject us from our homes."

"I know that's what you believe." Lothian looked at Pistachio. "Not to beat a dead horse, but you still haven't told us what you heard."

Pistachio stopped and swiveled his head around, glaring daggers at Lothian. "They were talking about how the swamp was a great opportunity, that they could make money by draining it and selling off the land. They wanted to do it quickly and didn't care who got in their way."

"You, yourself, heard this?" I asked him. "You heard Lillian Thornton and Chief Daniel Harmon say they didn't care who got in their way?"

I was annoyed at Harmon and wasn't thrilled Mayor Mom had pulled a gun on me in Punktex, but I couldn't picture those words coming out of their mouths.

Pistachio let out a frustrated sigh. "What does it matter?"

Uh huh.

I thought so.

"That's a no, then?" I asked.

Pistachio shot me an annoyed glare, his bushy

eyebrows knotted in displeasure. "No, I didn't hear it myself."

"Okay, then, who did you hear it from?"

"I heard it from the other pixies who had snuck out to look at what was happening. When they returned to the cave, they were all panicking, saying that the mayor and her boyfriend were plotting something against us. It's a good thing they did."

"Oh?"

"Of course." Pistachio started walking once more, concern deeply etched on his face. "It's a good thing they came to us. Thanks to them, we could get in gear and buy the swamp when it came up for auction."

The timing.

It was all wrong.

"You're sure this all happened six months ago?" I asked him.

"Yes, why?"

"Because my sister told me the land was bought at auction seven months ago," I told him. "And I don't see how you all would have bought the land seven months ago based on a repeated conversation you claim made it back to you six months ago."

Pistachio skidded to a standstill, his eyes wide

with alarm. "No, that's not right." The pixie frantically scanned the murky swamp as if hoping to find some other soul who could dispute my statement. "That can't be right."

"Look, Chief, I'm just pointing out that the two pieces of information don't jibe together. Unless my sister was wrong about the auction date—and I doubt she was—your explanation of events doesn't make sense."

"We didn't even look into buying this land until after the other pixies showed up, and those other pixies didn't come to our swamp until six months ago. I'm sure of it."

"How sure?" Lothian asked.

"Very sure! I'll admit Alice is far more focused on things like calendars, dates, and paperwork than I am," Pistachio said, "but six months ago was Halloween, and I most certainly remember that most holy turn of the wheel." He shook his head in disbelief and continued walking, only it was slower and more deliberate. "I don't understand. What you claim does not make sense."

As I was about to suggest that we look at the paperwork when we got back to Arden House, I heard a loud shout.

"Hey! You there! What are you doing on our land?"

I looked up and saw two figures silhouetted against the lights from the gas station parking lot about a city block away from us. One figure had the distinctive filling station cap on and was far too tall to be Ayla's friend Melvin Platt. "Bill?" I called out, assuming it was Melvin's father. "Is that you?"

"Your land?" Pistachio asked before they could answer. "I think not."

As we watched, Bill and the man with him stepped out of the shadows and full into the pathway's safety light, revealing the other man as interim mayor Daniel "Littlefeather" Caldecott.

* * *

"Ah! You must be Lothian and Pistachio," Caldecott said in a smooth voice. "I've heard so much about you two." His gaze moved from me to Pistachio, sizing us up with a calculating look. "It's good to meet you both in person, finally."

Who would Caldecott have heard information from that included tales of a pixie chieftain and a werewolf?

"What did you mean, your land?" Lothian demanded.

Daniel smiled benignly and shrugged his shoulders. "Well, when I say mine, I don't mean mine personally, of course," he said casually. "This land is for the people of Cassandra." He gestured around him with an expansive sweep of his arm.

Pistachio stepped forward and glared at Daniel. "What are you talking about?" he asked incredulously. "My girlfriend's company owns this land."

Daniel flashed us a grin. "Yes, she did. Or she thought she did," Daniel replied smugly, looking around at us with a satisfied smirk. "Unfortunately, poor Ima Nelson owed Cassandra a huge pile of tax money for this swampland, so she shouldn't have sold it. Personal property is subject to seizure for paying a delinquent tax, penalty, and interest. Didn't you know?"

"You're lying." Pistachio's face turned red with anger. "What court order gave you the right to seize this land?" he demanded, his voice rising. He stepped forward, pointing an accusing finger. "Show me the paperwork!"

Pistachio Waterflash, chieftain of the Central Florida pixies, knew little about calendars—but he was apparently super familiar with Florida asset seizure law.

Bill Platt watched the exchange with a confused expression, still unsure what was going on. "Mr. Caldecott, sir, I know these folks, and they were just using the path," he said. Bill glanced around at the other people present: Lothian, who looked determined; Pistachio, who seemed ready to fight; and Daniel Caldecott, whose smarmy grin made him look like a snake oil salesman. Finally, his gaze rested on me. "Astra, do you know what's going on here?"

"I'm honestly not sure how to answer that, Mr. Platt," I told him sincerely.

Bill's expression made it clear he knew he was missing something important here—something crucial to understanding what was going on with this very polite confrontation. "I'm not sure I understand what's going on here, but I know these folks don't mean any harm, Mr. Caldecott. The public can walk the path any time."

Daniel smiled at him condescendingly and said, "Mr. Platt, perhaps you should go back to your filling station and wait there while we sort this out. I'm sure Pistachio and Lothian can handle it without your help." He waved Bill away dismissively as he turned his attention back to us. "Run along, now."

"What's your game, Caldecott?" I asked, point blank.

Caldecott cleared his throat and looked around at us with a satisfied air. "This is my land now—well, the land of Cassandra. You are all standing on the grounds that were once owned by Ima Nelson and now belong to Cassandra. After tomorrow, they'll belong to my business partners and me." He smiled again, but there was something sinister about it this time—as if he was daring us to challenge him.

Bill Platt—who hadn't left—cleared his throat as well. "Mr. Caldecott—"

"Oh, are you still here? And it's Mayor Caldecott," the interim mayor correct. His gaze was fixed on Bill with an expression of cold superiority that made it clear he believed himself to be better than the gas station owner. "Or Littlefeather."

Bill's eyes narrowed as he gazed at Caldecott with a haughty expression. "Mr. Caldecott, I was born here and have lived here all my life, so I know what it means when someone claims something as their own without understanding the implications or responsibilities that come with it."

Caldecott laughed at Bill's statement, a deep, hearty chuckle that echoed off the trees. "You have to admit, Mr. Platt, that your stance is quite amusing," he said, a bemused expression on his face. "You think you know so much about this place, and yet here you are being taught lessons by outsiders." He waved his hand in an exaggerated gesture of dismissal. "It's just business, Mr. Platt. As head of the Merchants Guild, you must have some respect for how I've maneuvered, at least."

Caldecott was so open about his maneuvering, so obvious in his machinations, that I again marveled at how obviously villainous he was. "You're pretty comfortable admitting to some shady tactics here, Caldecott."

Caldecott shrugged.

"If you think we are just going to stand here and let you take away our land without a fight, then you are sorely mistaken." Pistachio's eyes were as wide as saucers, and his usually-rosy cheeks were now drained of color. "We have been living on this land for generations and will not be pushed out of it without a fight. This is our home, and we will do whatever it takes to protect it."

Caldecott just stared at Pistachio with imperiousness, then slowly began to laugh. "You naive dimwit. You seem to think that you can stand up to me like I am some bully and prevail because you have some moral entitlement to it, but that isn't how the world works. I'm not a bully. I'm a businessman. This is business." I could feel the tension in the air as everyone stared at Littlefeather. "And it's done."

CHAPTER THIRTEEN

$\mathcal{W}$e watched as Daniel Caldecott strutted up the path toward his car in the gas station's parking lot, completely at ease and oblivious to the concerns of anyone else in the predicament he'd created.

I turned to Pistachio—who was seething.

"How can he be so callous and behave like it's nothing? How could he speak of something so heinous with such ease?" the pixie sputtered. "He spoke with no shame, no hesitation! His audacity was staggering—"

I placed a hand on his shoulder. "Calm down."

"Calm down? When phrases so vile—"

"Yes, yes to all of that," I said, waving my hand in agreement. "But the most puzzling aspect of all this is the timing. Caldecott being so forthcoming about his actions," I explained to Pistachio. "He mentioned the transfer of the property to his organization or company or whatever it is will take place tomorrow. Yet he chose to tell us tonight. Why give us advance notice, as if inviting us to try and prevent it?"

Lothian's head drifted downward in a nod of grim acknowledgment. "That guy radiated an almost supernatural level of confidence that his scheme's going to work out just like he had planned," he said.

"Well, gods know Lothian would know what that looks like," I said.

The werewolf glared at me.

"He did seem pretty sure of himself," Pistachio admitted.

"Who's helping him? Someone has to be." I watched Daniel march up the winding path with an iron resolve, his chest puffed and his chin lifted in pride. "He's confident. He's got no worries about this all falling apart even though it's not done. Even though we told him we'd stop him." I looked around. "Where's that confidence coming from? We could find Lillian Thornton. We could pull a political maneuver to unseat him.

I could blast him with lightning. But he's not worried. What am I missing?"

Bill Platt squinted his eyes at us, a crease on his forehead as he watched us argue our points. The confusion was written all over his face. "What are you all talking about?"

Pistachio stared at Bill, his expression one of disgust. "Like you don't know. You came out here with that pretender." He spun around without waiting for a response, facing me again. "Helping him? You think someone is helping him?"

I nodded. "Someone has to be. Did that guy look like a man concerned about a plan falling apart to you?"

Pistachio thought about this for a second, then slowly shook his head from side to side. "No, he didn't," he said. "But if that's the case, how are we going to find the one person in Cassandra that helped that snake plan and plot this?" He glanced around. "The ghosts are saying nothing."

That would be a first.

"Why are you assuming just one person?" Lothian asked.

"Who could keep this a secret?"

"And why just automatically suspect Cassandrans?" Bill asked, his hands firmly planted on his hips. "I've heard tell you have a bunch of new pixies running around in the marsh. You vet all of them or throw open the doors and let 'em pile in one after another?" He shook his head in disbelief.

"Why would pixies plot to hand their own swamp to treacherous psychic humans or cut-throat resort developers?" Pistachio asked, his voice echoing off the trees like a thunderclap. "That's bonkers! Have you lost your marbles?"

"That, and the chief said Caldecott was selling off buildings in town," I added.

Lothian stepped forward, his expression serious. "Hold on there," he said. "Don't rush too hard into things. We already know what Caldecott's plan is. We gotta figure out who helped him, so we can try to stop it."

Pistachio looked at him. "Thanks for the recap, Captain Obvious."

Bill paced along the edge of the sidewalk, his arms crossed tightly. "I thought you all were looking for Lillian Thornton. At least, that's what Mel told me. Now we're standing here talking about land deals and politics." He stopped pacing and glanced at us with a knowing look. "You think the mayor's disappearance has to do with this land brouhaha?"

"Bill, why did you come out with Daniel Caldecott?" I asked.

"How do you know him?" Lothian added.

"Are you allergic to answering questions?" Bill asked, frustration creeping into his voice. "You seem to dodge every question I ask, yet have no qualms about asking your own. Fine, I'll play along." He gestured up the dark path toward the brightly lit parking lot of the gas station. "That's my property. I own the gas station and a few other structures behind it," he said, his voice trailing off as his gaze became distant. "Hold up. Caldecott approached me a few weeks ago, expressing interest in purchasing it."

"Did you agree to sell to him?" I asked.

"No." Bill Platt appeared lost in thought, as if something troubling had just occurred to him. "I declined, but Featherhead didn't seem bothered by my decision." He looked off toward the parking lot, his face troubled. "He didn't seem bothered in the least."

"It's clear now that Caldecott has bigger plans than just this swamp, Pistachio. What do you think he's up to?" Lothian asked, his voice heavy with suspicion.

"I know what he's up to. He and his people have taken over four spiritual communities already," I told Lothian. "This is the fifth. They come in, buy everything, or buy enough that the other people feel pressured to sell, and then they turn it into a high-end new age spiritual retreat for rich people."

Bill shook his head slowly from side to side. "And whatever he's put into play culminates with the property transfer tomorrow."

"A property transfer he could only sign over as the mayor," Lothian said.

Bill stepped forward cautiously. "Which means he has to have something to do with Lillian's disappearance."

Again, I felt like I was going in circles—with everything obvious and nothing clear.

Pistachio frowned and crossed his arms over his chest as he mulled this over. "Look, it sounds like someone is planning on making a quick buck off Cassandra, doesn't it? That would explain why he wanted your property, the swamp, and the other buildings. But we know all that. We need to find someone who knew what Caldecott was up to before he started making all these moves."

"Why's that?" Bill asked.

"The only way I can see to stop this is to get Mayor Thornton back," the pixie said. "If she's the mayor, there's no transfer of property, and if there's no transfer of property, she can start to unwind Caldecott's plan."

* * *

WE STOOD outside Ima Nelson's house.

"Before we go in, tell me about her," I said.

Bill nodded. "She's been living here since before I was born."

The night was thick and humid, the shadows creating eerie silhouettes as they flickered around us. In the distance, the faint chirps of crickets and other night creatures formed a gentle chorus that accompanied Bill's voice, creating an eerie but calming atmosphere. A few streetlights broke through the darkness to lend a little sense of security while we stood on the sleepy street in the small psychic town of Cassandra.

Bill murmured, his words almost too low to hear. "She was alone after her husband passed, but her son stayed with her until he left for some fancy college up north. Time passed, and she got older and a little more withdrawn, but everyone knows her here. Especially the mayor." He had a good-natured laugh. "You should've seen the fights she had with Lillian!"

Lothian asked what her job was in Cassandra, and Bill told us she worked for the Administration office as a clerk. "Ima was always so organized. I think that's why they kept her on, even though she was getting older and slower. She used to keep track of all the town records, from birth certificates to marriage licenses to property transfers. You could always find her at the office, quietly filing away and making sure everything was in order."

"You said she didn't get along with Lillian Thornton. Why was that?" I asked.

"Cassandra's a town, but it's more than a town, you know?" Bill said. He paused for a moment, his gaze distant. "It's a community. Because of who we are and what we are, the whole town is different. Like a privately run town. Kind of like Disney World."

"Meaning what, exactly?"

"I mean, I own my gas station and the land on it, sure—but if I decide to leave, the town will repurchase it and resell it to another resident in Cassandra. Well, probably. They have that first-refusal option. They always take it."

"Is that legal?" Lothian asked.

"Sure. Have you ever heard of a company town? In the early twentieth century, there were thousands of them. They weren't outlawed. They just went away as this country got wealthier and the standard of living got better. Well, most of them went away." Bill pointed around him. "Not all of them. If it isn't legal, no one's complained about it yet."

I looked at the old house in front of us. It was a single story with white siding and a large porch around the entire building. Thick wooden shutters framed the windows, and I could make out a small garden on one side of the house. A large oak tree stood tall in the front yard, its branches arching over to provide shade during the hot Florida days.

"How old is she?" I asked.

"Oh, I'd guess she's midseventies, maybe eighty," Bill responded.

The quaint old Florida cottage exuded a certain charm and appeared well-kept, despite its age. The paint looked fresh, and not a single shingle was out of place on the roof, despite the powerful hurricane winds that often raged through the area. I wondered if Ima Nelson had undertaken the upkeep herself or with the help of her son. Either way, it was evident that she held great pride in her home and wanted to preserve its beauty for as long as possible.

The hair on the back of my neck prickled up. I had the feeling that Ima Nelson was watching us from inside. The curtains were drawn tight except for one showing a chair in an old-fashioned kitchen next to a wired telephone with a rotary dial.

"Well," Bill said finally, "we probably need to go in and talk to her. She's not getting any younger and might have some information to help with your questions." He started up the walkway toward the porch steps and motioned for us to follow him.

* * *

"He came down here not too long ago looking for me! Sayin' as how he wanted my help! Said he was gonna make a fortune down here and get rid of all the lousy locals while he was at it!" The old woman's voice was soft and weathered like a worn-out quilt. "I didn't know him from a hole in the wall, but he brought two pixies with him in his pocket," she said and poked a bony finger toward Pistachio. "Like him, only tiny."

Pistachio's eyes widened in horror. "He had pixies in his pockets?"

"Two pixies?" I asked.

Ima nodded slowly. "Tiny ones, like I said."

Pistachio shifted nervously on his feet. "The only explanation is that he must have kidnapped them," he said, his voice quivering slightly. "Or maybe he's a powerful wizard or something, and he's controlling their minds."

"They looked like they wanted to be here, and the man—a very kind Indian man named Caldecott—didn't seem like he had them doin' his bidding like little automatons or anything. The little things said he would buy the swamp and turn it into a resort next to the town. They were quite excited about it. Bless their hearts."

I exchanged a glance with Pistachio.

"Ima, when was this?" Bill Platt asked.

"Ah...I want to say Labor Day or Memorial Day. One of those. The one in September?" Ima said, her voice suddenly feeble and quivering. She paused to think, rubbing her bony fingers across the wrinkles of her face. "I told him the mayor wouldn't be too keen on some city slicker coming into town and changing things up, even if I did sell him my swamp, but he didn't listen. He said he had it all figured out."

Two months before Halloween, when the California pixies emerged from the shadows and asked that Pistachio give them asylum. Eight months. Not six. If Pistachio was telling the truth, in any case.

I looked over at him.

The chieftain's furrowed brow, tense shoulders, and quivering lip told me he understood what Ima's information meant—he looked like someone punched him in the gut. It was clear that the possibility of betrayal hurt Pistachio, but he met my sympathetic gaze with a stoic strength I couldn't help but admire.

"Well," Pistachio said finally, "It looks like the California pixies were in on it from the start." He looked around the room, his gaze settling on Bill Platt. "Did you know about this? Did any of you know about this?"

Bill sighed heavily and shook his head. "He didn't come to my house with tiny fairy-like creatures tucked away in his coat."

Ima Nelson lowered her gaze, examining her pants intensely as she plucked at lint and fuzz. A scowl had settled on her face, and her hands worked furiously—as if the task had taken on a significance well beyond its mundane purpose.

"We're not fairies," Pistachio said. "Well then. What do we do now?"

Bill cleared his throat and stepped forward. "I know I'm late to this shindig, but we need to take action before it's too late. This fiend has to be stopped. He wants to turn Cassandra into a playground for the rich, but we'll all be worse off if we don't act. We'll lose our homes, our jobs, and worst of all, the souls that rely on our town for guidance won't get the help they need."

"Well, technically, they'll still be able to get it. It just sounds like most won't be able to afford it," Lothian said. "You live in this town. What do you think our next step is?"

Bill nodded. "We'll need to unite and work together if we are going to have any chance of stopping this man. The top priority is finding Mayor Thornton," he said, "so we can get her to reverse Caldecott's plans for the town."

Ima scoffed, her eyes ablaze with anger. "You're assuming that she will!" The old woman rolled her eyes. "You can't be sure of anything with that woman! She's dating a cop from another town! It's not even a psychic town! Or a psychic cop! She's—"

Lothian cut Ima's rant off before it could escalate further. "I agree with Bill—we must come together to find a way to stop this guy. Maybe someone else knows where they're hiding the mayor, or they have a lead on her that we haven't picked up on yet—"

"Pixies," I interrupted. "We now know pixies are working with Caldecott. That means they could have pixie-dusted Thornton, put her in their pocket, and walked right out of the house with her in the middle of the night." I looked around. "How do we find a possible six-inch kidnapping victim?" I looked at Pistachio. "Sorry."

The chieftain shrugged.

"That's a good question, and I don't know the answer," Lothian said. "But even before that, we need to spread the word of what this man is trying to do—if enough people know about it, maybe we can monkey wrench the works up enough to slow him down."

Pistachio nodded. "It's as good a plan as any. Let's give it a shot—we don't have much time left before tomorrow's transfer. You go out and spread the word around town about what this guy is trying to do," Pistachio told Bill, "and try to gather whatever information on those land transfers you can get your hands on."

Bill nodded. "I'll get Melvin to help."

"Astra, we'll return to the swamp and find a California pixie."

"First, we need to run back to Arden House. I need to talk to the chief."

Pistachio didn't look happy, but he reluctantly nodded.

I looked at Ima, and it suddenly struck me that no one had asked the woman the most important question of all. "Ima; why did you decide to sell the swamp in the first place?" I asked. "And why did you do it by auction instead of selling it back to the town?"

The old woman's shoulders sank, and her voice was barely audible. "The truth is that I have been struggling financially ever since my husband passed away. He left behind a mountain of debt, and I was desperate for money—the swamp was all I had left. Selling it seemed better than nothing at all."

When Ima spoke, something about her tone felt unbelievably artificial. I was sure something was hidden underneath her sweet-old-grandma mask, and the discordant mismatch sent a shiver up my spine.

Lothian, though?

Ima's (possibly) devious attempt at feigning innocence and helplessness worked magic on him. He nodded and said, "It sounds like you were only trying to make the best of a bad situation, yet your decision has led us down a problematic path."

"I didn't mean for this to turn into such a mess," Ima said. Her cheeks flushed a bright scarlet.

I shuddered again. Something about how she spoke sounded hollow.

And false.

"It is my fault," Pistachio told the old woman. "Pixies can be extremely persuasive, and obviously, you assumed that we approved of the sale. How could you not? Caldecott brought members of my clan with him. Or at least what seemed like my clan."

Ima let out a heavy sigh and slowly shook her head. "We're completely out of solutions," she said bleakly. "We can try to talk to him and reason with him, but I don't think it will do any good. He's determined to take Cassandra from us, and I don't think our pleas will move him. At this point, we need something more, something that will make him realize the foolishness of his actions, something that will break the bond between him and Cassandra. But what could persuade a man like that?"

What bond?

Daniel Caldecott didn't have a bond with the swamp.

Caldecott was a rich dude, and he wanted to be a more prosperous rich dude.

It wasn't that complicated.

"We need to find Lillian," I said. "That stops this. She's the priority, and before everyone gets distracted again, I'd like to point out she could be in serious trouble."

Ima Nelson quickly nodded and added, "Oh, dearest. Undoubtedly so!"

Bill nodded firmly. "I agree with Astra. Finding Lillian is the only way to stop Caldecott's plans for sure. You three need to focus all of your efforts on that."

We left Ima's house silently, as if we all feared that Caldecott might overhear our plot.

As we walked out of the gate and onto the street, I looked over my shoulder and saw Ima Nelson talking frantically on the phone through her window. Our eyes met, and she frowned, dropping the curtain closed after a few moments, hiding her conversation from my sight.

A feeling of dread descended upon me with that curtain drop, like a fog that I could not shake. This all seemed so simple, yet my instincts told me things were not as they appeared.

CHAPTER FOURTEEN

*P*istachio, Lothian, and I walked down the sidewalk toward my Jeep, lost in conversation, when Archie suddenly plummeted from the trees overhead. He circled us, hooting in distress, before finally coming to a halt just ahead of us.

"What's wrong?" I asked, concerned.

"I saw something strange," Archie said, slowly letting his wings fold back. "Like, super weird. This whole town is made up of boring homebodies that couldn't find Rex's dance club with an iPad and a pin dropped right on the whiskey side of the bar, right? Yet a handful are slinking around people's backyards toward one person's house. Two blocks away."

"How many are a handful?" Pistachio asked.

"And who's house?" Lothian asked.

He scurried closer, an expression of disbelief upon his face. "What do I look like, the town mapmaker? A surveillance expert? The phone book? How should I know whose house it is and how many people went there?"

We exchanged apprehensive glances, our eyes darting around for any sign of danger. The moon was reaching its apex, the gentle light reflecting off the mica in the asphalt streets like jewels from a tiara. The night air was filled with chirping from the crickets and the frogs, their song lending a sense of calm.

"Well, I think we should go check it out," Lothian said.

I turned to him. "Thanks for sharing, but no one asked you."

"Do you always just decide without considering all the possibilities?"

"We all heard your suggestion, but we need to get back to Arden House so I can talk to the chief and read the jail that was sent to me," I said firmly. "We can look into this later. Archie can watch the place from the trees."

The owl looked annoyed. "Did I say there were trees?"

I looked down. "Are there trees you can perch in to watch?"

"Well." A pause. "Yes."

"There we go." I looked at Lothian and pointed to Archie. "Problem solved."

"I don't know. It's not that I don't trust you, Archie," Lothian said, shifting uneasily on his feet. He glanced at Pistachio, who was standing and watching us with his head tilted. "I feel like a group gathering isn't a good thing now. There's so much going on, and if there's another conspiracy brewing, I'd like to know what it is before we walk into it." Lothian leaned forward. "It's just one house two blocks away. What could be the harm?"

"It's not about harm. Bill's dealing with Cassandra. I can text him, and he can check it out. We agreed that our top priority was getting back to Arden House."

"No, you said that's what we needed to do. Again, the house is only two blocks away," he argued, stepping closer to me. I could feel his breath against my cheek as he spoke.

"Back up, dog."

"Tone down your attitude, witch."

Pistachio stepped between us then, his expression unreadable as he regarded us both.

"We can't start fighting among ourselves." After a tense silence, he added, "Perhaps we could investigate very quickly? Just drive by on the way out. That could satisfy Lothian's curiosity before we return to your home."

"No," I replied, stepping back. "We have a plan. We need to stick to it."

Lothian stepped up to me again, throwing his hands up in frustration. "Come on, Astra. You're being ridiculous. We should at least look before returning for your place."

"I'm being ridiculous? None of this has anything to do with you!"

Pistachio stepped between us with more force as he pushed Lothian back a few steps. "Stop it," he said sternly. "Astra is the leader here, and if she has a plan? Well, that's what we are doing. No more arguing about it."

"She is? She's the leader?" Lothian stubbornly crossed his arms and glared at the both of us, unwilling to give in. "When did that happen?"

The pixie rolled his eyes at Lothian, his expression looking weary. "When we all found out the witches in Forkbridge were demigods, werewolf," Pistachio sighed. "That tends to put a damper on any notions of challenging them. Don't you think?"

Ouch.

Archie jumped on my shoulder and flapped his wings in agreement. "Finally, someone gets it. It wasn't enough that I was sent from Athena. It wasn't enough that Astra carried around an ancient goddess's power and could sizzle anyone like a steak on a barbecue. No, you numbskulls only cared when the baby daddies showed up."

"Ugh. Jeez, Archie, don't call them that." I shuddered.

Lothian looked at me, then Pistachio, then back at me. He sighed and nodded, conceding defeat. "Okay, okay," he said, waving his hands in surrender. "You're right. The last thing we want to do is attract the attention of Astra's father. We'll go straight back to Arden House."

A bitter taste of disappointment filled my mouth.

The people around me suddenly disregarded my autonomy and capabilities because I happened to be the offspring of a god. I felt betrayed by Lothian and Pistachio's false respect.

I refused to accept this treatment, determined to make clear that my opinion mattered and that I deserved respect, not because of my father but because I was a strong, accomplished witch with years of experience.

"Look—" I started, seething with anger.

"No, wait." Lothian swallowed hard.

"No, I want to say something—" I started again.

"Please, let me finish." Lothian turned to me, his expression softening as he realized he had been out of line (for all the wrong reasons.) "I'm sorry," he said. "You're right; we should go back to Arden House. Bill can take care of dealing with this mess in Cassandra. He knows the people here better than we do."

Just as I was about to unload on him and Pistachio, we stopped in our tracks.

As we rounded the final corner, we spotted a gathering of people in front of my Jeep, their faces stern with rage. There were at least a dozen of them, probably more, carrying a motley assortment of weapons—pickaxes, pitchforks, and even a few shotguns. A select few had makeshift weapons, like sticks and stones—clearly not wanting to be left out of the fun due to a lack of sophisticated weaponry.

"Oh, look," Lothian said. "The mess in Cassandra has come to us. Well, that solves everything."

My heart skipped a beat as my adrenaline kicked in, and I felt my star powers tingle on my fingertips. I glanced over at Pistachio, who watched the mob with a wary eye.

Lothian stepped forward, his werewolf senses on high alert.

"What do they want from my truck?" I asked quietly. The street was a chaotic mass of movement, bodies pressing in from all sides. The wall of angry faces and raised weapons stood in a broad semicircle, almost blocking the Jeep from our view.

Pistachio raised an eyebrow. "Do we go talk to them?"

"I don't know," Lothian said. "But I don't like the looks of this. Do you see that?" he said, pointing down the street. "This is escalating. I know what a pack on the hunt looks like."

I followed his gaze, and my stomach dropped.

About a block away, the street was filled with another mob coming to join the first group, all carrying torches and yelling. There was a collective intensity in the air that could only get worse once the two groups converged.

"Come on," I said, yanking Lothian and Pistachio into a run as Archie launched himself into the sky. We ran ahead and ducked into an alleyway, taking shelter behind an ice cream shop's dumpster. "At least we're out of sight here."

I could make out a few faces in the crowd, some of whom I'd seen around Cassandra. People I would never have guessed were into part-time early evening membership in a weapon-wielding barbarian horde.

"What do we do?" Pistachio whispered.

"We have to get out of here," Lothian said. "If they see us, we're going to have to defend ourselves, and if the three of us defend ourselves?" He frowned. "People are going to get hurt. Badly."

"What do you want us to do, Astra?" Pistachio asked.

Lothian narrowed his eyes at the pixie. "What's the matter with you? Don't you have ears? Not able to comprehend what I'm saying? Auditory processing problems?"

"What was that, wolf?" Pistachio asked with an edge to his voice, barely hiding his irritation. "Did you say something?"

I looked at Lothian and Pistachio and then back at the mob.

The pulse of power in my veins was strong, and I knew I could use it to protect us. But I also knew that if I did, Lothian was right—someone would get hurt. Probably a lot of someones.

Instead, I reached for my phone, quickly dialing the number for Bill Platt.

"Bill?" I said when he picked up. "We have a problem."

* * *

MAYOR CALDECOTT'S voice boomed through the throng, his expression livid as he jabbed a finger toward my Jeep. "This evil witch murdered Lillian Thornton!"

"Does he think Astra can shape-shift into a Jeep?" Lothian whispered.

"Maybe. The guy doesn't strike me as very intelligent," Pistachio whispered back.

The crowd of angry citizens had become a veritable mob. Mayor Caldecott punctuated his speech with exaggerated gestures, his outstretched arm singling out my Jeep as some odd symbol of all the town's woes.

"She murdered Lillian Thornton!" he roared. "It was her, no doubt! We have feared this wicked witch ever since she slunk into town. She used her dark sorcery to bewitch and destroy Jason Bishop and then took his beloved mother's life! We must all stand together now to prevent her from taking more innocent lives!"

The mob erupted into a mad frenzy, and my stomach churned.

This was not going to end well.

Daniel "Littlefeather" Caldecott raged, his fist pumping skyward, a menacing finger pointing directly at my Jeep. "This chariot of evil is hers!" he shouted. "And it's here in our town tonight of all nights! We must raze it to the ground and incinerate it until there's nothing left of its wickedness!"

"Oh, hell, no," I said, pushing myself up. "No one's laying a finger on my Jeep, especially not some two-bit Indian faker like him."

Before I could take a step, Lothian grabbed me and pulled me down. "We have to keep hiding," he whispered. "The mayor will do whatever it takes to get rid of us. You can't go out there."

"Wow," Pistachio, who had been staring at us with a mischievous glint in his eye, said with a chuckle. "You fight like an old married couple."

Lothian and I both turned to him with looks of disbelief.

"What?" Pistachio asked, feigning innocence. "It was just an observation."

I took a deep, cleansing breath to clear my mind before returning to watch the interim mayor and the mob outside my Jeep. They were growing increasingly agitated, and I knew they would do something drastic if someone didn't intervene soon. "If they so much as scratch my Jeep, I'm walking away from this whole mess. Let their town get made into a resort."

"No, you're not," Lothian said quietly.

I calculated our chances of getting the mob away from my Jeep long enough for me to jump inside and drive away—without hurting anyone.

My chances to get my Jeep?

They were great.

Of not hurting anyone in the process?

Well, those probably weren't good.

We were woefully outnumbered, and the mob's rage was contagious. At any moment, they could choose to lash out in an act of desperation. If it came to it, we'd have no choice but to fight back, and if that happened, no doubt one or more of those Cassandra psychics would be left motionless, sprawled out on the asphalt.

I knew we couldn't just hide here and hope for the best.

At some point, we'd have to take action to save my Jeep and protect the throng from its crazed chief's directives.

But how?

I was at a complete loss.

"It's all right, everyone." The mob was instantly silenced by Bill Platt's deep baritone. All eyes were on the filling station owner and the two hulking mechanics from the shop who accompanied him as he confidently strode into view.

"Mayor Caldecott is oblivious to the accepted conventions of Cassandra, I see." Bill's eyes narrowed as he turned to face an old woman brandishing a tire iron. "Bertha Brady! What has gotten into you?"

"But she killed the mayor!" Bertha responded.

The mob of townspeople looked confused and unsure who to follow.

"Did she?" Bill asked. "Are we sure about that?"

"Yes!" Mayor Caldecott bellowed with righteous indignation. "It is time we bring an end to this heinous evil! We must eradicate this abomination before that wicked witch can cause any more suffering!"

I blinked.

That was a pretty weird statement.

"That's enough!" Bill Platt stormed forward. "We don't stand for this behavior here in Cassandra. We value peace over chaos and resolution over destruction. Surely, if we all pause and think clearly, we can find a more suitable answer than setting someone's car ablaze."

Yes, let's not set my vehicle ablaze, please.

"Why is it so important to him that the mob torch my Jeep?" I whispered.

Pistachio raised an eyebrow. "Because it's fun?"

The crowd swirled with low murmurs, their faces filled with indecision. Mayor Caldecott's scowling features deepened as he reluctantly stepped back, granting Bill Platt the platform to speak.

"Bill's got more of a bond with these people than Caldecott does," Lothian whispered. "I don't think this went the way Caldecott hoped."

"No. He hoped they'd torch my Jeep," I whispered back.

"Let's talk this out," Bill said authoritatively. "We can all agree that this isn't a desirable situation, but it doesn't require us to act hastily or irrationally." He paused for effect before continuing. "We can find another way—a better way—to handle this situation. For example, if none of you have anything to do, why aren't you out looking for Mayor Thornton? Is this the best way to spend your time?"

"She's dead!" a voice from the crowd screeched. "The ghosts can't find her!"

"It must be magic!" another shouted.

"We have no evidence whatsoever that she's dead or that magic or witches have anything to do with what's happened to her," Bill insisted. His expression was incredulous as he looked out over the townspeople. "None. Please think of how often we've been blamed for things people don't understand. You want to do the same to the witches?"

A silence descended upon the crowd as they lowered their weapons.

"Go search for Lillian. Or go home," Bill added. "But stop this. We're better than this."

* * *

THE ANGRY PROTESTERS QUICKLY DISPERSED, leaving Bill and Mayor Caldecott facing off in the deserted street. Pistachio, Lothian, and I remained concealed behind a nearby dumpster, observing the men and eavesdropping on their conversation.

"I'm not talking to you with them standing behind you like hired assassins." Caldecott pointed toward the two mechanics.

Bill nodded, and they turned and left.

"Thank you. Now, what do you know?"

Bill replied casually, "I know enough."

Mayor Caldecott scowled, arms rigidly crossed. "Enough to what? I thought we agreed—you wouldn't obstruct me if I refrained from rash decisions. You appear to be implying something else now."

"Your memory has holes bigger than a sinkhole," Bill said with a steady glare. "I heard nothing of burning Jeeps, Cassandra mobs, or mayors taken when you gave me your city improvement speech. You told me the pixies approved of the sale of the swamp—it's obvious that's a lie. Honestly, what have you done to help anyone but yourself?"

Mayor Caldecott seethed as Bill spoke but said nothing to refute any of his assertions. "You'll be exorbitantly wealthy when this town is wiped off the map and reborn into the premier vacation destination in Florida. So just shut up and collect your money. It's done. It's over already."

Lothian and I looked at each other.

"Yeah, no idea where he got that delusion of grandeur," the werewolf whispered. "I think you could fit this town in one of the Disney parks ten times over."

"Nothing is done." Bill stared at Mayor Caldecott with open disapproval. "Nothing ever ends in Cassandra. Don't you know that?" he asked. "Not even lives. Not even death makes things go away."

"Oh, shut up with your spiritual gobbledygook. This is your fault."

Bill raised an eyebrow. "My fault?"

Caldecott seethed with anger, his eyes blazing with fury as he scowled in the direction where the mob had been just moments before. "You! All of you!" The veins in his neck stood out in stark relief. "Your ridiculous guru and his spiritual mumbo jumbo. You can't focus on what's happening because the afterlife consumes you. Do you see? Do you see how quickly I worked this town into a hysterical state? And yet still, you cling to your delusions of creepy messages and prophecy."

"What is he talking about?" Lothian asked, confused.

"I'm sure it doesn't make sense to you, Mr. Caldecott. If you had lived here longer than six months, you'd know that already. But, this town, Cassandra, has a connection to the afterlife. We see ghosts and visions and omens. It's why we think intangible things can still be real. That understanding and belief are what make Cassandra distinctive. What makes its people unique. What makes it home."

"Home? Home?" Caldecott turned away and laughed an evil, mocking laugh. "How little you know people here, William. How little you understand this place." He shook his head and started to walk away before stopping and looking back, his expression hardening. "Now stay out of my way—I've got a town to take over."

As the interim mayor moved away, his bony knuckles knocking ominously against my Jeep like a funeral march, I asked myself again what was happening in this strange town.

What did Caldecott mean when he said that?

Was there something else going on that we couldn't see?

Was there another side we weren't seeing?

I wasn't sure what to make of it, but whatever it was, it appeared to be a problem for everyone in Cassandra if the mayor got his way.

CHAPTER FIFTEEN

*P*istachio, Lothian, and I scrambled out from behind the ice cream shop dumpster, and I cautiously breathed in the crisp air to rid my nostrils of the confusing, cloying scent. It had an intense bouquet of sweet, sugary ice cream and waffle cone mix, but it was strangely laced with the pungency of decaying waste. It was almost unbearably powerful in its potency yet strangely entrancing simultaneously.

It was like Daniel Caldecott: alluring and repulsive at the same time.

"Thank goodness you got here in time," I told Bill, nervously glancing around as we stood in the middle of the road. I could make out a large group of people far down the street gossiping to one another in hushed tones. "He's up to something," I muttered, furrowing my brows as I took a few cautious steps forward. "Like, more than what we think. Something else is going on."

"No kidding, Captain Obvious. Anyway, thanks for calling me." Bill looked around at the center of town. "If he believes he can take over this town, he is mistaken. And I'm not going to let him get away with it. When I first met him, he seemed perfectly normal. For Cassandra, at least." He looked back toward my Jeep. "If I thought he could turn into whatever this was on display tonight, I'd never have given him the time of day."

I could sense the tension in the air, a palpable mistrust in the atmosphere that left me uneasy. "I can only hope no one saw this coming."

Bill raised his eyebrow.

"You're saying Caldecott's different than he's been?" Lothian asked him.

Bill nodded.

"What was he like before?"

"When Caldecott showed up in Cassandra a few months ago, everyone liked him," Bill began. "He was friendly and outgoing. The guy had an upbeat attitude and was always willing to help in any way he could. He was always available to lend a hand with anything from carrying groceries to unclogging drains. Everyone had nothing but good things to say about him."

Lothian nodded in agreement. "If that's the case, I can see why the town trusted him. It's almost like he flipped a switch or something when he was elected mayor."

I threw a sidelong glance at Pistachio. He stood there, stiff and uneasy, hands fidgeting with his coat lapels. "Did you know Caldecott before he became mayor? Did you get any sense that this might be coming?"

The pixie took a step back. "Of course not. No, I never expected any of this. As Bill said, he seemed like a nice guy. Even helped Ima Nelson with a ride to a few of the meetings when we were negotiating to buy the swamp—"

My neck whipped around so abruptly that it felt like my head might come off. "Wait, what?"

The pixie looked confused. "Wait, what?"

I raised my eyebrow.

Pistachio blinked a few times. "I mean what to your what. I'm not mocking you."

"Ima and Caldecott knew each other before she ever sold you the land?"

Pistachio rubbed his chin in thought, his gaze meeting mine. "Yes, he knew Ima prior to her selling the swamp," he said. His brow furrowed slightly. "Interesting, now that I consider it, that does seem a bit strange, doesn't it?"

Oh, dear gods.

"More than just odd," I corrected. "If he knew Ima and wanted the swamp, why not purchase it from her then?" I asked, directing my gaze toward Bill. "He has the funds, correct? He's a wealthy developer from California. If that's the case, why sit back and observe all the negotiations, the switch to an auction sale, only to become mayor six months later and reclaim the land?"

Bill and Lothian both looked confused, but Pistachio pondered this with a slow tilt of his head. "Maybe he just wanted to ensure he got the best deal possible."

"Maybe." I crossed my arms tightly, my eyes narrowing in suspicion. "Or maybe there's more going on here than we're cluing in on."

Pistachio's eyes widened. "Do you think he was behind the auction? Did he rig it so we would win?" He scratched his brightly colored head. "But that doesn't make any sense, does it?"

"Not if he just wanted the land. But clearly, that's not all he wants. He wants something else."

"The whole town, I thought." Bill's shoulders rose and fell in an indifferent shrug. "Again, I thought that was pretty obvious. Or maybe he just wanted to be mayor?"

"No, I don't think so." I glanced back at the group of people farther down the street, their muffled voices still floating through the night air. "He's out to destroy this town, and he's gone to a lot of trouble—and taken a lot of time—to take it down all at once."

Six months of meticulous plotting. Of spying, sucking up to the town, lurking in the shadows, and biding his time to ensure everything would unravel as he planned. Ima could have quickly sold the land to Caldecott if he had just asked. But this wasn't about the land—or not just about the land.

But what?

I turned back to face Pistachio and Bill, my gaze darting between them. "What else do you know about Caldecott?"

Bill shrugged. "He always kept his personal life pretty private. I know he moved here six months ago and started buying up small businesses and empty buildings. He did talk pretty openly about building a fancy resort here but never mentioned a specific location or what it would look like. No one seemed bothered by it."

My forehead creased as my eyes narrowed. "Surely he must have mentioned something more than that? Why would someone move to this small town out of the blue with no explanation? And why would none of you question that? You're a town of psychics, for goodness' sake."

"We're a town of mediums," he said.

"Fine. Mediums." I threw my hands up in the air. "The ghosts never said, 'hey, this guy might be bad news?' or advised you to look at him more closely?"

Bill ran his hands desperately through his hair like he was grasping for the answers. "How the hell would I know?" he shouted at me, his voice echoing off the surrounding buildings. "I'm not the guru! I'm not a medium, and I don't talk to ghosts! So please explain to me how you expected me to figure that out. I only care about my gas station, not the rumors that float around from beyond the grave."

Lothian gestured dismissively with one hand. "You obviously cared about what he was doing, or he wouldn't have thought you were in his corner. Astra's right. It is odd that he would move in without explanation or back story and that none of you would ask about it."

Bill's shoulders tensed in annoyance as he

spoke. "Maybe a little. You two forget that he has plenty of money and clout to do whatever he pleases. Regular people don't question rich people to their faces." He slowly turned to me. "This is getting us nowhere. So what do we do? Do we approach Caldecott with our suspicions? Tail him around town? What's the plan?"

I sighed before answering, knowing whatever action we took had to be calculated and precise if we were going to get the answers we needed without raising too much suspicion or tipping off Caldecott that we were onto him. "I have to get back to Arden House. My sisters have been looking into the paperwork. The chief is there, and the little house is there." I turned to Bill. "I'm going to leave my Jeep here against my better judgment."

"Why?"

"Because he wanted it torched a little too much. Since that didn't work, my guess is he'll send someone to set it on fire or destroy it once the street looks empty—I want to know who he sends. Grab them, and we'll be back to get some information from them." I started to walk away, stopped, exhaled a breath of resignation, and looked Bill in the eye. "Please don't let this guy torch my Jeep. I love my Jeep."

* * *

THE ROAR of Lothian's motorcycle was deafening as we tore down the open road toward Arden House, and I thanked my lucky stars Lothian was thoughtful enough to provide me a helmet that dulled some of the tremendous roaring sounds.

After a sprinkle of shimmering dust, Pistachio was safe inside a pouch attached to the loop of my jeans.

I hoped his tiny eardrums didn't explode.

"Slow down!" I yelled over the thunderous peal of Lothian's brutally loud exhaust.

"Stop yelling. I can hear you just fine. There's a microphone in the helmet," Lothian laughed. "I thought that was the point of this ride, Astra? To go fast? To get there soon?" He eased up on the accelerator, but it still felt like we were flying over the pavement. "Come on, live a little! You can't tell me you don't enjoy this at all." He cast a mischievous glance back at me, his crooked smirk daring me to say otherwise.

In spite of myself and my arms being wrapped around Lothian, I did enjoy it. The biting wind whipped against my skin, sending shivers throughout my body and stirring a sense of life within me that hadn't been present since the death of my mother and Jason.

So, sure. I enjoyed it.

A little.

But that didn't mean I wanted to get killed in the process.

"Hold tight," Lothian said, the microphone humming over the sound of the wind. "We've almost reached Arden House."

The motorcycle roared fiercely through the streets of Forkbridge at a relentless pace. Lothian expertly navigated us around sharp bends and cut through the busy roads with reckless abandon, as if he were performing a stunt from an action film. My knuckles were white, my grip on him tight as my heart raced.

"I hate you," I muttered.

"No, you don't. You don't like when someone else is in control."

"Does that mean you'll let me drive?"

"Nope!" He punched the accelerator.

"You're such a jerk."

Lothian chuckled as his motorcycle rapidly maneuvered around the corner. The town blurred past—the red awnings of shops, orange lampposts, and tall pines—like an abstract painting. And then, as we whipped around the corner, an inky park appeared with an empty playground in shadows; Lothian grinned and shouted as he opened the throttle, and we raced toward the city park. "You okay?"

"Are we there yet?" I responded.

Lothian said nothing, absorbed in the thrill of roaring through the winding roads. His eyes would flash mischievously back at me as his lips curled into a smug smile, only adding to the air of mystery that seemed to surround him as he deftly maneuvered the bike around sharp turns and sudden curves.

"Watch the road!" I shouted.

Lothian didn't answer.

The town flashed by in a blur of colors and shapes, with houses and buildings blending into one long stretch of color. We flew up the driveway to the colonial after hurtling out of the street near the city park. I smelled Arden House before I could see it, decorated as it was with a kaleidoscope of roses twirling around the trellis casting an aromatic barrier around the house.

Lothian deftly brought the motorcycle to a halt in front of the house, and I stumbled off, my legs still shaking from the adrenaline coursing through my veins. I hadn't been on a motorcycle in years, especially one that moved at such speeds.

He shut off the roar of the engine and jumped off the machine. With a twinkle in his eye, he said, "I told you we'd be just fine!"

I locked eyes with him. He had a smug, devilish smirk on his face that made him appear even more handsome, yet his smirks only served to infuriate me further. I was not too fond of his arrogant attitude—as if he was so sure his coy behavior and disarming smile would make any woman forgive him anything.

That calculating crap didn't work on me.

"You are utterly infuriating," I told him.

Lothian let out a hearty laugh and leaned against his bike. He bowed low, his eyes twinkling. "My pleasure, milady."

"What's your pleasure? To be infuriating?"

"Well, I have been ordered to protect you, and it's my honor. Just tell me what you need me to be, and I'll do my best to make it happen." He ran his fingers through his hair, a beaming grin creeping onto his lips. "To be a guiding light, a rock in the storm, a beacon of hope. Whatever you want me to be. Whatever you need." A burst of soft laughter accompanied his words, and the werewolf's gaze shimmered with amusement.

My stomach roiled with nausea.

"Oh, dear gods, please stop." I sighed deeply and glared at him as he straightened up and moved toward me. "I mean it. Stay back. Stop. Dial it down."

Lothian halted in his tracks. "As you command, milady."

My fists clenched as I gritted my teeth. "I really want to punch you in the face."

"That could be fun," he said as he stepped back.

I could feel the heat rising in my cheeks as Lothian's gaze lingered a beat too long.

Lothian Pennington had an infuriating way of being insufferably flirtatious—a thing I could usually ignore but would occasionally make me blush like an idiot schoolgirl. I both resented and reluctantly (privately, secretly) sometimes enjoyed it in equal measure.

I would never let him know that.

Well, that I enjoyed it.

The resentment and annoyance I was happy to heap on him by the shovelful.

"Come on," I hissed, gripping the door frame. "Let's get in there and get this over with. The sooner you can return to your pack and leave me alone, the better."

I took a few determined steps toward the house, but Lothian was at my side before I could go any farther, his lopsided grin stretched across his face. He leaned in close and whispered, "After you, milady."

I yanked away. "I honestly couldn't despise you more."

"Oh, Astra. You don't mean that." He reached out and tucked an errant lock of hair behind my ear. "Not deep down, anyway. You only wish you hated me." His smirk only widened. "And I promise, that's not the same thing."

* * *

WE OPENED THE DOOR, and it was chaos.

Serena Bliss was standing tall and resolute, her fists clenched as she stared into the blazing eyes of the towering Chief Harmon. They were roaring back and forth like a raging storm, each trying to out-shout the other.

"It had nothing to do with me! I have no idea who this guy is!" Chief Harmon bellowed. "How dare you accuse me of participating in the kidnapping of my girlfriend! I don't care what hippie dippy magic you think you got, you're wrong, and you're an idiot!"

Serena's eyes narrowed as she scowled at him, her lips pursed together tightly. "You're a police officer, and your woman disappeared from your bed. Do you think we should find that believable?" Her voice was dripping with sarcasm, her blond brows raised in disbelief.

My sisters were nowhere to be found.

Then again, if I had to deal with these two for more than five minutes, I'd probably run to the restroom for a long while, too.

Lothian forcefully cleared his throat. "Ah, excuse me? We just got back from Cassandra and... well, can someone tell us what is happening here?"

Chief Harmon whirled around, a look of disgust on his face when he spotted Lothian and me. "Oh, great, now we've got werewolves traipsing around. Wonderful! I see you've returned without Lillian!" He spat the last word and crossed his arms, scowling at us.

"Because you disposed of her body expertly!" Serena spat, her face contorted with fury. Harmon stepped toward us, but Serena raised her arm like a barrier, pushing him back. "Don't you dare walk away from me, you deceitful pig!"

Chief Harmon froze, his eyes widening as he stared down at Serena. His fists clenched at his sides as he struggled to contain his anger, his cheeks flushed as Lothian opened his mouth to speak again.

"What is going on here?" Lothian demanded, his voice like a crack of thunder in the room. Everyone in the room stiffened, eyes widening at his voice's underlying hint of authority.

Or perhaps it was because those werewolf men possessed chiseled, godlike physiques, as if born from a union between Jason Momoa and Dwayne Johnson. Even I couldn't deny that their imposing figures made them appear nearly indestructible.

Yeah, it had to be that.

Serena audibly exhaled, her lips twisted into a knot as she spoke angrily. "Astra's sisters invited me over here to discuss the disappearance of Lillian Thornton, and when I stepped into this house, I found the killer before me, spewing poisonous words to them!"

Chief Harmon's eyes flashed with fire as he turned toward me. "Remember how you thought this woman was nuts during that arson thing?" Harmon asked me. "You were right. She's nuts. And it's probably her fault that Lillian's missing—"

Serena's face contorted in a fury, her eyes

narrowing to slits as she launched into her tirade against Chief Harmon. "You are so blind and ignorant to the supernatural world!" she spat, her hands curling into fists. "And now, you've taken away our only chance to find out what happened to Lillian!"

"What do you mean?" I asked Serena.

She stared at Harmon.

I looked at Harmon. "What does she mean?"

Harmon merely shrugged his shoulders and crossed his arms, his expression growing defiant. "She'll say anything to keep people from realizing she'll move up in power if Lillian's dead." A sneer curled up one corner of his mouth as he looked at Serena. "Won't you?"

Lothian, watching the showdown between the two silently until this point, finally stepped forward. "Enough. Where are Astra's sisters?"

Serena pointed to the room across the way, her face still tense. "Her siblings are in there stirring up some concoctions. I believe they found all the squabbling and bickering too much and decided to remove themselves from the dispute."

"Shocking," Pistachio's tiny voice squeaked from my hip with a chuckle.

The two immediately began bickering again.

"No wonder they decided to move to another room," I sighed, rubbing my temples.

"Are you all right?" he asked, concerned.

I nodded. "Fine"

"Okay." Lothian walked toward the door, but I stopped him with a hand on his arm. "Wait. I should—" I glanced back at Harmon and Serena before glancing at the pouch attached to my belt loop. "Or should I?"

Lothian looked down at me, glanced at my pouch, and seemed to catch my drift immediately. "It might be better if those two don't know that you have what's in your pouch," he responded in a voice almost too low to hear. "People might speak freely."

I gave a silent acknowledgment, and we moved toward Althea's potion chamber.

As I walked beside him, an unfamiliar feeling of contentment overtook me. Was it because I knew I could turn to him in times of need, or was it because I was relieved our obligated time together would soon be over?

I didn't know.

I pushed aside my jumbled thoughts and focused on the task at hand: finding out what happened to Jason's mother.

That was my top priority.

CHAPTER SIXTEEN

$\mathcal{M}$y three sisters surrounded the table, the solitary candle at its center casting shifting shadows across their faces. They were silent, seemingly captivated by the flickering light, their eyes fixed in a dreamlike trance. Jason occupied the fourth seat, his mirror enabling him to take the place of the fourth participant.

As I approached, I caught his gaze in the mirror, but he quickly looked away, avoiding my eyes.

Interesting.

I wondered what the heck that was about.

Althea's potion room closely resembled an alchemist's lab from a "Harry Potter" film, with bubbling cauldrons, peculiar glass flasks and beakers, obscure herbs, and tinctures. Crystals and runes were arranged along the shelves, serving either as ingredients or as ornamental decorations. The room was heavily scented with sage, lavender, and rosemary, giving it a mystical, otherworldly atmosphere.

Ami, still staring at the candle, spoke first. "You're finally home."

Ayla sighed. "Serena and Harmon have been driving us up the wall."

Cerberus barked in agreement, his tail wagging rapidly.

"Ayla's being generous. Serena and Harmon have been driving us to the brink of insanity." Althea threw her hands up in the air and then gestured around her potion room. "I reluctantly let everyone come here to hide and hope for the best. I figured they'd either work it out or kill each other."

"It took some convincing, but this is the only room that's soundproofed in the whole house," Ami added. "You know, since Thea blows things up occasionally."

"Not in months," Althea said as she made her way around the table. Her delicate fingers gripped a dropper, precisely adding a few drops of a white liquid into a flask. "Where's Archie?" she asked, not looking up from her task.

"How do you know he's not here? You haven't even looked up."

"Lily informed me," Althea said. The crow's talons curled around her shoulder comfortably as it raised its head and looked at me with sparkling eyes. "We can communicate telepathically."

Jason cleared his throat loudly, the sound echoing in the room like a shockwave from the underworld. "So, what have you discovered?" he asked, the uncertainty of the unknown palpable in the air.

Lothian slightly nodded. "That your hometown is weird."

"Oh?" Jason's eyes flared as his demeanor instantly shifted from confusion to agitated anger. "Good thing I wasn't asking you, then."

Lothian's jaw tensed, his eyes narrowed, and his anger rose to match Jason's agitation. His stony silence spoke volumes, as if he was trying to express his wrath without speaking in front of me.

Though they existed in vastly different worlds, their animosity was palpable, bridging the divide between them.

"There has to be something here that we're

missing," I said, trying to interrupt before tensions between them boiled over. "Let's go back over what we know."

So we did.

My sisters and I agonized over the mystery, frantically tossing ideas and strategies around. Jason listened intently and shared sage advice whenever possible while Lothian and his vexed, brooding presence loomed over us like a storm cloud.

"Did you say that Caldecott and Ima Nelson knew one another before the land went to auction?" Jason asked from the silvery surface of the mirror, his features blurring every so often in the hazy mist.

"I did."

Ayla crossed her arms. "You guys keep acting like that's a big deal. I don't get why that's a big deal."

I glanced at Jason, but when he didn't answer, I did. "Because Caldecott's group is trying to get the swamp land through this political coup when he could have just bought the land from Ima Nelson directly months ago."

"Yeah, I get that, but then Ima wouldn't have the money Alice paid her for the swamp." Ayla scratched Cerberus's head haphazardly. "If

Caldecott confiscates the land tomorrow for some reason, does Alice get her money back from Ima for the sale? Pistachio hasn't said anything about it. And he would know, wouldn't he?"

Jason's figure was slightly distorted, giving an otherworldly feel to his words. "They're taking it for unpaid taxes. I think you'd have to sue to get the money back, but honestly, this whole thing sounds like a legal spaghetti mess."

Althea snorted derisively. "Cassandra's itself is a legal mess. Even the county folks practically run in the opposite direction when they hear its name."

"Here's the other thing bothering me," Jason said, his hands shimmering in a bluish fog. "Where's Irving in all this? You would think Ima's kid would have a vested interest in his mother not selling the property. It would have been his inheritance, after all."

Althea raised an eyebrow.

"Who's Irving?" Ami asked.

"What are you talking about?" I shook my head. "Ima doesn't have any kids."

"I remember playing with a kid called Irving when we were growing up. From what I could tell, he was Ima's son, her only child. Then one day, he just left town, and no one ever heard from him again. Rumors spread about him getting into trouble and being forced to go somewhere far away." Jason looked around. "I swear. The kid came to my eighth birthday party and knocked over the cake."

There was a beat of silence as we digested this new information, the puzzle looming over us like an unanswered question.

"That's it," Lothian said, his voice low.

Ayla looked at him. "What's it?"

"That's where the missing piece of the puzzle is." He looked around the room, his gaze settling on me. "We need to find Irving."

Althea exhaled loudly, her eyes rolling dramatically. "We don't even know if there is an Irving." She then turned to Jason in the mirror, her eyebrow (and her crow's eyebrow) raised in matching looks of disbelief. "You may have school kids mixed up in your addled dead person memories. Nelson is a common name, and it could be a different kid—"

"But it's not," Ami spoke up softly, low but confident. She turned the laptop in front of her around and showed the rest of us the flickering screen. "Look." She pointed. "Irving's the son of Ima Nelson."

"Huh." I squinted. "Does that say he currently lives in California?"

"It does. Why?"

Lothian and I locked eyes, and our faces mirrored the same understanding for the briefest of moments. His eyebrows lifted slightly in acknowledgment, and I responded with a slight nod.

Jason's jaw clenched as his arms folded protectively across his chest, his body flickering with flashes of red light. "Oh, for crying out loud —can you two put your hormones in check for one second? My mother is still in danger!"

His words hit me like a ton of bricks, and my mouth dropped open in shock. "What was that for?" No answer. "What on earth or in Hades is wrong with you?"

Jason huffed, his reflection wavering in the mirror. "Forget it. Just forget it."

Taking a deep breath to keep myself from kicking—and shattering—the stupid mirror, I cleared my throat and spoke in a steady, firm voice. "Can you guys give us some space? I need to speak to Jason privately."

"You want us to go back out there?" Ami asked incredulously.

"With them?" Althea added, her voice layered with many levels of disbelief.

"Yes, that's probably best," Ayla said, rising from her chair swiftly. She reached the door and motioned for the others to follow her out of the room. "Let's go. They need to talk."

My sisters and Lothian shuffled out, leaving only Jason and me in the potion room, our gazes fixed on Ayla's receding figure.

* * *

JASON'S ARMS were still crossed tightly against his chest, his expression one of apprehension. He sighed deeply and frowned like he was trying to make sense of what was unfolding before him. His voice was distrustful and wary when he spoke. "It's clear you have something to tell me. So spill it already."

I paused as I collected my thoughts. "I feel like you might have something on your mind, Jason. Lothian and I weren't flirting. We both simultaneously came to the same idea—that maybe Caldecott is Irving Nelson."

Jason shrugged as he averted his gaze. "Maybe. But what does it matter? That doesn't bring us any closer to finding my mother." His voice was flat, revealing none of the emotion he'd been flinging all over me just moments before.

"You're right, it doesn't bring us any closer to finding your mother, but it does help us understand what's happening. Everything we understand brings us closer to figuring out what's happening." I felt like I was gently explaining logical thinking to an elementary school child.

Jason grunted and diverted his gaze, his arms folded as if fortifying a barricade between us. His eyes brimmed with frustration, and I guessed it was jealousy of Lothian—I could sense a torrent of emotions surging beneath the surface.

This was ridiculous.

I could barely contain my disdain for Lothian on most days.

I mean, sure. Occasionally he was helpful.

Occasionally.

"Fantastic." Jason's voice echoed against the walls in a way that suggested the emotion he'd been trying to contain was now pouring out. "At least you're acknowledging me now. That's better than trailing behind you and Lothian and being completely ignored."

Is that what this was about?

Really?

I dramatically rolled my eyes and threw up my

hands. "What were you expecting me to do? Use that tiny hand mirror like a walkie-talkie? I brought it, and we tried, but it was impossible to hear you! That thing was way too small."

"You barely tried."

"I did!"

Jason shrugged his shoulders and turned away, his voice heavy with disappointment. "Sure. Okay, Astra. It's not a problem. I had nothing useful to contribute about the town I grew up in or the townspeople I've known since I could talk. You and Lothian had it all handled. You were clearly prepared."

"So this is about the werewolf?"

"Of course, that's what you'd focus on." Jason's tone was flat, and his gaze focused on the wall behind me instead of directly on me. His expressionless face and tight-lipped frown made it clear whatever anger he had over me was still front and center in his mind.

He seemed to be hurtling daggers my way with every icy glance, and I didn't know how to bridge the gap between us. He was like a statue, so distant and unapproachable. So unlike the warm and funny Jason Bishop I remembered. If not for the occasional blink, he would have been a corpse—

Okay, that wasn't funny.

I tried once more. "Jason, Lothian was just trying to help."

"Lothian is trying to take my place." He glared at me with jealousy burning in his eyes once again. "So you two are working together now? Is that what this is? Just you and him, solving mysteries like some crime-fighting duo?"

"Jason, what has gotten into you?" I raised an eyebrow at him. "The day you died, you were this roll-with-it guy, all happy to be moving on in your afterlife, all cool about our relationship and your feelings. Now you're more jealous than I've ever seen you, alive or dead. What the heck happened to you?"

Jason seemed taken aback by my question. "You want to dive headlong into this now? With my mother who knows where, the future of Cassandra about to be derailed by some developer, and your father guarding some cursed spring in the swamp—with all that happening, you want to talk about why I'm a little sour about how you've treated me since I died?"

Whoa.

"Jason, I want your help, but I'm not sure you can see through your rage or misguided suspicions to provide it. And that could put your mother at risk."

"Misguided suspicions?" he asked, disbelief and annoyance evident in his voice.

I could sense that he was still hurt from being left out of the conversation earlier, and he had a point - I didn't put much effort into making Althea's spray work in the field. I felt a twinge of guilt for not giving him more opportunities to contribute, but at the same time, I wasn't sure how to handle him. The thought of asking for his help never even crossed my mind.

Upon reflection, this seemed to be a recurring theme in our relationship.

No wonder he was so upset.

Well, that and the fact that his mother had been abducted.

Not everything was about me, you know.

Jason and I locked eyes for what felt like an eternity. I saw a storm of emotions ripple across his face as his expression slowly softened into one of resignation. He turned away briefly, then raised his head again to meet my gaze. Although I could still sense some underlying tension, I was relieved to see that the anger in his eyes had somewhat dissipated. "I just don't want to be forgotten," he said, his voice laced with sadness.

I moved closer to the looking glass. Desperately yearning for the comfort of his embrace, I did the next best thing and spread my fingers palm down on the mirror's cool surface. "I could never forget you. I don't want to forget you."

He smiled in return and reached out to place his palm against mine. "I'm sorry. This being dead thing? It's not easy sometimes. Especially not when dealing with the living."

I was relieved to see him smile, but I couldn't shake off the feeling that we'd dealt with absolutely nothing.

* * *

"So," Ayla said, her eyes widening with amazement as she delicately cradled a miniature owl, no bigger than a thumb, in the palm of her hand. "Althea can make him big again, but we all thought you would want to see him like this first. Because it's freaking adorable."

"Archie?" I exclaimed in surprise.

The tiny owl had a fierce expression on his teeny face as he looked up at me from the center of Ayla's palm. "A foolish pixie threw a handful of dust at me, and now I've shrunk down to this

284 | LEANNE LEEDS

size!" he exclaimed, flapping its tiny wings. "Make me big again! This is embarrassing! Mortifying!"

I was momentarily stunned, unable to respond.

Ayla chuckled, her fingertips brushing against my arm before she handed the owl to me. "He's been ranting and raving since we found him on the back porch, but I think he's just upset in general. Once we return him to his normal size, maybe he'll be able to provide us with better information."

I took Archie carefully in my hands, scanning him for injuries as best I could. His feathers seemed fine, and his eyes were bright. He did not appear hurt or injured, just worn down and meeker than usual. "It's okay, Archie. We'll get you back to normal soon."

He huffed and nestled closer, the fear and rage in his eyes fading slightly.

Ayla grinned. "I told you he was adorable. Maybe we should leave him this way for a while."

"Shut up! Stupid pixies," Archie grumbled from my hands as Ayla pushed Jason's mirror through the potion door into the living room. "They chased me down the road by your Jeep. Then through the woods! Throwing handfuls of pixie dust at me! I thought I was done for!"

I glanced down at Archie, his little owl face frowning up at me in anger. His features were so small, yet I could feel the intensity of his anger radiating from him.

"My pixies would never have chased down an owl," Pistachio protested from the pouch at my waist, his voice rising in disbelief as he eavesdropped on our conversation. "Are you sure they were pixies?"

"Come on." I opened the top of the pouch as Althea rolled her eyes. "Look at him. What else would have done that to him?"

The pixie stuck his head out. "We still don't know who shrunk the chief, do we?" Pistachio pointed toward Harmon and Serena (who were still going at it in the ritual room alcove.) "So whoever sent him here probably shrunk Archie, too."

"Hey!" Archie exclaimed, his talons violently digging into my palm to hammer in his point. "They were pixies. You can dance around the fact that you people are the only ones with sparkly shrinking dust like there's some other explanation, but I'm telling you. Pixies shrunk me." His eyes blazed with fury, and his eentsy-weensy wings were outstretched, quivering angrily.

Pistachio pointed his finger at Archie, his face contorting with pique. "My pixies would never have done something like this!" he snapped. "We are a peaceful tribe, and don't go around shrinking innocent owls!"

Archie snorted. "Well, you'd better check your people because whoever did this to me intentionally did it."

Pistachio clamped his arms across his chest, scowling and silently fuming. He opened his mouth to talk, but Althea cut him off with a sharp gesture before he had a chance to speak.

"Enough bickering," she said, her eyes sharp and jaw clenched tight. She placed the mini-jail in front of me with a thud and slowly surveyed the room like a lion sizing up its prey. "Whoever shrunk the chief and sent him here got us all involved. I want to know who that is. After listening to the two of them bicker for an eternity, I have one heck of a thank you planned for them."

Ayla stepped toward the alcove, rapped on the entryway, and cleared her throat. "My sister's right. Enough. Let's go." The two kept arguing. "Do I have to send the dog in to stop the two of you? He's an American Bulldog." The arguing continued without pause. "Their bite force can easily crush bones and break teeth."

Harmon and Serena stopped mid-argument and stared at Ayla.

"You wouldn't," Serena said.

Ayla shrugged.

"We need to return Archie to his normal size, have Astra read the mini-jail, and some quiet to do both would be nice," Ayla called to them. "You two have had your fun—it's enough. I suggest you both work with us to get to the bottom of this."

Serena and Harmon looked at each other defiantly as if in a silent battle of wills. They stared at each other for a long time until they finally turned away and walked to the living room to join us.

Althea presented a thimble of amber liquid to my tiny owl. "Here, Archie," she said. "Drink it, and you'll be back to normal."

My feathered friend cocked his head and peered at the contents. "Does it taste good?"

Althea chuckled as she pushed the thimble closer to Archie. "It doesn't matter, Archie. So I'm not going to answer that."

"It's awful," the crow squawked.

CHAPTER SEVENTEEN

*A*rchie gulped down the potion and quickly started to grow, his feathers becoming more prominent and thicker and his beak longer and more pronounced. In a few minutes, Archie was his regular size with bright eyes and strong wings.

"Good," Althea said, handing me the mini-jail. "Let's get to work."

I took the small box and closed my eyes, sensing its magical signature. It had the faint aroma of pixie magic, lighthearted energy with an undercurrent of dark humor, and a mischievous twinkle scented like cotton candy. "It's pixie magic," I murmured, my eyes still shut.

"I can sense it. I don't need to look at the scene to know that."

"That's impossible!" Pistachio, the pixie chieftain, jumped out of his pouch on my hip, shimmied down my leg like a salamander, and shouted up at me, waving his tiny fists into the air. "You're wrong!"

"I'm not, though."

The pixie seemed to swell with fury, almost as if his anger had fed him and spurred his growth. He enlarged and magnified until he was of human size. His eyes shone fiercely, blazing like red-hot coals, and he seemed ready to take on the world—starting with me.

Lothian responded instantly, hurling me behind him and out of harm's way with a menacing growl. His muscles were tense and ready to spring at a moment's notice, his face a portrait of unbridled determination.

"Are you insane?" I asked in absolute shock.

"I have my orders," Lothian snapped back.

"Oh, for heaven's sake—" Althea moved closer, her eyes fixed on the pixie as her mouth formed a hard line. "Don't. Just don't. It's not a fight you want to pick. Not in this house and not in this company. Don't be an idiot."

"And let's be honest, it looks like you're the

SCRIES LIKE AN OWL | 291

main culprit here," Ayla proclaimed in a voice full of accusations. "It would be foolish of you to do anything more to incriminate yourself."

Cerberus barked in agreement and then wagged his tail.

"It's not necessarily him," I told them, but no one heard me.

Pistachio was a lot of things. He was overconfident and cunning to the point of being occasionally disingenuous. The guy had a terrible sense of humor and was far from being the most competent leader the pixies had ever chosen.

But I didn't think he was a kidnapper.

I clenched my teeth and closed my eyes, blocking out the cacophony of muffled arguments as I searched again for a magical link to the jail. At first, I could only feel the familiar hum of pixie magic, but soon another power grew in my awareness. It appeared to be reaching out to me and pressing against my mind. A force that seemed intent on concealing something from me, cloaking what I wanted to know in darkness and cutting off my connection—

It was disconnecting me.

I opened my eyes with a shudder.

Pistachio dramatically stepped forward, his voice shaking with fury. "We would never do anything like that! That note on that jail made a godly claim—we're not fools! We would never pretend to be gods or do anything to attract their attention. We are in the midpoint of existence—not cursed by any god, but not especially blessed by any of them." He thrust his arm forward for emphasis. "Besides, we are divided into tribes based on personality and action. My pixies? They would never do something like this."

I blinked. "Run that by me again? Tribes based on personality and action?"

"So what did the witch government know about us? Anything?" he asked sarcastically.

I raised an eyebrow. "You want to discuss a government that no longer exists?"

"And it's clear why it no longer exists," Pistachio said, pausing for a moment before continuing. "Look, pixies are divided into four groups: Protectors, Explorers, Dreamers, and Warriors. The Protectors handle threats from outsiders, the Explorers look for new land to expand our borders, the Dreamers use their creative magic for research and study, and the Warriors want action. Period. All of them do what they do best."

"And what are you? Or your tribe?" Lothian asked.

"We are Protectors." Pistachio punctuated his explanation with a wave of his hands. "I'm saying this kind of thing—snatching some poor sap off the street—isn't our idea of a good time. We stick to our code and wouldn't bring dishonor on ourselves by doing something like that."

I raised an eyebrow and queried, "Okay, so who?"

Seemingly unbothered by the tension in the air, Pistachio announced, "Humans." His voice was a flat monotone, reverberating off the walls.

"Oh, stop. You and I both know what I'm asking." I pushed Lothian to the side with a shove. "Would any of these tribes you mentioned ever take a human mayor captive?" He didn't answer. "Pistachio, if they felt they had cause, would they be willing to do it?"

The chieftain squirmed under my stare, but he reluctantly spoke after a few moments of silence. "The Warriors," he admitted. "They are the most hard-headed, battle-hungry bunch I've ever seen. Their craving for power and action often leads them to cross lines."

"Often, huh?"

He nodded and then shot me a glance, almost as if he knew what I thought before I said it.

"So, what about those California pixies you took in?"

Everyone was silent, their eyes wide as they watched the exchange between Lothian, Pistachio, and me. Some were standing, some were sitting, but all had their eyes trained on Pistachio, waiting for his response. Even Archie stared intently at Pistachio, his body eerily still, waiting.

"What about them?" he asked.

"What kind of a tribe are they?"

The silence that followed was heavy with tension, and all the while, Pistachio's gaze still held mine. "Warriors." His voice was stern and resolute but with a hint of sadness. "They are Warrior clan. But I still don't believe they did this —it doesn't fit their code of honor, either. I can't think of any reason they would do something like this," he finished in an uncertain tone. It was as if he was trying to convince himself more than me.

"What happens if you break your code of honor?"

The chieftain shifted uncomfortably and sighed, his voice stern. "Well, it's not right," he said, his gaze locking with mine. "It would be beyond disgraceful. Pixies shouldn't be doing stuff like that."

I sighed, realizing the answer. "In other words, nothing."

Pistachio stared back at me and then nodded.

Lothian gazed down at me. "This is major. Somebody wasn't just trying to get rid of the mayor. They wanted Pistachio gone, too. That's two powerful leaders taken out of the game."

Ami mulled over the strange situation. "Whoever sent him here must not have known that Astra would free him. Everyone here knows she helped Alice with her business issues that time. But why would they lie and say it was from her father? That doesn't make any sense." She looked at me with a puzzled expression, then continued. "You could just call him and confirm it isn't true."

Ayla snorted. "How many people even know that a god is living in the swamp near here? Even if they knew about our fathers, would they think we can give them a call and have them answer our questions?"

Ami met her gaze and sighed. "I still can't."

Ayla hugged her.

"How many people know about our fathers, anyway?" Althea asked.

"Not many."

"Everyone in Cassandra does," Jason said, his

voice echoing across the abyss. He shimmered in the mirror, a bright blue haze surrounded by the darkness of the underworld. "My mother told everyone. She wasn't pleased about what happened, and she blamed the gods as well as all of you."

"She had every right to be upset, Jason," I said, breaking the silence that had fallen over the room. "You're her son—"

* * *

My brain felt like it was on fire, the pieces of this twisted puzzle connecting with lightning speed. Ima Nelson's son was Daniel Caldecott. Ima, Cassandra's town administrator, had been at loggerheads with Mayor Lillian Thornton, and now, Lillian was gone—

"What does a town administrator do?" I blurted out.

All eyes stared back at me in confusion.

"Like, in general? What do they do?"

Ami tapped on her laptop. "A town administrator is a professional overseeing a town government's day-to-day operations. They work to ensure that the town is running smoothly and efficiently and that its residents are receiving the services they need," she read. "This can involve tasks such as managing the town's budget, overseeing the hiring of town employees, coordinating with other government agencies, and working with the town council to set priorities and make policy decisions. The specific duties of a town administrator may vary depending on the size and needs of the town, but their overall goal is to help the town government run effectively and serve its residents." Ami looked up. "Want me to read more?"

"But that's not what Ima did for Cassandra," Serena Bliss said, speaking up for the first time since she and Chief Harmon stopped screaming at each other. "That's what I do, but that's not what she did."

"Then what did she do?"

"She was more like a town clerk," Jason said from the mirror. "She issued licenses and permits and maintained official records like contracts and ordinances. You know, stuff like that."

My eyebrows rose. "Property transfer records?" I asked.

"Yes," Serena said. "She maintained records of who owns each property in the town, including any changes in ownership over time. She'd collect transfer taxes and facilitate the transfer process."

Serena stood next to Jason's mirror. "Astra, why are you asking these questions?"

"Because who better to help facilitate the takeover of a town than the town clerk?" Lothian asked Serena. "She has access to all the property records; she knows who's late on taxes and who's transferred land recently and how much they paid."

Serena's jaw dropped, and her eyes widened as if she'd just seen a ghost...well, not a ghost.

Because she was used to that.

"Ima Nelson wouldn't do that to Mayor Thornton," she said, her voice barely a whisper. But as reality sunk in, the color drained from her face. "It can't be. We wouldn't do something like that to one another."

"Really? Didn't you guys have arsonists in your town last year?" Althea asked.

"But they were new," she sputtered in disbelief. "They were outsiders who had joined us. Ima was born here. She has lived here and served all her life."

"Seems like all of you are sure no one you know did any of this," Ayla said with a toss of her head. She looked pointedly at Pistachio and then at Serena. "I'm betting both of you are wrong."

"Ayla's right," Lothian said. "Someone would

have had to know the town very well to pull off what Daniel had done in just a few days. This plan didn't come together overnight."

Serena violently shook her head, mascara-streaked tears coursing down her cheeks. "No. She could not have helped him! She wouldn't do something like that! How could you think that Ima—"

Jason reached out to wrap his arm around her shoulders comfortingly and then frowned when he realized he couldn't touch her. "Astra and Lothian think that Daniel Caldecott might be Irving Nelson," he said softly. "If it is, and he's back, you know as well as I do that he would be capable of something like this. You're a walking encyclopedia regarding the town's secrets."

Serena's eyes darted between Jason and Lothian as the displeasure of what they were saying sunk in. She sighed, resigned. "Yes," she said. "I see what you mean. Irving was always so ambitious and always wanted things he didn't earn—it wouldn't surprise me if he had devised a plan like this. And his mother did have a lot of connections in the town. People trusted her."

She gritted her teeth and shut her eyes as if trying to stave off the sorrow. "Ima would never do something this cowardly. No amount of money, no promises, no threats—none of it would be worth more than her honor and her loyalty to the people of this town. Nothing would make her act against us. I have to believe that."

She could believe what she wanted, but I was pretty sure her beliefs would come crashing down around her pretty little blond head shortly.

I'd seen Ima's expression through the window as we left.

My confidence in her town loyalty was not as high.

Lothian gave a quick nod and peered out the window toward Cassandra. "Maybe he forced her," he said, his voice low and doubtful. "Or threatened someone close to her." He shook his head and faced us with newfound determination in his eyes. "We'll uncover the truth about Ima Nelson soon enough. But for now, we have to neutralize Daniel."

"Which comes down to finding Lil," Chief Harmon reminded us.

"Which we are no closer to doing," Althea pointed out.

* * *

I SNAGGED Chief Harmon by his arm and tugged him away from the group.

"Pistachio said he stumbled across you and Lillian in the swamp with a couple of surveyors about six months back."

Harmon narrowed his eyes at me. "So?"

"So it seems that the overheard conversation was the catalyst for this situation," I said, glancing back at Pistachio, who was engaged in conversation with Lothian and Serena. "He claimed to have heard the four of you talking about expanding, discussing the draining of the swamp and how to lay foundations there. Does that sound familiar to you?"

Chief Harmon stilled, his eyebrows furrowing in confusion. "Of course it sounds familiar," he said in a low voice. "I recall it vividly, but I don't understand what you're implying. How could that conversation have set all of this in motion?"

"He thought you were talking about developing a resort. The exact thing that Daniel Caldecott or Irving Nelson or Feather-whatever is trying to do now," I asked, arching an eyebrow. "Is that what you were talking about doing? Was the mayor trying to oust the pixies?"

Harmon's eyes widened, and his voice rose in disbelief. "Of course not! Jeez, Arden, what the hell do you take her for? How could you think that of her?"

"After she held a gun to my head in aisle five? I have more questions about some of her behavior than I used to."

"She didn't hold it to your head, Arden." Chief Harmon's face softened, and he gave a subtle nod. "Fine. We were looking to block off some of the swamp and dam up portions so no one could get there. Stories started swirling about—strange occurrences, people behaving oddly after getting splashed with swamp water. Lil thought better safe than sorry."

Persephone's well, I thought. "What kind of occurrences?"

"It was as if their wires had been cut. They used to care about careers, spouses, kids, pets, you name it, but it just didn't register with them anymore. Weirdest damn thing. Lil traced it back to that area in the swamp."

It was Persephone's well.

It had to be.

He peered out the window. "We had no clue what was going on," he said, "but we were sure it had something to do with pixies and that swamp. We figured it had to be some spell or cursed enchantment, but we didn't want to start any trouble."

"It's a goddess's fountain. My dad bought a place near the swamp, and now he's pumping out as much of the magical water as possible, right into a stone fountain in his backyard. But he didn't show up here six months ago. He came three or four months back, right after the spring was discovered." I glanced toward the living room. "Hey, Pistachio!"

The pixie swiveled his head in my direction, quickly excusing himself from whatever conversation he was having with Lothian. He walked over. "Yes?" he asked, in a voice that said 'What fresh hell is this, Astra?'

I gave him the run down of what Harmon and I had been discussing. "So, my question is this: did you know about the spring?"

Pistachio Waterflash, leader of the pixies, stood rooted to the spot, his knuckles whiter than snow from the death grip on his hands. His gaping mouth and bulging eyes were proof enough that he was utterly shocked.

"I take it from your expression that's a no?"

"I didn't know," he muttered in complete disbelief. "My patrol was supposed to tell me everything, but it…it makes sense now why they never did." The fury in Pistachio Waterflash's eyes was unmistakable. "I swear, I didn't know. But I should have."

"Why's that?" Harmon asked.

"Let me guess," I said. "The California Warrior pixies?"

He angrily jerked his head. "When they arrived, they volunteered to take over the patrol duties in the swamp."

CHAPTER EIGHTEEN

The three of us—Lothian Pennington, Chief Harmon, and I—stepped out of the car and into a ghost town. The night was still and eerily quiet, with not a sound to be heard. No cars, no barking dogs, no television sounds from open windows. It was as if the stars had taken a break from twinkling.

"So far, so good," Lothian said, breaking the silence.

Harmon snorted in response. "Silence isn't good. It's suspicious. It means people are hiding and plotting in secret."

I gazed toward the window and saw a slender figure illuminated through the sheer, gauzy curtains. It was Ima Nelson, peering out with wide, unreadable eyes. It was a surprising moment for a supposed medium, and I wondered why her ghosts hadn't warned of our approach.

The werewolf turned to Harmon. "You're quite a suspicious one, aren't you?"

"My girlfriend might have been abducted by magic and miniaturized by pixies," Harmon replied. "What do you think?"

The two exchanged a look, and we continued our march to Ima Nelson's door. Despite all we had learned, I still wasn't sure what we would find on the other side. I hoped it was Lillian Thornton. I was tired of coming up empty-handed in my travels between Forkbridge and Cassandra.

We knew what Daniel was up to, more or less. We knew about Persephone's well. We had a good idea of what the California pixies were doing. We suspected Ima Nelson was assisting Daniel/Irving with his plan, but after a few tarot card readings, Ami wasn't completely certain.

"I'm getting the Three of Swords for her," she had announced, holding up a tarot card featuring a red heart pierced by three swords in a cloudy sky with rain pouring down. "It symbolizes emotional suffering, betrayal, and being at odds with others. And it's crossing the Empress," she added, showing another card featuring a woman dressed in a glamorous gown and flowing cape. "It speaks to motherhood. If she is helping her son, I'm not sure she's comfortable with it."

I hoped to talk to Ima, piece together the clues, and retrieve my Jeep on the way to finding Lillian Thornton. However, the unknowns were piling up. We still didn't understand Ima's involvement in the secret scheme, and we still hadn't found Lillian Thornton. Our only option was to take precautions and head back to Cassandra.

I raised my hand and pounded on Ima Nelson's door. The sound echoed through the street, seeming to reverberate off the old red brick of her home. "Come out, Mrs. Nelson!" I called. I could hear Lothian breathing just behind me as I listened for a response. "I know you're in there. I saw you through the curtain while we were walking up."

"She's probably hiding in a closet," Harmon guessed.

"It's possible," Lothian replied, pressing his face against the window and inhaling deeply. "I have her scent. She's close."

"And what does an old lady smell like, exactly?" Harmon asked tartly.

"Like mothballs and peppermint tea," Lothian replied.

"Yeah, I wasn't serious," Harmon said.

"Then next time, don't ask," Lothian shot back.

I rolled my eyes and pounded on the door again. "Mrs. Nelson!" I yelled. "We know you're in there! Come out and talk to me!"

The door's hinges squeaked in protest, and Mrs. Nelson's weathered face appeared in the crack. Her body trembled in the faint moonlight that cascaded through the doorway. "What do you want?" she demanded, her voice wavering. "It's late. Have you no mercy for an elderly woman?"

Mercy? The irony was not lost on me.

"While you left us out here banging on your door, I touched your front door and read who's been coming and going," I said, my voice firm as I used my foot to prevent her from closing the door on me. In reality, I hadn't done that. I didn't want to close my eyes in hostile territory. But she didn't know that.

Her expression changed. A mask of scorn and outrage covered her face, and she stepped back. "That's a flagrant disregard for my rights!"

"The front of your house? No, it isn't," I

pointed out. "It's open to the public. I didn't want to break down your door if I was mistaken. As you say, you're an old lady, and I'm not a complete jerk. But you know who I am and what I can do. I could feel the traces of everyone who had come and gone beneath my fingertips." I wiggled my fingers at her. "And do you want to know what I discovered?"

Apparently, she didn't.

"What do you want?" Mrs. Nelson asked, her expression guarded.

I heard a muffled thump from inside, as if someone had stumbled away from the door. "Is that one of your California pixie friends?" I asked. "One of the pixies your son Irving brought back to Cassandra so you two could take over?"

"No," she snapped, her gaze darting around like a frightened rabbit. "I don't have any idea what you're saying. I swear I don't know anything about pixies." Mrs. Nelson's face contorted into a menacing expression. "Leave me alone. You have no idea what you're talking about."

My voice was like a hammer, "Yeah. You've been helping your kid with his shady plan, and you know the whereabouts of Lillian Thornton. You'll spill it, or we'll make sure you spend the rest of your life in jail as an accessory."

"We don't use the justice system in Cassandra," Ima hissed.

"I don't live here," Harmon retorted. "If I don't find Lil in perfect condition—having been treated well and given anything and everything she needed—so help me, Mrs. Nelson, I will spend the rest of my career making anyone who had something to do with any level of her discomfort pay for their crimes. I'll look up laws that most people aren't even aware exist. And if they fire me for being vengeful or abusing my position, I'll spend the rest of my life punishing you people using whatever illegal means are available to me. And if I am killed for that? Or if I die? I will haunt every one of you. Forever." He locked his gaze on her. "Do you want me to repeat any of that?"

The chief's vow of retribution hung heavily in the air.

Lothian's gaze was determined as he extended his arm, hand balled into a fist, toward Chief Harmon. "Respect," the werewolf said in a deep voice

The chief simply nodded and returned the gesture, culminating with a delicate bump of their knuckles.

Oh, for goodness' sake.

The gesture of machismo solidarity between

man and werewolf would have normally called for a rousing round of snarky commentary on my part, but we really didn't have time for me to do it justice.

In our silence, the older woman stared us down, her gaze bouncing between us as if trying to extrapolate our motivations. The tension grew thicker with each passing second as she considered Harmon's words. As I watched her consider his threat, I held my breath, not wanting to be the one to break the silence.

Finally, she pulled the door wide.

"Get yourself inside here this instant and stop making a ruckus. I won't have my neighbors eavesdropping on your nonsensical babble." She glanced outside. "I've been living here for as long as I can remember, and these people know me. They know you were responsible for Jason Bishop's death, so your wild speculation would mean nothing to any of them. All of them would love to see you burn."

"Rude," I muttered, but her statements were contradictory. Either my assertions meant nothing, and no one in Cassandra would ever believe them, or they did mean something, and she didn't want anyone overhearing them.

It couldn't be both.

As soon as I stepped over the threshold, I felt the oppressive energy of the pixies hovering in the air. The sweet aroma of spun sugar filled my nostrils. It felt like peering eyes were concealed in the room's dark corners.

"Do I smell candy?" Lothian asked, his nose wrinkled.

"So, you're here. Let's cut the crap. What do you want to know?" Ima snapped, her words tinged with resignation.

"Where's Lillian Thornton?" I asked once more. "That's all I want to know right now. Where is she? You've known her all your life. Just tell me where she is."

"Somewhere far away from your meddling hands!" a tiny voice cackled.

* * *

THE SHOUT CAME from a tiny figure in the corner of the room, a slim figure no taller than a paint can. His voice echoed confident and sure despite his size, sending shimmering dust of blues and purples to drift around the room. It settled like stars hanging in the air.

"A California pixie, I presume?" I coughed, trying to clear away the pixie dust in the air.

That's when I noticed it was him—the pixie I had bumped into while walking in the park.

"We'll finish this conversation once you morons shrink down to a proper size," he said, his arms spread wide. "That way, I don't need to shout."

Lothian, Harmon, and I looked at each other with amused expressions.

"What was that?"

"What was what?" Harmon asked.

"What was that peculiar expression?" the tiny pixie shrieked, gazing up with alarm as Ima Nelson contracted to the size of a pixie, but we remained our full, human sizes. (Lothian being, more accurately, a giant mountain of muscle).

"Not sure if you know, but my sister's a potion master."

"It didn't taste good, but it does work," Harmon added.

"What works?" the pixie demanded, his eyes flashing with fury.

"What we're talking about is—oh, never mind. The punchline is that we won't shrink," Harmon told the angry pixie.

"Nope," Lothian said, his tone harsh. He leaned down to address the pixie. "I'm sorry for you, that is. And my boots," he added, stomping his foot for emphasis. The pixie's gaze shifted to Lothian's feet, and the tension in its body grew. "I'm worried about my boots. If I step on you, will your innards be a normal color or are they luminous? You know, like your hair?"

The pixie gulped, his eyes darting around the room.

I stepped between Lothian and the pixie, giving them both a stern look. "We are not here to squash anyone," I said firmly, aware that despite my words I had been accompanied to this place by the small town Chief Punisher and Stomps the Werewolf. I crossed my arms and raised an eyebrow, trying to maintain an even tone. "We're here to ask questions. So, who are you?"

The pixie from California, who said his name was Amadeus, sighed deeply. "This is very embarrassing. Warrior clan pixies do not get caught flat-footed like this."

"Did you know that being caught flat-footed came from the phrase 'caught on the flat of one's foot,' which was used to describe someone slow to react or respond to a situation," Archie's muffled voice called from outside, his large, round eyes looking in from Ima's window as he perched against the glass. "It is thought to have originated in the late nineteenth or early twentieth centuries."

I looked through the window at the owl.

His eyes widened in the darkness as he tilted his head toward me. "Helpful?"

"No?"

The owl cocked his head sideways. "Fair enough."

I turned back to Amadeus. "Where is Lillian Thornton? That's all I care about right now. I want to find her safe and sound." I did not point out that in finding her, we would undo everything else these morons had done, and I hoped he was so focused on whatever his mission was that he wouldn't put two and two together. Pixies could be like a dog with a bone when they wanted to get something done, but they had a nasty habit of focusing on it to the exclusion of everything else. "Where is she?"

The pixie clenched his jaw, avoiding Harmon's gaze.

"You know, we can make this easy on you," the chief said, stepping closer so he loomed over the tiny man, "Or we can make it very unpleasant. Your choice."

The pixie's itty bitty Adam's apple bobbed as he swallowed, and his eyes darted to each corner of the room before meeting Harmon's gaze. "Look, she's fine, all right? Obviously, you figured out what was happening because you're here and ingested some magical defensive potion, so I can't shrink you. You confronted Ima Nelson, so you obviously know who Daniel really is. If you get all that, you must realize I won't tell you where Lillian Thornton is. Certainly not today."

Harmon exhaled, relieved. "She's all right, then?"

"Yes, yes, of course. We may be a bunch of morally bankrupt capitalists that don't have any qualms about lying, cheating, stealing, or even kidnapping, but we are not, and have never been, murderers. She's safe and sound." The pixie paused. "Most likely."

"Most likely?"

Amadeus stood tall, his chest puffed out, throwing his words into the air like a challenge. "No, no, no, I'm sure she's fine. We mustn't jump to conclusions. I mean, sure, we're no saints. Regardless of the methods, we'll do whatever it takes to get what we want. But killing? That's a line we draw. We're no murderers. It's one thing to be corrupt, but it was quite another to be a murderer," the pixie explained with a sense of grandeur and entitlement as if he expected applause simply for not taking the final plunge into the rock-bottom depths of unabashed depravity.

"Okay, let's back up," I said, and the pixie stepped back toward the hallway. "Hold it right there! That's not what I meant, and you know it." I took my hand and scooped up Amadeus and Ima with a feather-light touch to not break their tiny bodies in my grasp. I looked at Lothian. "You have it?"

Lothian nodded and placed the mini-jail on the coffee table.

* * *

"Oh, this is just embarrassing," Amadeus complained as I gently pushed them through the jail door and shut it firmly with a tiny clang. He held his chin high, holding on to that hint of arrogance in his gaze as he looked around the cell. "Hoisted by my own petard, as it were. Ridiculous."

"Did you know," Archie began from the window, "that hoisted by my own—"

"It's from Shakespeare!" I said, arching an eyebrow. "You know you're supposed to be keeping watch for anyone on the street. So did you develop eyes in the back of your head, or what?"

The owl cocked its head to one side, clearly annoyed at being cut off. "No, but I can rotate my head up to 270 degrees in any direction to—"

I held up a hand, stopping Archie from speaking. "No more. Let's focus on getting Lillian back, and then we can return to dismantling Daniel's plot," I said. I lowered my head and studied Ima Nelson, my brow furrowing. "Mrs. Nelson, how did no one in town realize that Daniel Caldecott is your son?"

Ima's jaw dropped, and her hand flew to cover her mouth. "Why would you think that?" she gasped.

I pointed at the pixie sitting next to her. "Because he just told me."

Her gaze shifted to the impish pixie beside her on the jailhouse bench, and her eyes widened in realization. "You idiot."

"No way!" Amadeus bellowed. Suddenly, he froze. His fingers lingered by his chin as he scratched his light stubble, and his eyes widened in surprise as he realized what he had done. "Oh, goodness me. I certainly did, didn't I? Whoops." He gulped and turned to Ima with a sheepish expression. "Perhaps in retelling our misadventure to Daniel, we can leave that part out?"

Ima's face twisted in disgust as she snapped back, "I doubt there's any need for that. I'm sure my son already knows what a fool you are."

"He didn't hire me for my brains, that's for sure," Amadeus agreed.

Ima looked up at me. "I doubt there's any need to explain why he had to leave. My son can't be allowed to forget what he did as a teenager in this town, especially when the mayor still sees him as a potential threat. Everyone knows."

Harmon, Lothian, and I exchanged a silent look of confusion before I finally spoke up. "Ima, I don't think we know what you're discussing. Something happened when Irving was a teenager, but I've never heard specifics. Jason and Serena didn't seem to know."

Ima's expression was puzzled, and she glanced between us. "Fine. The reason no one recognized him is that once Irving turned eighteen, he changed."

"Changed how?"

"He was ready to go out into the world and make his mark after spending years in reform school, and I wanted him to do something great with his life, so I sent him to school in California.

I also warned him that he should build a life somewhere else and never return." She looked down. "He could never escape what he'd done as a teenager, and the mayor would never let him forget he was a threat to her."

I blinked slowly, unable to imagine what kind of childhood experience would still be causing him such pain decades later. "What could he have done as a kid that could have haunted him that long?"

Ima heaved a heavy sigh, and her gaze detached as if her eyes could no longer bear the memory. "He had a rap sheet since before he was a teen. He was already well-acquainted with the wrong side of the law, always wanting things he didn't earn, but stealing Lillian Thornton's car? That was the last straw. The mayor had...had the ashes of a citizen in the passenger seat," she said, her gaze meeting mine. Her expression seemed to echo the sorrow in her voice. "He wrecked the car, and the ashes went everywhere. The ghosts were appalled, the guru furious at his disrespect."

Oh, dear.

"Jason didn't tell me that's why Irving was sent away."

"Jason didn't know. Lillian didn't tell him," Ima admitted, wiping tears from her eyes. "Jason never did understand our town's justice system and never agreed with it. Without thinking, he called the sheriff instead of using Cassandra's justice to report the car stolen, and that started a host of consequences for Irving. To protect Jason, though, everyone that knew what happened stayed quiet. Including me."

"Protect Jason?" I asked with an eyebrow raised. "I don't understand."

"He didn't go to the guru," Ima said. "He went to the county. We don't do that."

"And if people do that?"

"Lillian would have had to step down as mayor," Ima Nelson replied, her voice heavy with resignation. "They might have been asked to move away or even been banished from the community."

Lothian gasped in disbelief. "This town is a cult," he said. "He was your son. You went along with that?"

Ima was taken aback by the harshness of the question. "I'm sure there are things about you wolves we would have a hard time understanding," she said defensively. "In any case, when I visited him in California, he was different. He'd bulked up and changed his diet, but the biggest difference was that he'd had plastic surgery to change his features completely. He'd also legally changed his name."

Lothian's brow furrowed in confusion. "Why would he do that?" he asked.

"He wanted revenge," I replied for Ima Nelson. "He adopted a Native American persona, knowing that most people in this community wouldn't know the difference. He used it as a way in. He knew about the pixies from living here, so he set out to find them. With their help, he educated himself on the various communities he wanted to destroy."

"Why the other ones?" Harmon asked.

"Practice?" I raised an eyebrow. "Money?"

Lothian furrowed his brow. "Speaking of money, where did he get enough to do all this?"

"It's not hard to find investors in California," Amadeus pointed out. "Ever heard of Theranos?"

Theranos was a privately held health technology company founded in 2003 and dissolved in 2018. According to various reports, the company raised over $700 million from investors despite never having a working prototype of the product everyone was throwing buckets of money at.

The founders wound up in jail.

The $700 million vaporized.

So, yeah.

The pixie had a point.

Ima's chin quivered as she glanced up at us with a look of stubborn determination in her eyes. "I never meant for this to happen, but when he strolled back into town six months ago, no one knew who he was. He was finally the son I always wanted. He fit in, made friends, joined the church, and even held a public service job. I was so proud of him...but I didn't see what he was doing until it was too late. How could I turn him in? How can I betray him twice for this town?" Ima's brown eyes were distant when they met mine. "Maybe he's right. Maybe it's time for it to go."

I swallowed hard and looked at Ima, her face anxious and drawn. "Ima," I asked quietly, "do you know where Lillian is?"

Ima's chin quivered like a clamped hold on a taut rubber band. Her voice trembled as she said, "No. But I know he has her somewhere. He wouldn't hurt her." Ima's lip trembled and she turned away, but not before I saw the tears welling up in her eyes.

The woman he thought had orchestrated his exile from the place he called home? Naw, he'd never hurt her, I thought sarcastically. Whatever consequences of Cassandra's past Irving was bringing to bear on the town, one thing was certain.

This was far from over.

And my damn Jeep was right in the middle of it.

CHAPTER NINETEEN

*L*othian confidently led us through the town's quaint streets, while Harmon and I trailed behind. We were headed toward my Jeep and, hopefully, to catch up with Bill Platt again—who was, hopefully, protecting my Jeep from the town. The lights in the windows of the buildings we passed flickered, casting an eerie and haunted glow upon our faces I felt like we were being watched from the shadows with every step we took.

We turned a corner, stopped, and stared.

"What is this?" Harmon asked.

"Voodoo Ceremony!" Amadeus's tiny voice exclaimed with awe.

It wasn't, as the pixie claimed, a "Voodoo" ceremony.

In the heart of downtown Cassandra—right smack in the center of Main Street and perilously close to my Jeep—stood a crackling bonfire at least ten feet tall, its orange and yellow flames illuminating the figures of the gathered crowd. That crowd, a group of around twenty masked revelers, awkwardly swayed in time to the beating of drums and the clanging of cymbals.

The sight of the bonfire and the revelers made me feel uneasy. I had always been skeptical of Cassandra's odd beliefs and practices, but this one seemed especially bizarre—and not normal for the town.

"This isn't Voodou," I told them.

"How can you tell?" Harmon asked.

"The masks." The masks they wore were of all shapes and sizes, some resembling animals, others whimsical and lighthearted paranormal creatures, but all added to the festive and joyful atmosphere of the night. "They're not right. And Voodou practitioners—well, the person leading the ritual, at least—would be dressed in white," I explained, pointing. "There should be a shrine set up with offerings of food, drink, and candles. There's none of that here." Despite their lack of coordination, the revelers seemed to be having the time of their lives.

"You're really creepy sometimes, you know that, Arden?" Harmon asked.

"It's quite surprising, Chief Harmon, that you, as the police chief of a Florida city, are so uninformed about the alternative religious groups in your area," I said, my concern clear in my voice. "It's not the 1700s anymore, and being ignorant about these communities can lead to problematic situations."

Harmon looked taken aback by my statement. "We don't have any Voodoo people in Forkbridge," he said, his tone defensive.

"And you just made my point for me." I struggled to keep my voice level, despite the chief's incredulous expression. "That may be your perception, Chief, but I assure you, Voodou communities do exist here," I said, gesturing widely with my arms. "Citizens of these communities pay taxes, run businesses, and raise families, just like everyone else."

"Our purpose for being here tonight is not to culturally educate the chief. Let's stay focused on the task at hand." Lothian's words were like a whip cutting through the buzzing conversation. He fixed his gaze on Chief Harmon.

Harmon's shoulders relaxed and the furrow between his brows disappeared.

I gave a slight nod.

"Does anyone see Caldecott?" Lothian asked, looking around at the crowd.

"No," I said, scanning the clothing and hairstyles of the people around us. "At least, I don't think any of those folks are him. Caldecott tends to wear high-end clothing that's a bit out of place in a small Florida town like this."

Harmon grunted.

I took that as a no.

Despite their uncoordinated movements, the revelers were clearly having a blast, and the late hour didn't seem to deter them in the slightest. Oddly, no one from the surrounding homes came out to tell them to quiet down. I continued to search the crowd, hoping to catch a glimpse of Caldecott's distinctive sense of expensive style.

"This feels like we stumbled into a small town version of Children of the Corn," Harmon muttered under his breath, his tone uneasy.

Lothian shot Harmon a withering look. "Did you even read the books, Harmon? The town was Gatlin, Nebraska—not exactly a metropolis. And your comparison is off-base—the town was filled with demonic children. This is a small group of manipulated old people." The werewolf rolled his eyes in exasperation. "You really need to think before you speak. It would do you a world of good." His face swung toward me. "This is your town's top cop? Really?"

"All right, settle down. Let's not turn this into a Film 101 class," I said, trying to steer the conversation back to the task at hand. "As you so eloquently snapped at us, we have a job to do, and bickering about movie trivia isn't going to get us anywhere. Let's focus on what's important."

"I see a bunch of people dancing around a bonfire and drumming without any sense of rhythm," Lothian said. "Caldecott's nowhere to be seen. Are we just going to stand here and wait for him, or do you want to go get your Jeep? Because if we're going to stand here and do nothing, I'm going to talk about whatever I damn well please."

The day felt endless and I was ready for it to be over.

I wished my father had used his magic god-hand to move the darn water from my backyard so none of this would be happening. What gods settle down in Central Florida, anyway? Palm Beach I could understand, but here?

On top of that, I was plain tired of these Cassandra people. I wanted them to go home, slather on some Ben-Gay, and crawl into bed. None of them had the stamina or the physicality to join Caldecott's little cult, and none of them had the brains to realize they were signing the death warrant on their town.

Where were the ghosts? The army of spectral guards and nosy busybodies these people counted on to protect them. Granted, I couldn't see them like Ayla could. But if they were here, wouldn't they have told the town's mediums that Daniel was Irving (and just a little bit evil?)

Most of all, I wondered where Caldecott was and where he'd stashed the real mayor—

Wait a minute.

I squinted.

"Look," I said, pointing.

Lothian and Harmon followed my gaze. On the sidewalk next to my Jeep, two figures were deep in conversation, their heads bent close together. I looked up into the branches above them and saw Archie, frozen in place just a few feet from the tops of their heads.

"I think that's Caldecott," I said.

* * *

HARMON SQUINTED, trying to get a better look. "Yes, that's him. Let's go."

"Well, now, wait a minute." The scene was chaotic and unruly, with people of all ages and sizes talking, shouting, and gesturing, but not so crowded that we wouldn't be spotted right away. "The moment the bonfire of the insanities over there spots us, they're likely going to come after me again. Who's that with him? Can anyone tell?"

His conversation partner's back was to me but I could see he had broad shoulders and a slim waist, their dark hair shining in the firelight. Whoever they were, they stood confidently as they talked with Caldecott, their posture reflecting a comfort with the fake mayor that I didn't like.

"What do you want to do, then?"

"Let's just stay here and wait for a minute," I told Harmon, my gaze still lingering on the mysterious figure. My old military sense tugged in the back of my mind telling me something was about to happen. "Something's about to change."

"What?" Lothian shrugged. "Why not just go find out?"

"Just wait."

As soon as I finished telling Lothian to wait, the drums became faint and then stopped altogether, leaving a tense silence on the street in its place. I glanced over at Lothian and tried to silently convey my smug vindication with an exaggerated eye roll and pursed lips. It wasn't good enough. "I don't know why you bother to argue which me," I whispered.

"Because sometimes, you're not lucky," he whispered back.

Daniel Caldecott stepped forward, his booming voice carrying over the crowd.

"Tonight, I make a promise to you all," he declared. "Tomorrow this town will be what it was meant to be—a place where people can come and escape their past pain, just like you all have done. A place of safety and peace. A place where the ghosts of the past are banished. Together, we will make sure none of us ever feels lost or alone or abandoned again."

The crowd erupted into cheers.

I frowned. "What did he mean by that?"

"By which part?" Lothian asked.

"This town," he continued, "has always been blessed with ghosts—we all know them, for they are part of us. Now we have been blessed with water that helps us to let go. Let go of pain! Let go of toxic relationships! Let go of concerns! This is not a place for the forgotten with forgotten dreams—this is a city with honor, ambition, and vision! Yes, you, too, can believe in these things and make them come true!"

And there it was.

Daniel had been using the water to control the people of this town—to make them follow him and his ideas, no matter how far-fetched they may have seemed. He disconnected them from anything that would get in his way, anything that bring attention to the fact that the emperor had no clothes.

Or, well, he had clothes.

And he planned on stealing more of them.

Their feelings about the town, their relationship with the ghosts. This wasn't about bringing anyone's pain to a close—it was about controlling them, making sure that everyone followed his vision.

Harmon sniffed. "Is he about to sign them up for an MLM?"

The cheers of the crowd continued as Caldecott spoke. He was obviously a master of rhetoric, and his words seemed to be hyping the masked followers up.

The fake mayor continued to speak about the promise he was making to the town – that it would become a safe haven where everyone could find their purpose in life and strive to make things happen. He reminded everyone that everyone was important, including those who didn't have a voice or weren't seen—they were all part of this new beginning, too. And if they didn't want to be, well, anyone could release their attachments with one shot of the water and a sustained thought.

I'd heard enough.

"What about Lillian Thornton?" I called out, stepping out from behind a parked station wagon. I hoped that I was making the right move, and that my instincts were leading me in the right direction—and I wasn't just tired of hearing his yapping.

"Astra Arden has joined us!" Daniel stepped out into the street, a smug and confident expression on his face. I knew right away that he didn't want these people to think my presence threatened anything he was trying to accomplish. He was in command, and he made sure everyone knew it. "Do you think she'll come to join us on our mission of unity and peace, my friends?"

"What about Lillian Thornton?" I asked him again. "Where is she?"

"You really think he's just going to tell you?" Lothian asked, his tone skeptical.

Harmon said nothing.

Caldecott looked at me for a moment before speaking. "Our town has been blessed with a great many things," he said, gesturing around him. "Including the disappearance of the mayor. For without that disappearance, would any of this be happening? All things, my friends—all things have a purpose!"

"Your son's got them wrapped around his finger," Amadeus's tiny voice told Ima Nelson. His laugh echoed from the jail. "He's so awesome! He doesn't care about anybody, he barrels into these plans with reckless confidence, he can manipulate people like no one's business. What a man! No guilt, total disregard for your normal human—"

"You're describing a sociopath," I told the pixie, cutting him off.

"You've been listening to the wrong people, Astra," Daniel Caldecott called to me, his voice relaxed.

To everyone else he may have looked self-assured, but I noticed his movements were slow and methodical. His eyes laser-focused on me, as if he was assessing my level of threat and drawing conclusions beneath the smug facade.

"You don't know who I've been listening to.

We need answers, Caldecott," I said, my voice firm. "And we're not leaving until we get them."

"I suggest you go back to Forkbridge and keep your opinions about Cassandra to yourselves. You don't need information about anything. None of you belong here."

"That's rich coming from someone that was run out of Cassandra on a rail, isn't it, Daniel?" I asked him. "Or should I say Irving. That is your original name, right?" I tilted my head. "Daniel, Irving, Featherhead—"

His lips tightened, his nose wrinkled slightly. "Littlefeather."

"More like Littlefinger," Lothian scoffed.

"These three individuals are responsible for Lillian's disappearance!" Daniel said, pointing a finger at us. "Harmon had access to the mayor and is obviously in league with the witch. They both came here with a werewolf, so we can assume their intentions aren't peaceful!"

"Speciest twerp," Lothian growled.

I glanced at Daniel, standing there so confident and smugly sure that he held all the power here. He thought he could spin this story any way he wanted—that he could manipulate people into believing whatever he wanted them to believe.

But how? Why was he so confident?

"No," I said firmly, stepping forward into the street so they'd all hear me loud and clear. "You have it wrong, Daniel—or Irving, or whatever your name is." My eyes bore into his as I continued speaking calmly but loudly enough for all present to hear my words. "You kidnapped Lillian Thornton. You have her somewhere, and we're here to find her so she can stop you."

He remained still for a few moments, assessing me. I could see the silent calculations taking place on his face as he weighed his options. Finally, he sighed and said, "You're not going to leave, are you?"

"Nope."

Daniel spoke in a low voice, his eyes cold and calculating. "Take them. Find out what they know about Lillian," he commanded.

The masked revelers slowly moved toward us. Their faces were hidden by the eerie animal masks and their movements were slow and steady, like a pack of wolves closing in on their prey.

Harmon was the first to speak up. "What are we going to do?"

"We have to fight them off!" Lothian said fiercely, moving to push me just behind him protectively. His body language screamed courage, and I might have been more impressed by his gallant show of authoritative defense if I wasn't sure the people under the masks were middle-aged citizens that had last seen a gym thirty years ago in high school.

I held up the jail. "Come one step closer, and I throw this to the ground," I threatened. "I have your mother and Amadeus in here. I doubt they would survive the landing, but we could see."

Daniel's barked command stopped the crowd in their tracks.

He took a step forward, and I could see a hint of worry on his face mixed with a great deal of fear. He reached into his pocket and pulled out a flask, taking a long drink before addressing us once again. "You think you can frighten me?" he said with a sneer, eyeing the jail in my hands. "I don't care what you do. Let them go or throw them down—it makes no difference to me."

"Oh, wow, dude," I breathed, taken aback by his actions. "Your mother holds so little value in your eyes? And what of the pixie ally who aided you here? Are they so insignificant to you that you'd disconnect from them both? Seriously?"

"What?" Amadeus asked from inside the jail.

Irving/David's words were bold and his expression betrayed no fear.

But I'd seen it there.

I was sure of it.

It was there until he banished it with one swig.

I cast a quick look at the revelers, who continued their leisurely progression toward us as if they didn't have a care in the world. As if it didn't matter whether I brought Ima Nelson crashing down to the ground.

"This town went from a place that cared about everyone, living or dead, to a place that cares about no one—"

I stopped and stared.

The shadowy figure that had been talking to Caldecott on the sidewalk stepped off the curb and into the street. Bill Platt, his face illuminated by the swirling firelight, stepped out of shadows near the bonfire and into the light. "Just go home, Astra!" he called out. "Save yourself and your friends."

"He was working with Caldecott the whole time?" Harmon gasped.

"No, he wasn't. Bill Platt's not that conniving."

"It certainly looks that way, Astra," Lothian added.

I shook my head. "No," I said. "He wouldn't. Whatever Bill Platt is or isn't, he's devoted to this town. There's no way he would support an outsider coming in and changing it." I lowered my voice. "It's the water."

Irving chuckled, but it was a forced, uneasy sound. "People change," he said. "Sometimes quicker than you can even blink."

"Or quicker than you can gulp," I retorted, facing him with a fierce determination of my own. "You're using the water from Persephone's well to make these folks uncaring. They don't care about the town, Lillian, their lost loved ones, or each other. You're using it to sever their ties to what matters most to them." And then, all at once, it finally made sense to me. "But you couldn't do it to Lillian Thornton, could you? My sisters and I warded her. You couldn't manipulate her the way you could everyone else."

"Persephone's well? Is that what you witches call it?" Irving squinted his eyes at me for a beat before finally nodding, gesturing for the revelers to halt their advance. "To be honest, it doesn't really matter whether you know or don't know—everyone here has drank the swamp water. They are indifferent to their guru, this town, or their ghosts. But you were mistaken about one thing."

"What's that?"

"They care about the mayor, whom we all still believe you kidnapped."

In other words, he kidnapped her, but they still think I did it.

Archie flapped his wings and swooped down, landing on my shoulder with a graceful touch. He leaned in closer and regarded me with inquisitive eyes. "This seems very unfair, doesn't it?"

"Of course it's unfair, Archie," Lothian commented with a roll of his eyes.

Astraea, the goddess's who's power Athena had entrusted to (okay, forced on) me was known for her strong sense of justice and her unwavering commitment to righteousness. Athena had kind of deputized me with the star power of her long-gone sister to dispense justice the way she saw it—with fairness, impartiality, and equity.

Or so my mother had claimed.

Astraea was believed to have the power to balance the scales of justice as a guardian of the moral order. To ensure that the guilty were punished and the innocent were protected. My mother had claimed that if I simply allowed the power to flow, it would do just that—act on its own accord.

To safeguard the innocent.

To unleash justice.

"He's right. I agree with Archie," I said. "This seems a bit unfair."

"Unjust, one might even say," Archie said smugly.

"Do you have any idea what they're talking about?" Harmon queried.

I dropped down to a low crouch, my hand pressed firmly against the pavement. The air around me hummed with electrical intensity and then, with a flash of light and a burst of color, a surge of potent energy surged out from my palm.

CHAPTER TWENTY

The brightness was blinding, and I had to close my eyes briefly until they adjusted. Once I reopened them, I noticed that the surroundings had changed. Everywhere I looked was bathed in a soft golden glow emanating from the air itself. The shadows were gone, and the entire area pulsed with a revitalizing energy that sent shivers down my spine.

I couldn't help but grin, basking in a feeling of power and control that was almost dizzying. Moments like these made me feel fully alive and reminded me of the boundless potential within me.

A potential that I rarely tapped into.

But, well, every once in a while, it came in handy.

Like now.

"Don't get too drunk with power, there, Witchy McStardust," Archie snapped, bringing me out of my moment. "That's not the end of it."

The dense cluster of people around the bonfire quietly removed their masks, revealing their faces and gazing at each other in bewilderment. All of them looked lost, not one of them understanding the strange events that had just occurred.

"What have you done?" Daniel demanded, his voice tinged with hostility as he crossed his arms defensively across his chest. His eyes darted to the jail, still gripped tightly in my other hand. "Seize her!"

The atmosphere grew heavy with dread and panic as the revelers huddled in uncertainty. Despite getting a hefty dose of my power, Daniel stood firm and silent, his gaze unwavering.

"What just happened here?" an older woman asked. One hand clutched her chest, and the other still gripped the mask. "Why am I out here?" Her wrinkled hands shakily dropped the mask to the ground. "Daniel?"

Before he could give the woman a reply,

Lothian stepped forward. His expression was inscrutable, but I could sense the tension radiating from him. "You've been hoodwinked by a swindler, and Astra—the one you all targeted and the same person that man just instructed you to go after once more—rescued you. You're welcome," he ground out through clenched teeth. "Now, where is the mayor?"

Daniel gulped and backed away, his eyes darting around indecisively. As he weighed his options, the thoughts that were likely flooding his mind were almost palpable.

Thanks to Persephone's well, whatever he'd suppressed in himself was now resurfacing for him the same as it was for everyone else. Although he was doing better than they were because he understood what was happening to him, it was clear that he was at a loss for what to do next.

"I am the mayor!" he told Lothian!

"Why were you so insistent that we torch Astra's Jeep?" Bill raged as he marched up to Daniel/Irving in a fit of anger. "If you'd bothered to learn anything about the subconscious mind, you'd know that people can't be manipulated into doing something they wouldn't normally do. Swamp water cannot override a person's free will or personal beliefs, you imbecile!"

"They weren't hypnotized, you nitwit!" Daniel shouted back.

"Wait a minute, wait a minute, wait a minute," I said as I walked over to my Jeep, still parked across from the entrance to the park. "Why did you want them to torch my Jeep? That's been a major focus of yours all day. You've been insistent. Why are you so insistent?"

Daniel's face blanched, and he seemed to be at a loss for words.

"Is there something special about my Jeep?" I asked.

Daniel shook his head. My blast of star energy seemed to have disconnected Daniel from the Machiavellian part of his brain, and he was having trouble figuring out what to say next.

One of the revelers stepped forward and spoke up. "Daniel wanted us to torch your Jeep because he said it was the only way you could escape responsibility for your murder of the mayor."

"But it's not Daniel, is it?" Melva Platting, a mother of two, stepped forward, her face twisted in unhappiness. "I remember from before—you're Irving. Irving Nelson." She frowned. "We went to school together, you and I. Well, until you had to leave."

Daniel's face contorted with anger. "I didn't have to leave!" he shouted. "You all rejected me and broke your own rules! We were supposed to go before the guru, but no—precious Jason called the police, and I went to jail for a joyride!"

"Irving, Jason was just a kid—"

"He knew the rules! I knew the rules! We all knew the rules!" Irving snapped at Melva, his face contorted in a fury. "My mother refused to allow me back home once I got out! That's what you people did to her! This stupid town and its stupid beliefs ruined my life!"

"Not for nothing, Irving, but you seem to be doing pretty well for yourself," Bill told him. The citizens nodded in agreement and began murmuring about how well Daniel was doing. "You got a college education, you—"

He whirled around to face Bill, his eyes blazing with anger. "Oh, really, Bill? Do you think I did well for myself? Do you really believe that?" Irving's face crumpled like a rejected child's, his cheeks flushed with rage. "I had to do well for myself—it was the only way I would ever have access to enough money and resources to destroy

348 | LEANNE LEEDS

this town! Raze it to the ground! It's been my sole focus. My only goal."

"You used us to ruin our own community," Melva whispered, her voice barely audible. The people behind her silently nodded in agreement. "You made us assist you in betraying our people."

"I didn't force you to do anything!" Irving roared. "You're a naive group of imbeciles who think this town, sitting in the heart of a Central Florida swamp, is a whimsical land of sunshine, rainbows, and pixies. Well, I have news for you— the pixies are locked in conflict and can be bought for a plot of land, and the sunshine and rainbows are reserved for the privileged few allowed to live here." He folded his arms across his chest. "You deserve to be manipulated."

"Enough!" I shouted. "Irving, where is the mayor? Where is Lillian? You people can work out your political disagreements later. Where is she?"

* * *

It was only a fraction of a moment.

A quick shift in his gaze.

A subtle redirect of his attention toward my Jeep, followed by a swift turn away to avoid drawing attention to the fact that he'd looked when I asked the question. The question about Lillian's location.

"Oh no," I whispered, taking off in a full run.

The ideas collided in my mind, each pounding into my consciousness as my boots hit the still-shimmering ground. The pixies had undoubtedly reduced her size, as a five-inch tall mayor was much easier to conceal. But where could she be hidden? Daniel's persistent demand that the townspeople burn my Jeep to ashes finally revealed the final piece of his scheme to me.

If the Cassandrans set it ablaze and she was concealed within, poor Lillian would perish small, but her body would revert to its full size upon death. In one fell swoop, Irving Nelson could implicate me, the townspeople, or all of us. Even the pixies in the swamp who initially shrunk poor Lillian. Because no one would know Amadeus and his California clan were at odds with Pistachio and the original pixies of the Florida swamp.

"She's in the Jeep!" I yelled as I ran. "Probably in some kind of container! Find her! Hurry!"

Another problem was the longevity of the pixie dust's effects. It lasted for a few hours, possibly six, perhaps twelve, but definitely not more than eighteen. Bones can snap, and flesh can be punctured by engine parts. And despite all the Hollywood movies that depict a human growing from five inches to five feet in five seconds as a safe and uncomplicated process, it was far from safe when you were confined within a vehicle like a Jeep.

"Wouldn't your magic have healed her?" Lothian asked, panting as he caught up to me. "You released it all over everyone and everything."

"Tires!" I yelled as we reached the Jeep. "The rubber is electrically resistant!"

We scrambled around the cab, throwing books, clothes, and other objects that had accumulated on the floorboard everywhere. Lothian tugged at a small black box hidden under my driver's seat and shouted triumphantly.

We both stared at it with a mix of anxiety and hope.

I delicately accepted the box from him, my fingers trembling with anxiety. I could feel the subtle energy within it, but I had to ensure it was what we thought it was. Summoning all of my courage, I closed my eyes and inhaled a steadying breath before wrapping my bare hands around it.

In a quick mental flash, I saw Lillian Thornton scream.

That was all I needed.

"Stand back," I told Lothian.

I slowly crouched down and gently placed the small container on the road. A strange sense of anticipation filled the air as I closed my eyes and released the star magic once again to do its work. Suddenly, a bright flash of light burst upward, illuminating the surrounding area, and a few moments after that, a thin tendril of smoke started to rise like a spiral out of the container. It curled and billowed in the air, and when it dissipated, standing in its place was a full-sized Lillian Thornton.

"Welcome back."

Lillian looked at me, her eyes wide in surprise. "Astra, is that you?" she asked, her voice barely above a whisper.

Before I could answer, Harmon ran to her, scooping her into his arms and kissing her wet cheeks. Everyone nearby breathed a sigh of relief.

Everyone, that is, except Irving.

"Are you all right?" the chief asked.

Mayor Thornton nodded and kissed him once more. "I knew you'd find me. I never gave up hope. I had all the faith in the world that you

were turning every rock over, and you'd save me."
She kissed him a final time. "I love you."

"Yeah, he didn't," Lothian told the mayor.

Harmon glared. "Is that really important right
now?"

"No, no, of course, you're right. We'll let the
mayor believe you were the day's hero. No need
to tell her that I found her. Or that Astra—the
one she wanted to shoot—was the one that
narrowed down where we needed to search and
that you didn't help us. Oh, or that she used her
magic to make the box disappear—"

"Okay," Harmon said. "We get it."

"—and then broke the pixie dust's effects. But
yeah, no, you helped, too. I'm sure you played a
part." He rubbed the back of his head. "I just can't
quite recall how at the moment."

Mayor Thornton and I locked eyes, the
tension between us palpable. For a moment, I was
transported back to better days, just months ago,
when I wondered if she would wind up my
mother-in-law. It seemed like something had
shifted in her expression like she recognized that
no matter what had come before, she'd made it
through because of me.

Harmon cleared his throat after an awkward
silence descended upon us. "Astra deserves all the

credit for finding you and breaking the spell on you. It's true. Without her help, we would never have been able to find you in time."

"I see," was all she said in response.

Not "thank you."

Just "I see."

Well, you can't win 'em all.

Daniel/Irving tried to sidle away from the group, but he was quickly stopped by Bill Platt's firm grip on his shoulder. "This is Irving Nelson."

"Irving...Nelson? The young man that stole my car so many years ago?" Lillian Thornton looked gobsmacked. "Ima's son?"

"Yes, ma'am." Bill presented Mayor Thornton with the decree making Daniel/Irving interim mayor until Mayor Thornton could resume her duties with full authority. "Did you sign this? I'm figuring no, but I have to ask."

The mayor read over the decree with a scoff before tearing it into pieces and tossing it onto the ground at Irving's feet. "Of course not." Looking up at him coldly, she said, "What kind of game were you playing here?"

"He thought he could use your absence to take over our town and destroy it." Bill's voice grew louder and more forceful with each word. "He thought he could manipulate the people and bend them to his will. He underestimated the strength and resilience of this community," Bill said, his tone filled with pride. "We stood up to him, we fought back, and we won."

She took a step forward, her eyes never leaving Irving's. "Well, let me tell you something. This town may be small, but it's full of strong, capable people who will never bend to the whims of a con artist like you."

"Mayor, he just wanted to belong," Melva said, her face torn. "His mother did tell him not to come back."

"He wants to belong? That won't be a problem. Serena and the guru will prepare a place for him until he faces the town and will no doubt return him to it after his trial. He'll belong here for years. Just not in the way, he would have wished." With a final glare, Mayor Thornton turned and walked away, leaving Irving standing in Bill Platt's iron grip, defeated.

* * *

PISTACHIO AND ALICE arrived from the swamp, thanks to Archie, and Serena returned thanks to a quick phone call to my sisters. Once everyone was there next to the bonfire, everything was organized far more quickly than one might have expected, given the convoluted situation we'd found ourselves in.

Bill Platt and Chief Harmon relocated Ima and Irving to Cassandra's "Serene Sanctuary of Transformation and Redemption"—an involuntary lodge that doubled as their jail.

"What happens now?" Lothian asked.

Bill explained that the Nelsons would answer the town in a meeting tomorrow, and the town itself would pass judgment. "Even the ghosts get a vote."

"What do you think will happen?"

"Oh, I suspect they'll go for chakra cleansings and soul realignment," Bill said.

I raised my eyebrow. "That sounds like a spa treatment."

"Nope, it's definitely not. They undergo those daily until the town feels they've worked. While those happen, they'll be guests in the SSTR until they take." Bill shrugged. "They can petition the town for release once Jupiter or Venus is supportive in relation to their natal charts. They only need 4/5ths of the town to forgive them."

I had no idea what he meant about Jupiter or Venus, but I nodded like I did. "Of course."

Within minutes of Serena and Lillian

Thornton's arrival, they discovered that Irving had pumped Persephone's water into the town's drinking supply. With a few quick disconnections and blasts from my buzzy hands, we detoxed Cassandra and cleared it of ill effects.

Pistachio assured me that he and Alice would deal with the California pixies.

I didn't ask how.

I didn't want to know.

"How are you feeling?" Lothian inquired, propping himself against the open window. "You look relieved to be back in the driver's seat."

Cloaked in the darkness of the night, I could feel the coolness of the air and the warmth of the leather on my hands. My grip on the wheel was firm, and the whites of my knuckles were visible in the dim light, illuminated by the stars and the soft glow of streetlights. "I'm fine. Why wouldn't I be fine?"

"I don't know how your magic thing works." Time seemed to stand still momentarily as Lothian Pennington looked deep into my eyes. "Think of it as my last duty of care to you. I got you through this without so much as a scratch. I'd like everything to stay on the rails to the end, you know? No tripping in the end zone."

The audacity of this guy.

"You got me through this, did you?" My voice dripped with honey, but my tone had a razor-sharp edge. "It's like saying you scored the winning touchdown just because you happened to have a ball in your hands."

"That's why I like you, Astra." He stepped away from my Jeep and grabbed his motorcycle helmet off the side of his bike. "You're so unapologetically confident in yourself. You don't need anyone's help to get things done; you just do it. You don't need sisters. You don't need friends. You don't need anyone. Right?"

"I think you're describing yourself. Arrogance isn't an attractive trait, Lothian," I quipped.

"I am a pack member," he countered, straddling his bike and revving the engine. "I know where I belong and where my loyalties lie. As much as I enjoy our little exchanges, it's getting late, and we should get back. I'll follow behind you just to make sure no one else tries anything funny on the way back to Arden House."

Lothian pulled away, his bike wheeling around in a swift and tight loop before settling in behind me. I accelerated slowly, my eyes trained on the road ahead, searching for any signs of trouble. I could feel Lothian's reassuring presence in my rearview mirror, his watchful eyes a constant reminder that I was not alone.

As we made our way back to the safety of Arden House, I kept a steady pace, my mind alert and focused. I couldn't shake the feeling that danger was lurking just around the corner, and as much as he annoyed me, I was grateful for Lothian's company.

Especially when he was far enough behind me that I didn't have to talk to him.

CHAPTER TWENTY-ONE

Sleep.

It was glorious.

I was lying on the bed, my head resting on the pillow. I'd barely opened my eyes and stirred when Archie decided it was time for me to start my day.

"Did you find time to sleep, or did you just stay up all night trying to make your hair look that bad?" Archie asked from his perch in front of the open window. Behind him the sky was a luminous blue with wisps of white clouds. The temperature was humid and warm—as usual— and a chorus of birdsong filled the air. "Because that looks like it took actual effort."

"Why can't you be like those birds?" I asked,

my finger pointing toward the open window. "Hear that? They're singing. Happy to be alive. Cheerful. You could be like that."

"You have no idea what those birds are saying. None."

Okay, he had me there.

As I pushed myself up, I felt the sheets slipping away from my body. My toes curled against the hard wooden floor of the bedroom, and I let out a sigh as I took in the new feeling of being out of bed and ready to start my day.

"Are you sighing already?" Archie asked.

Standing in front of the mirror, I stared back at my reflection. My hair was tangled and mussed, and my eyes droopy with exhaustion. I took the brush in my hand and began to bring it through my hair, smoothing out the knots and tangles until it looked presentable.

"There." I turned to the owl. "Better?"

"Much."

"I agree," Jason said.

I turned back to find Jason's ghostly reflection within the vanity mirror, ethereal and flowing with a faint luminescence. "Morning. How's your mother doing?" I put the brush down. "Does she still hate me or did that whole saving her life thing change her attitude a little bit?"

Jason reveled in being a shrugger, and apparently death hadn't changed his habit. "She and Harmon did a lot of talking last night, and while I don't think she's come around enough to join your fan club, she probably won't be pulling a gun on you in Punktex any time soon."

"Again," I corrected. "She won't be pulling a gun on me in a Punktex again. Because she already did that once. Pull a gun on me. Not sure if you were aware."

Jason's laughter bubbled out of him and his eyes sparkled with amusement.

I sat down on my bed. "You stayed around and listened last night?"

"I did."

"Okay, I have a question. What on earth happened to the ghosts?" My brow furrowed. "Your home town supposedly has this fancy ghost alarm system that spies on everyone and knows everything and prevents forest fires and all that." Jason's lips stretched in a slight smirk. "They totally missed the boat with this. Why?"

"Persephone's water," Jason explained.

A puzzled expression crossed my face as I tried to make sense of his answer. "What about the water? You mean the folks in Cassandra didn't care about the ghosts and what they had to say? Any one of them could have come here and told Ayla. Or you. And you guys could have told us."

"Persephone is the goddess of the underworld —that means her magic can affect the dead and the afterlife," Jason explained. His hands moved in purposeful, emphatic motions, and he looked exactly like the teacher he once was. "Persephone's water made dormant whatever you were thinking about the moment you came into contact with it."

"How do you know that?" I asked, surprised.

Jason looked at me, a hint of a knowing smile playing at his lips. "Astra—I'm in the underworld. Hades and Persephone are here. I can just go up to them and ask them things," he said, his eyes twinkling with amusement.

"You just strolled in and asked Hades?"

"I could have. Though in this case, I did not. I asked your mother, and she did some digging," he added, his tone turning serious.

"My mother, huh?"

"Well, who better to ask than someone who's tried to avoid Persephone's wrath her entire life?"

"Fair." I looked at him. "Turn around."

"Turn around?"

I held up my clothes. "Yes. Turn around."

He did.

I slipped off my nightshirt and pulled on a pair of faded blue jeans, tucking the cuffs at my ankles. I followed it with a black cotton shirt, feeling the soft fabric settle against my skin. "You can turn around. Another question—how did Irving know about the water to use it?" I asked as Jason turned to face me.

"Ima Nelson."

I blinked. "Ima?"

"Who do you think my mother went to about the land ownership when she first realized there was an issue with the water?"

"Ima. Because she was the town clerk."

Jason nodded. "She had no reason not to trust her with what was going on, so she told her. And then Ima must have mentioned it to Irving, and then Irving decided the time had come for his revenge on the town." Jason dropped his shoulders and glanced down at my vanity. "Which really was revenge on me for calling the police." He looked up. "Ironic that I was dead by the time he showed up, huh?"

"You were a kid, and you made a mistake. Kids that don't live in Cassandra rebel, too, Jason. You were a teacher. You know that. You rebelled by calling the police because that wasn't done in the town you grew up in. Most people's teen rebellion doesn't get a small town turned into the new age Four Seasons."

His shoulders were slightly slumped, as if the weight of his regret were too heavy to bear. "I guess."

"Your posture says you don't buy it."

"I don't, but you don't need to worry about it." His eyes were sad, filled with longing and regret, as if he were lost in his own thoughts and struggling to find a way out. "Lots of time to work through past regrets down here."

* * *

I WALKED DOWN THE STAIRS, taking in the sight of my family at the breakfast table. My three sisters were chatting and laughing while my aunt stirred her coffee. The aromas of bacon and eggs wafted softly through the air.

Archie launched from my shoulder as soon as he smelled the bacon and was headed straight for the table. As I watched, he swooped low and then landed softly, plucking the bacon from the serving dish with swift precision. He flew back to my shoulder before anyone could stop him.

"You're getting grease on my shirt," I told him.

The owl's sharp beak snapped at pieces of bacon, quickly tearing them into small pieces and swallowing them whole. His eyes glinted with determination as he devoured it, not wasting a single morsel and not caring one whit for the talon-sized grease stains he was leaving.

"Nice, Archie."

He ignored me.

Aunt Gwennie handed me a plate of fried eggs and sizzling bacon while my sister Ami passed me a warm cup of coffee. "We thought we'd let you sleep, dear," my aunt told me with a nod. "You got in very late last night."

"I didn't think you'd be up for hours," Ayla said with a nod.

"I'm impressed that you're up at all," I said to Ami. "You look so much better than you did a couple of days ago."

"Thanks. I think." She had a gentle expression on her face with a hint of a smile, and her bright blond hair framed her face, making her look more serene than I'd seen her in a while. She nodded slightly. "I've been talking to Mom a lot in the mirror the past day. It's helped a lot, I think."

"Well, it's good that Mom has the capacity to help." My tone was sharp and cutting, conveying my disapproval. "You wouldn't think so considering the mess she made of everything, but maybe a leopard can change it spots."

"Astra," Aunt Gwennie snapped, a heavy frown on her face.

"No, you know what, Aunt Gwennie?" Ami's voice was soft and her words were careful. "It's okay that Astra's angry. Mom did some terrible things, and maybe she didn't let the three of us do anything, but she practically banished Astra for not living up to her expectations. Mom didn't even live up to her own expectations." She spoke with an air of authority, but also with a sense of kindness and understanding. "You don't have to defend Mom from our feelings any more, Aunt Gwennie. We all need to work through how we feel. That's the only way we'll heal."

Aunt Gwennie's eyes widened, her mouth agape as she looked at Ami. Her face was a mixture of admiration, satisfaction, and disbelief, and it was clear that she was shocked by what she had just heard. The wrinkles on her forehead softened as she slowly nodded in approval.

I looked at Althea with a raised eyebrow. "Do we have a new high priestess?"

"No," Ami answered for Althea. "I'm not a high priestess, and we're not a coven. We don't serve.

We're a family." She looked around the table. "No one has to worship some god to belong here. No one has to be only one thing or they're kicked out. We're just four sisters, one aunt, and some animals. We love each other, and we support each other. That's who we are and what we do."

"What have you done with my sister?" Ayla asked.

"Let's not forget one of the animals is illegal," Althea said as Archie skittered across the table once again and snagged more of the bacon. "And if that illegal animal doesn't leave bacon for the rest of us, I swear, I'm calling the authorities."

Archie had one talon clasped around a piece of bacon, while it stared at Althea with an intense, unblinking gaze. "You wouldn't." His head shifted from side to side as though studying her intent. "You know I can pluck your stupid crow from the sky, right?"

"Just try it, bird brain," Lily, Althea's crow, cawed from her perch.

Cerberus barked.

"Aw, family," I sighed and grabbed my own bacon from my plate before Archie laid claim to it. "What would we do without family?"

The morning sunlight filtered through the window, casting a warm glow over my family gathered in Aunt Gwennie's kitchen. Maybe we could finally accept our pasts, forgive those who had hurt us, and move on with our lives.

By working through it, though.

Not by drinking a potion or Persephone's water to hide it.

It felt like we made a promise to each other that day to always stay connected as a family no matter what happened. I left that breakfast feeling like we would look out for each other and always have a shoulder to lean on when times got tough.

It was unsaid, but I could feel it.

After months of danger and chaos and gods and ghosts, it felt like the world might finally taking a break from all the madness.

* * *

WE DECIDED to take a trip into Cassandra and check on its recovery.

It was, shockingly, the same as it was before Daniel Caldecott.

As we walked down the streets, I saw people bustling about their daily errands, heard children laughing as they played with each other, and caught glimpses of business owners working diligently in their shops. The atmosphere was filled with hope and optimism—a far cry from what it had been last night around the bonfire.

"Boy, people really bounce back, huh?" Ami asked, breaking the silence between us.

The sun was just beginning to dip behind the horizon, painting the sky a deep pink and orange as we approached the edge of town. I couldn't help but glance up at the fading colors, savoring the calm atmosphere of this place. It felt like a sanctuary, a safe haven from the outside world.

Just as it should.

With a deep sigh of contentment, the four of us turned away and continued our journey toward my Jeep. I felt safe and secure in the knowledge that—for now at least—everything was okay.

* * *

THANK YOU FOR READING!

I hope you enjoyed Scries Like an Owl. Please think about leaving a review! Astra, Archie and the whole Arden family continue their adventures in Book 12, Owl Berry Mysterious.

KEEP UP WITH LEANNE LEEDS

Thanks so much for reading! I hope you liked it! Want to keep up with me?

Visit leanneleeds.com to:

Find all my books…

Sign up for my newsletter…

Like me on Facebook…

Follow me on Twitter…

Follow me on Instagram…

Thanks again for reading!

Leanne Leeds

FIND A TYPO? LET US KNOW!

Typos happen. It's sad, but true.

Though we go over the manuscript multiple times, have editors, have beta readers, and advance readers it's inevitable that determined typos and mistakes sometimes find their way into a published book.

Did you find one? If you did, think about reporting it on leanneleeds.com so we can get it corrected.

ARTIFICIAL INTELLIGENCE STATEMENT

Portions of this book were created with the assistance of AI tools used for editing, proofreading, and refining the text. However, the ideas, storyline, characters, and overall creative vision remain my own original work.

While some aspects of the cover image were generated using AI tools, it was done so under my creative direction and curation.

I want to acknowledge the use of these technologies as part of my creative process, while affirming that the essence of this work comes from my own imagination and effort.

Leanne Leeds

www.ingramcontent.com/pod-product-compliance
Lightning Source LLC
Chambersburg PA
CBHW021432240626
47153CB00001B/118